SISTERS

OF THE

SWEETWATER FURY

A NOVEL

KINLEY BRYAN

Blue Mug Press

Copyright © 2021 by Kinley Bryan

Blue Mug Press
Hilton Head Island, South Carolina

Cover design by Tim Barber, Dissect Designs
Book Layout © 2017 BookDesignTemplates.com

Sisters of the Sweetwater Fury/ Kinley Bryan. -- 1st ed.
ISBN (paperback): 978-1-7379152-0-1
ISBN (ebook): 978-1-7379152-1-8

For Mike

[T]hose grand freshwater seas of ours,—Erie, and Ontario, and Huron, and Superior, and Michigan,—possess an ocean-like expansiveness...they are swept by Borean and dismasting blasts as direful as any that lash the salted wave; they know what shipwrecks are, for out of sight of land, however inland, they have drowned full many a midnight ship with all its shrieking crew.

—HERMAN MELVILLE, *MOBY DICK*

THURSDAY
November 6, 1913

Black River, Lorain, Ohio

Only fools and shipping bosses would boast of safety before the boats were in winter layup, but the sailors were keenly aware how few fatalities 1913 had seen: only nine—ten—men lost, with mere weeks to go. Word of the tenth reached the *Titus Brown* as Sunny Colvin stood in the galley, scooping the cores from green apples. Cleve, the porter, had heard from a dockworker how it had happened. Over in Detroit, a first mate had been reaching a pole from his whaleback steamer to the mail boat pulled up alongside it when he'd lost his balance and toppled into the river.

Sunny let out a sigh, wondering who the man had left behind, a widow perhaps, or grief-stricken parents or young children. To those hardest hit by this awful news, there was no consolation in the fact that losses on the Great Lakes this year were fewer than usual. The sad truth was, with thousands of vessels working the lakes, carrying iron ore to Cleveland and coal to Duluth, limestone to Chicago and wheat to Buffalo, it was normal to lose a few ships and several dozen sailors in a single nine-month shipping season.

No fatalities had ever been incurred on the five-hundred-foot steel freighter *Titus Brown*. Though bad luck could befall even the best sailor, Providence tended to smile on the skilled, and Captain Hanna credited Sunny for his crew being, as he put it, the finest on the Great Lakes. The captain was a reserved man whose few hints of frivolity included the occasional pun and a fondness for ballroom dancing. At the end of each shipping season, he would implore Sunny to return to him in the spring. Her cooking and baking had no rival on the Great Lakes, and the best sailors clamored to work on his vessel.

"Herb can stay ashore," he would say, referring to Sunny's husband, the steward, "as long as *Huron* my boat come March, for you're *Superior* to any cook on the lakes."

Sunny would roll her eyes and groan at his puns and promise to return the following spring. She and Herb had sailed with Captain Hanna for ten years—her very first day at sea had been her twenty-third birthday. Five years later, in 1908, they'd followed the captain to his new berth, the just-launched straight deck freighter *Titus Brown*.

In less than twenty-four hours the crew would embark on their last upbound trip of the season. Sunny was in a foul mood. The supply boat was late, and if it didn't arrive this afternoon with the cinnamon she'd requested the day before, she wouldn't be able to make the captain's favorite snap doodle bread. The supply boat had come when they'd arrived in Lorain a day earlier, and Sunny and Herb had climbed down the side of the *Titus Brown* to select the meats, vegetables, and other ingredients they'd need for the twenty-day round trip to Fort William, Ontario. But there'd been something wrong with the cinnamon—there were big clumps in it, like it had gotten wet. The supply boat had just come from the *Schuck*, a freighter where a rival cook worked and Sunny wouldn't put it past that cook to tamper with a spice she was known for using. Fortunately, they were in port an extra day waiting on a load of coal, and there was time for the supply boat to return with more.

It had become a tradition to have snap doodle bread when setting sail on inauspicious Friday mornings. Captain Hanna liked it with his coffee. He wasn't superstitious any more than the rest of them, which was to say he *was* somewhat superstitious. He wouldn't whistle on deck lest he whistle up the wind. Nor would he say "goodbye" or, heaven forbid, "good luck." And while he'd rather not set sail on a Friday, the *Titus Brown's* schedule was up to the shipping company, not him, and he'd come to think of the bread as warding off the bad luck sailing on a Friday was thought to bring (Friday being the day of the Crucifixion). And as this was their last trip up the lakes this season—the season ending in early December when ice clogged the St. Marys River, making Lake Superior inaccessible from the lower lakes—Sunny didn't want to tempt fate.

An unseasonably warm breeze wafted through the open galley windows. Sunny put the cored apples into two large earthen crocks and covered them with cold water. In addition to her breads, Sunny was known for her desserts. Her baked apples were a family tradition and well loved by the crew. She wanted to get the apples into the oven before the supply boat arrived.

Herb poked his head in the galley doorway. "You want Cleve to get your cinnamon?" her husband asked, referring to the porter.

"The supply boat's here?"

"For about five minutes now."

Sunny threw up her hands. "Why didn't anyone tell me? You know I'm waiting on it." She untied her apron and hung it on a hook, the one hung lower than the others to accommodate her diminutive height. "If we lived on land I wouldn't have to worry about the store sailing away."

"You would go ashore and disappoint the Old Man?" Most of the crew, as on other lake freighters, referred to the captain as the Old Man.

"I know a third-rate cook who'd take my place quick enough." Not that she'd want to leave Captain Hanna in a bind. And she loved watching the crew tuck in to something she'd made, the way the men would get all quiet with the business of eating. Sunny wasn't immune to pride. "Will you help me with these apples, then? I'll get the cinnamon myself."

"Of course my love."

"Oh, you save that mush for your girlfriend." She was only teasing, for Herb was as true as they came. She told him what needed to be done: a cup and a half of sugar for every six apples before placing the crocks in the oven.

Sunny stepped onto the after deck. It must have been sixty-five degrees, and that was something for early November in Ohio. Well, the warm weather wouldn't last on the upbound trip, certainly not as far north as their destination. In Fort William, Ontario, they'd load up with iron ore for their final downbound trip, and then it was back to Port Austin, Michigan, where she and Herb spent winters living with her older sister, Agnes, and their mother, whom they all called Maman. Their younger sister, Cordelia, would come home from Cleveland for the holidays with her new husband, a Great Lakes captain whom Sunny had seen in port now and again, their boats owned by the same shipping company. While Sunny knew Edmund Blythe mostly by reputation (a fine sailor whose reticence was notable even for a lake captain), Agnes and Maman had never met the man, for he and Cordelia had eloped less than two months ago before settling in Cleveland. That was Cordelia for you: impulsive and romantic. Despite the sisters' different natures they got on well and she looked forward to being with them again. She was already planning Christmas dinner.

On her way to the ladder Sunny nearly bumped into Ernie, the assistant engineer, as he dashed from the boilerhouse—all cleaned up and carrying his sea bag. It was clear he had something on his mind.

"You jumping ship?" Sunny asked, although certainly Ernie had more brains than that. Why work all year just to duck out before the last trip of the season? You'd lose your bonus just as the holidays were coming.

"I am, Mrs. Colvin." Ernie, like all of the younger crew members, had a habit of calling her Mrs. Colvin despite her invitations to call her Sunny. She both appreciated the sign of respect and felt aged by it. She was only thirty-three, after all. And no gray strands in her hair yet, only reddish ones among the brown.

"But why? Just one more trip to go and we've got this nice weather."

"The wife needs me at home." Ernie sounded a touch defensive. "Anyhow I'm tired of sailing."

Sunny laughed as if he were joking. "Who isn't tired of it come November?" That didn't mean you could just walk away like that. There was no figuring some people. "Your family's in Detroit, right? You could ride with us and get off there."

"Nah, I'll take the train."

Sunny almost needled him some more, but the young man was clearly uneasy, so she softened instead. "If you're tired of sailing, then what are you going to do?"

Ernie shrugged. "It may sound silly..."

"Out with it."

"Well, Mrs. Colvin, I've spent the last few winters making cupboards. My customers like my work and I get more requests than I can finish in three months. So I've been thinking about starting my own business."

A cupboard-making business! The prospect of the assistant engineer—a kid, really—going ashore to start a business struck something at Sunny's core. "How long have you been wanting to do this?"

"Since last winter. One of my customers said my craftsmanship was top notch and that I could make a living from it. I thought he was crazy at first."

"And now?"

"The more I've thought about it the more I believe I can. At least, I want to give it a try. Plus I get to be my own boss, and be close to my family."

"And you have to leave this instant?"

"I have a cousin in Lorain and he's got a lathe for me. I figure if I don't go get it now I'll put it off and I'll end up spending another year on the lakes. So I made up my mind. I don't want to be a fellow who just thinks about doing something, you know?"

"No, of course not." She'd never told anyone, but Sunny had an entrepreneurial dream of her own: to open a restaurant in Port Austin. A café. She would serve breakfast and luncheon. Business would be brisk in the summer, when tourists flooded the area. In the winter the café would operate fewer hours and serve the locals. She didn't know when she had first dreamed it, but she'd had the dream for so long now it was as much a part of her life as any of the real things she'd experienced. "Well good for you, Ernie. It takes courage to start your own business. Not everyone could do it."

He shrugged. "I don't know. I'm more excited than anything. I figure I can always come back to sailing if things don't work out."

"I'm sure they'll work out fine. Better than fine." Sunny patted him on the shoulder. It was funny how people could surprise you. "But you will miss my baking."

"Oh I know it Mrs. Colvin. I know it."

"Wait a sec and I'll fetch you a snack for your trip." She ducked into the galley where oatmeal cookies were cooling. She tried one—perfectly done, if she may say so herself—then brushed the crumbs from her bosom, wrapped three in paper and took them onto the deck. The assistant engineer shifted his weight from his left foot to his right, back and forth, like he had to use the toilet.

"Wish I were going, too," Sunny confided as she handed him the cookies. "I've had enough of sailing for one lifetime."

"Why don't you, Mrs. Colvin? That is, if that's what you want."

Sunny let out a short, sharp laugh. "The Old Man will never let me leave this boat. And I mean *my* old man, not Captain Hanna!"

Ernie laughed, thanked her and hurried to the port bow.

Sunny watched until he disappeared over the gunwale. She shook her head, trying to clear it of the conversation. The assistant engineer's plans to go ashore had rattled her. It felt as if Ernie had taken the last of a scarce resource, leaving her with nothing. There was a pulling sensation in her belly and she grabbed the railing to steady herself. Why should she care in the least what Ernie did? Men came and went all the time. This was different, somehow. It was like her acquiescence to yet another trip up and down the lakes, her belief that she had no other choice, had been called into question. The assistant engineer, who might've been ten years younger than she, was leaving to start his own business!

She continued along the starboard side to the ladder. The deckhands were washing out the hold now, getting rid of the last bits of red iron ore dust in preparation for filling it with coal in the morning. She didn't much like walking on deck while the hatches were open. There were fourteen hatches, each one a rectangle spanning nearly the ship's width. Fall in there while the hold was empty and it was a good thirty feet down to the steel bottom. The coamings that reached up a foot or so around each hatch, built to keep water out or a hapless deckhand from stepping in, also seemed the right height for tripping a poor fellow into his doom.

Like it or not, the hatches would be open to the sky until they departed in the morning. Captain Hanna always left port as soon as the last bit of soft coal—or iron ore, or what have you—landed in the hold, and not a moment later. The deckhands wouldn't begin to close the hatches until the freighter pulled away from the dock.

Sunny gripped the lifeline and walked forward until she reached the ladder, where she climbed down to the supply boat, which, at perhaps sixty feet long, was a child's toy next to the 480-foot straight decker *Titus Brown*. Sunny, like most of the crew, took a certain pride in their boat's massive size— never mind that boats now launched in Lorain and Cleveland were a hundred feet longer! Sunny wasn't the strongest of swimmers, despite her late father's lessons. Nevertheless she'd always felt secure on the *Titus Brown*. She rarely became fearful, even when it pitched and rolled in storms, tossing anything unsecured onto the galley deck.

Sunny stepped into the supply boat's cabin. The captain had the fresh cinnamon waiting for her. As was the custom, he gave her an earful—bits of news and gossip he'd picked up from the many vessels he visited each day. He asked if she'd heard about the death of the mate in Detroit, which of course she had, the worst news always traveling the fastest. Then, in a cheerier voice, he described how some poor workboat captain in Toledo had passed beneath a closed railroad bridge and the superstructure was swept right off his sandsucker dredge.

"No one was hurt, excepting the dredge," the supply boat captain said. "And the captain's pride. Tell you what, if I were that poor soul I couldn't work in Toledo after that. Maybe not anywhere in Lake Erie, the way word travels!"

"And you make sure that word travels fast and far, don't you now?"

The supply boat captain raised his hands in a gesture of innocence. "It's what my customers like, ain't it? The news is free of charge."

Sunny allowed herself the momentary fantasy of messing up so terribly that Herb would insist she left the lakes for good. The temptation lasted only a moment.

After supper that evening Sunny returned to the cabin she and Herb shared on the port side of the boilerhouse. Like the other crew quarters aft, the entrance to their cabin was from an exterior passageway. It had a double berth with a curtain that could be drawn, two porthole windows to let in fresh air, railed shelving for drinking cups and toiletries, a closet, and, because she was the only female crew member, a private washroom. The cabin wasn't big but it was all they needed.

Sunny retrieved an envelope from the drawer beneath her berth. She'd received it a week ago, when the *Titus Brown* passed Detroit on its downbound trip from Duluth. She didn't get much in the way of mail, but each time the *J.W. Westcott* pulled up alongside their moving freighter to deliver bags of mail, laundered table linens, and officers' uniforms, she hoped to receive news of home. It could get dull on the ship, especially with no other women to talk to, and Sunny enjoyed the newsy updates from Agnes, her elder sister by three years.

It was one such letter Sunny had received the week prior, and now she read it a second time. The letter started cheerfully—Agnes's daughter Aimee was thriving at her secretarial school in Detroit; a nice young woman, the sister of the new life-saving station keeper, had joined her china-painting group—and then the tone turned somber. It was Maman. Now that Cordelia had left home to marry Captain Blythe, and Aimee had moved away for school, it fell solely upon Agnes to care for their widowed mother. The problem wasn't Maman's physical ailments. In fact, at fifty-five she was just as strong as she'd been a decade earlier. The problem, as Agnes wrote, although not in so many words, was that Maman drove her batty. Their mother expected Agnes to be at her beck and call, to eat every meal with her, and to run daily errands. Agnes was suffocating under the weight, not only of Maman's expectations, but also her incessant criticism. Agnes apologized for complaining and proposed no particular solution, only mentioning that she would be relieved when December came, when everyone would be together again in Port Austin.

There was nothing Sunny could do for her sister from the deck of the *Titus Brown*. She and Herb sent money to her mother, who lived with Agnes in the cottage where Sunny's father had been raised. Maman and Agnes also took in a boarder or two during the summer tourist season. What Agnes clearly needed—though she wouldn't ask for it directly—was someone to help with Maman.

But what had really gotten Sunny worked up was Agnes's news about the restaurant, the one Sunny had long dreamed of as hers: it had just gone up for sale. Located in the village of Port Austin, next to the hotel, the cozy café had a view of the lake and living quarters upstairs. If Sunny had been waiting for a sign, this was it. Years ago, Agnes had made the offhand remark that Sunny ought to open a restaurant in that location, but they hadn't spoken of it seriously, nor had they referred to it since. And yet in this letter Agnes told Sunny the asking price as if this was something they'd planned together all along. Sunny had saved almost enough to make a good offer. If Captain Hanna was as generous with his bonuses this year as he had been in the past, then she would be able to do it.

Sunny returned the letter to her drawer and began pacing the cabin—from the porthole window to the wall-mounted wash basin and back again. She had been waiting for news like this for a long time. What she hadn't expected was the feeling of dread that came with it: dread at the proposition—newly real—that she must tell Herb she wanted to leave the *Titus Brown* to open a restaurant. Now there were no excuses for not broaching the subject with him, and it terrified her for reasons she couldn't name. As she considered how to lay bare her dreams, dreams she'd kept to herself for so long, the cabin door opened. She stopped pacing and faced her husband. Herb's large frame filled the doorway; he'd been giving direction to Pug, the third cook, on preparations for the night lunch.

"What's troubling you?" Herb asked. "You're twisting your hair again."

Sunny uncoiled the tendrils at her temple from her finger. "It's just the letter from Agnes. I read it again and it's got me in a state."

"Agnes can handle your mother just fine."

"Maybe she can and maybe she can't. Maybe it'll be the death of her."

"Oh come on now, Sunny, don't get angry." Herb, who was six feet tall with a boyish face and wavy red hair, sat on the edge of their bed and removed his shoes. He rubbed his feet.

"The problem is, no matter how much Agnes does, it's never enough. And now with Cordelia married and Aimee moved away, she's all alone with Maman's sharp tongue." It really wasn't fair. Agnes was the kindest-hearted of the three sisters and this was what she got for it. But Sunny was dancing around the real issue. Agnes's happiness was a concern, of course, but Sunny wanted that restaurant whether Agnes needed her back in Port Austin or not.

"I feel sorry for your mother. She's lonely, maybe a little scared of the future. In any case this is between Agnes and her. Don't let your sister draw you into their arguments."

"I should be involved, though, shouldn't I? She's my mother, too, and Agnes needs my help." The scaredy-cat part of her thought she might convince Herb they should go ashore solely for Agnes's sake, and leave her own dreams out of it, for now.

Herb twisted and tilted his head this way and that until it cracked. "We'll be back in Port Austin by the end of the month."

"Yes, but that's only temporary. What will she do come March?"

Herb stared. "You want to go ashore. Is that what you're saying?"

"I just feel bad, that's all," Sunny said, retreating, and mad at herself for doing so. She retreated every time. Why didn't she just tell Herb what she wanted? Wasn't she allowed to want things? Men wanted things all the time—look at Ernie, leaving the *Titus Brown* to start a business like it was nothing! But there was no use having that discussion now. Herb would only tell her why opening a restaurant was a bad idea. He was a steady kind of man, which was one of the things she loved about him. Once he found something that worked, he was loath to change. He would say that sailing was a good living, that starting a business was risky. He would say that she had no experience running a restaurant and that she would lose all the money she'd saved. And if he said all that, she might let herself believe him.

If Sunny was going to convince him, she needed just the right arguments, just the right proof that this was what they should do (for she saw Herb running the restaurant with her). She wouldn't bring it up until she had fully prepared her case, like a lawyer going to court. Nor would she keep putting it off, however. She would tell him on this trip.

"Did you order more coffee mugs?" Her tone was sharper than she'd intended.

"Are we low?"

In his role as steward, Herb, in addition to being head cook and supervising the galley crew, handled all the paperwork, including the ordering of supplies.

"I told you before we left Duluth we barely had enough," Sunny said. "Cleve checked the wheelhouse this afternoon when he was making up the officers' rooms and he found a few but we're gonna have a hard time on this trip with what we've got. You said you were going to order more."

"It wasn't on my list."

She sighed. "Well that's too bad. I swear the officers just throw their empty mugs overboard rather than bother carrying them back to the galley."

"Now, now. The crew is no better."

"Why do you always take the officers' side? They expect you to keep to a certain budget, but do they help at all?"

"I don't take their side, Sunny." He reached for her hand. "The only side I'm on is yours."

Now that she was all worked up he wanted a peace offering. She wasn't feeling peaceful. She was irritated. Irritated at

Herb for being so content with this boat, these lakes, this life. For being the one who got to decide. "It's wasteful, it is. Thousands of years from now archaeologists will find trails of white china mugs, all up and down where the lakes used to be. And Cleve won't be happy. He'll have to wash the ones we do have more often."

Herb shot up from the berth. "Yes, I get it! I made a mistake! Why not toss me overboard and I'll get all those mugs at the bottom of the lake!" He put his shoes back on and said he was going on deck. He must have been really agitated because as he left, the door to the cabin closed ever-so-slightly harder than usual.

Sunny stared at the door. Overcome with a sudden heaviness, she sat on the berth and replayed their conversation in her mind. She hadn't meant to start a fight with Herb, certainly not about coffee mugs, of all things.

Alone in their cabin, Sunny tried to read a *Ladies' Home Journal* by the electric light mounted above their berth. As she skimmed an article on the benefits of a new "no burn" kettle bottom and an "up-to-date" noodle-cutter, cheers erupted outside the boilerhouse. She did her best to ignore the commotion and focus on the magazine, but the words became random and held no meaning and she kept going over the same phrases (*aluminum disk with a row of buttons, twelve sharp cutters in the form of wheels*) again and again. Her thoughts went to Agnes and her chest tightened. At this moment Maman was probably critiquing the way her sister washed the supper dishes. More yelling and clapping on the spar deck. And Herb—he'd taken for granted that she'd join him on this boat, ten years ago now. And at this very moment someone else could be buying *her* restaurant! A flush of heat passed through her body and she unbuttoned the top of her shirtwaist. Nevertheless she shouldn't have yelled at Herb about the mugs like that. The mugs weren't the issue. Tossing the magazine aside, she went to the porthole and slid open the metal cover.

Outside her cabin was the exterior passageway and the riverbank sloping up to the B&O Railroad's coal dock. The ruckus came from forward of the boilerhouse. From the sound of it, the crew was having another one of their wrestling matches. One of the firemen usually won, strong as they were. Then again, the new second watchman was surprisingly nimble and tenacious. Herb was probably watching the match. She ought to find him and apologize. He was such an easygoing man, which made it all the more unsettling when he was upset. Whenever they fought, which wasn't all that often, she always hurried to patch things up so she could be at peace again.

She fixed her hair, which she wore in a simple bun. Herb sometimes called her his "Gibson girl" though his perception of her appearance was surely clouded by affection. While her brown hair was of a substantial fullness and, if she was forced to consider such things, had a pleasing natural curl, she had about as much use for those grand hairstyles as she did for corsets that would mold her own ample curves into someone else's. She swung closed the portal cover and left the cabin.

Herb wasn't in the crowd gathered by the fourteenth hatch, where the second watchman was holding his own against a fireman. Sunny went to the stern. There on the fantail, Herb leaned against the railing, gazing at the Hulett ore unloaders near the mouth of the Black River. The tremendous machines were silent now, each one like a giant arm with its elbow pointed at the sky, a hinged bucket for a hand aimed at the ground.

Sunny stood silently alongside her husband, hoping he would speak first so she'd know by his tone if he'd forgiven her. She was contrite at losing her temper. Herb had done nothing wrong.

"Captain Hanna wants you to bake your gingersnaps," Herb said finally, a second later adding, "for delivery in Detroit."

"Detroit, is it?" Sunny said conspiratorially, for they both knew Captain Hanna had a sweetheart in the city. "You think he's going to propose?"

Herb didn't look at her. "I don't know. It's not my business."

Sunny drew back, chastened by his refusal to gossip. Why was Herb acting so high and mighty? He liked this sort of intrigue as much as she did—he was pretending not to only because he was sore at her. Why, it was just this past summer when Herb told her, as the *Titus Brown* docked overnight in Detroit, how Captain Hanna and his mates went to a ballroom dance where the Old Man foxtrotted with a woman with long red hair. Herb had overheard the mates talking in the dining room the next morning and come straightaway into the galley to tell Sunny.

A month later, Sunny had been asked to bake gingersnaps and box them up for delivery in Detroit. Herb suspected whom they were for, and his suspicions were later confirmed. The galley crew was quietly cheering for the Old Man, who'd been a widower for as long as he'd captained the *Titus Brown*. He never talked about his late wife. In fact, he rarely showed an emotion other than a detached cheerfulness. That he might have found love again was welcome evidence that sometimes life could surprise you for the better.

"I'll bake them tomorrow after breakfast, so they're ready," Sunny said, businesslike. Then, "I hope this lady treats him right. Captain Hanna deserves some happiness."

"I'm certain she will. We redheaded folk love as fiercely as we do faithfully." Herb put his arm around her.

Sunny relaxed into Herb's bulky frame. All was well again. The Black River flickered with moonlight as small waves peaked and flattened. High above the river, a well-defined halo circled the moon. Her stomach stirred.

Herb, who must have noticed her looking, said, "When halos ring the moon or sun—"

"Rain is coming on the run," Sunny finished.

Herb gently squeezed her shoulder.

"I'm sorry, Herb. I don't care about the dratted mugs."

He kissed the top of her head. "Tomorrow I'll telegraph the *Westcott* to bring us more when we reach Detroit."

Cleveland, Ohio

Cordelia Blythe willed the streetcar to move faster. She could picture Edmund now: standing at the *Marguerite's* bow, alternately watching the pier and glancing at his pocket watch, increasingly concerned and maybe even annoyed that she wasn't there. His leaving port on time was more important now than ever and if she made him late—well, it would be a poor start to their honeymoon. She leaned out the window to see if an accident was the cause of their slow pace. Finding none, she sat back in her seat, hopeful she would make it to the dock on time.

Then the streetcar stopped altogether. So did the other streetcars, pedestrians, and horses and buggies crossing the Superior Viaduct on their way downtown. Cordelia's stomach pitted. It would take another five minutes for the bridge's central span to swing open, allowing a waiting steamer to pass, and then swing back into place. If only she hadn't spent so much time this morning on her face and hair. She'd wanted to look pretty for Edmund, so that he'd be pleased to show her off to his crew. Perhaps she was trying too hard to make everything go right. It was just that she had gotten this second chance at happiness, and she didn't want to spoil it. Not keeping to Edmund's schedule, however, was hardly prudent.

Cordelia inhaled deeply, trying to slow her heartbeat. From her perch on the elevated roadbed, she took in the smokestacks rising up from the buildings. The Flats was a jumble of factories and railroad tracks, all of it dusted with a dark red film from the iron ore piled in dunes near the shore. If they sat there much longer, she, too, would be dusted with a dark red film. With a gloved hand she brushed the skirt of her olive travel suit.

Down below, a steamer and barge glided past the viaduct and along the Cuyahoga River toward Lake Erie. Docked just upriver from the viaduct was a grand steamship. Painted in white on its side was the name: *Seeandbee*. So that's what it looked like. Much fuss had been made about this new vessel, the largest passenger steamship on the Great Lakes: five hundred feet long, with four decks and four giant smokestacks in the middle. One of Cordelia's Lakewood neighbors had gone on a *Seeandbee* excursion that summer and it was all the woman talked about. The neighbor spoke breathlessly of the staterooms and parlors finished in mahogany and ivory, of the grand ballroom where a band played. Cordelia had tried not to be envious. Seeing it now, she had to admit it was a dilly of a ship.

Well, her neighbor's husband wasn't a ship's captain, now was he?

At last the bridge's central span swung back into position, and traffic started moving again. She tightened her grip on her valise. This would be the most time she'd ever spent with Edmund. She opened her pocketbook for a peppermint, for her mouth had gone dry. She found one and placed it on her tongue. That was better. There was nothing to be nervous about, really. A romantic adventure: that is what this would be. A chance to get to know Edmund better. There was so much she didn't know.

They crossed the viaduct and continued to Public Square, which was choked with streetcars carrying shoppers and workers. On one corner two ladies held a large sign: VOTES FOR WOMEN. Cordelia alighted from the streetcar. From here it was an easy walk to the pier. She made a quick detour to mail a letter to Maman. Her stomach fluttered. How many times had she watched a lake freighter in the distance from her hometown on the tip of Michigan's Thumb? The silent ships would hover on the horizon, almost like they weren't moving at all. She'd always wondered about the people on board. And now she would be one of them.

Cordelia's late-September elopement with Edmund was the most romantic thing she'd ever done: a courthouse wedding in Cleveland, followed by dinner and a night at the Statler Hotel. She and Edmund had decided then that she wouldn't accompany him on a journey up the lakes until next July, when she'd want to escape the oppressive summer heat blanketing the city. But this past week had been unseasonably warm and the new house was still strange. And, yes, an ignoble part of her wanted to tell her neighbor of her own romantic cruise—one with her husband at the helm. So when Edmund had arrived in Cleveland two days earlier she'd begged to join him on his last trip of the season. He'd hesitated, making some noises about unpredictable November weather, but when Cordelia caressed his cheek and said it would be their honeymoon cruise, he relented.

Now, as she arrived at the pier, the truth of it hit her: There was nothing romantic about the coal loading docks or the freighter itself. What a simp she was, for imagining otherwise. Coal dust hung in the air and a layer of it covered everything: the dock, the lampposts, and the shipping office. The five-hundred-foot freighter, which when out on open water and from a distance of several miles had seemed romantic, elegant even, up close was anything but. The *Marguerite* was a steel beast, its maroon sides scraped and scarred from years of labor. This ship was not her neighbor's luxurious *Seeandbee*.

Yet it was impressive in its own way. Up close, the freighter's size was breathtaking. The *Marguerite* towered over everything around it. If you turned the ship on its bow, Edmund once boasted, it'd be taller than *two* of the city's Rockefeller Buildings stacked one atop the other.

Cordelia crossed the railroad tracks and approached the dock. At both the *Marguerite's* bow and stern stood a tall white structure not unlike a two-story house. Separating the two "houses" was a long, flat expanse of deck where the holds were now being filled with coal. On the dock next to the *Marguerite*, a coal hopper car was pushed up an incline, lifted and then turned sideways. The car dumped its load into a large, funnel-shaped pan. The coal slid down the pan, passed through a chute and fell into the ship's hold.

Edmund appeared on the bow. He waved to her and then climbed down a ladder on the side of the ship. Of course he'd known precisely when she'd arrive.

"Oh Edmund," Cordelia said, after kissing him on the cheek, "It's going to be wonderful, isn't it? The weather is beautiful and I simply cannot wait to be out on the water. We're going to have a marvelous time." If she sounded like she was trying to convince herself, maybe Edmund wouldn't notice.

Her husband smiled and said he hoped the voyage would be everything she wished for.

"I'm certain of it! I know you have to work, too, and I've brought some books so you needn't worry about keeping me entertained the whole time. I have the latest Edith Wharton novel, although after *Ethan Frome* and the way it ended, oh it was too terrible to contemplate, but I have others, a short story collection and a Willa Cather—" She was prattling on again.

Maman would have scolded her. "What I mean to say is, I'm looking forward to our adventure."

Edmund nodded, then took her valise and motioned for her to follow him. It would be nice if he were a little more effusive, if he'd said how happy he was that she had joined him. It was their honeymoon cruise, after all. He didn't think she was in the way, did he? What, exactly, *was* he thinking? Clearly she had her work cut out for her: getting to know a man of this much reserve would not be so simple.

Edmund, having started for the ladder, stopped and turned back to where Cordelia stood, unmoving, her gaze fixed on the ship. The narrow ladder stretched up the freighter's straight steel side. She was going to have to climb that.

He gestured for her to go first, adding, "It's best if you don't look down."

The ship was flush against the dock. Cordelia stepped onto the first rung and began climbing. Her skirt, which reached down to her kid leather shoes, blew in the shore breeze. When she was about halfway up, the wind gusted and the cables holding the ship to the dock moaned and pulled. She felt the ship move away from the dock a little. And though she hadn't meant to, she glanced down and saw that where the ship had once touched the dock there now was a strip of dark water between. If she fell at that moment there would be no saving her.

Cordelia felt a rising panic as she saw herself falling into that band of water. Feeling somewhat outside of herself she continued, hand over hand, until she reached the top of the ladder and the metal grated landing on the other side.

Clasping the railing, she watched as Edmund climbed the ladder with only one hand, the other holding her valise. Though his chest and arms were muscular and thick, his movements were nimble as a dancer's. In one swift movement he was over the side and on the deck. He put his arm around her waist, and she took that to mean he was glad she was there. She lay her head against his shoulder. Being next to him made her feel safe. Secure. This, then, was the stability she'd long been seeking. She had done the right thing in marrying him—it hadn't been an impulsive, foolishly romantic decision as Sunny had said, an assessment with which Agnes no doubt agreed in her own quiet way. Maybe they thought she should have spent more time in mourning. Cordelia meant no disrespect to her late fiancé; she still loved Lewis and mourned his passing. She was just no good at being alone. Impulsive decision or not, Edmund would not regret marrying her; she would see to that. Even her sisters would notice the depths of her devotion.

Edmund led her to the forecastle at the bow. It had three levels. They climbed a flight of stairs to the second level, where he said his living quarters were located. They were about to go inside when a man descended the steps from the level above.

"May I have a word, Captain?" the man asked Edmund. He nodded at Cordelia.

"You must be Richard," Cordelia said, immediately hoping she hadn't made a mistake. Edmund had spoken fondly of one of his wheelsmen, a man from Sarnia, Ontario, whose people lived on the reserve near Parry Sound. But maybe there was more than one Ojibwe officer aboard. "I'm Cordelia Blythe."

"Mrs. Blythe," he said, offering a slight bow. "It's a pleasure to meet the woman who's put a smile on the captain's face."

Cordelia, pleased by Richard's comment and determined not to be in the way, excused herself so the men could talk. She walked to the railing and looked aft. Deckhands were moving the coal chute from one rectangular opening in the deck to another. There were twenty-four such openings in the long, straight deck. A coal car emptied its contents into the chute and then returned to the track upright. With a clang the next coal-filled car slammed into it, pushing the empty hopper car down the far side of the incline where it banged into a string of empty cars on a siding.

After a minute Edmund returned to her, having learned from Richard that the second mate had taken ill. The third mate, a man named Mack, would help cover his shift. Edmund led her inside to his small suite of rooms. Decorated in gold and green, his quarters were more elegant than Cordelia had expected, given the ship's no-frills exterior. She felt herself relax a little. The bathroom was paneled in dark wood and had a clawfoot tub and a checkerboard-tiled floor. In the bedroom, floral curtains hanging by the double berth could be drawn for privacy. There were two drawers under the berth, one of which Edmund had emptied for her use. There was also a locker where she could hang her suit and stow her valise.

Next to the bedroom was Edmund's office, which had a chart-case and desk built into the woodwork. An electric light hung above it and daylight came in through the full square window. A stairway led directly from the office to the wheelhouse above. Curious, Cordelia started up the steps, but Edmund stopped her. He said he'd take her to the wheelhouse when he returned from the shipping office next door, where he needed to sign some papers.

"Edmund," Cordelia said as he took his leave.

Her husband stopped at the door.

"Do you have to go right away?" she asked, immediately wishing she hadn't.

"If I'm late departing, I'll have to make up the time at sea."

"Of course." She'd only wanted to show her affection for him, but she should have realized he would be more worried about the time. He'd had some trouble with late arrivals that year and the shipping bosses would be paying close attention. He didn't want to lose his position on the *Marguerite*. She would stay out of his way. She'd convinced him to let her come on the *Marguerite* and she didn't want to give him any reason to think her a nuisance. On the contrary, she would make things easier for him. Somehow. She ran her hand down the thick curtain tied back from the berth and, before she could stop herself, said, "But you're glad I came?"

Edmund came to her and put his arms around her waist. "I'm glad you wanted to come. I just hope you aren't bored. I'm rather a dull fellow."

"You are not." She gazed up at him with a smile she hoped was reassuring. "You're a Great Lakes captain. The handsomest on all the lakes. You could never be boring. And besides," she added cheekily, "I've always wanted to see Duluth."

He kissed her forehead and left her to unpack.

Cordelia drew herself a bath in the clawfoot tub. She would feel better once she'd washed off the coal dust that had settled everywhere. Sometime tomorrow, Edmund had said, they'd pass Port Austin. But they'd be miles from shore, and while she might be able to see the shoreline, she likely wouldn't be close enough to make out the lakeside cottage where her mother and Agnes lived. Even so, she'd asked him to tell her when they passed, so she could wave.

After she'd been soaking in the bath a while, there came from outside a series of whistles and shouts. There was a high-pitched whistle from farther away—the tug, coming to take them out of the harbor. Cordelia closed her eyes and lay back against the edge of the tub.

Sometime later the ship rumbled with the start of its engine. A whistle blasted three times, low and deep. Cordelia dressed and went out on deck. The freighter had cleared the breakwater and was on open water. The deckhands were closing the hatch covers, which were made of metal and, when opened, folded onto themselves like a telescope.

Her adventure had begun at last. The Lake Erie shoreline west of downtown Cleveland was thick with oaks and maples and elms, all mostly bare now that it was early November. The warm breeze carried with it the scent of burning leaves. It was good to be moving again. Her ever-present restlessness began to quiet. The trees grew smaller as the freighter moved away from the land. The shore became a thin line between sky and lake. Almost nothing at all.

Port Austin, Michigan

Agnes Inby's fellow hobbyists sat around the table, their heads bent over their bread and butter plates as they painted the wild rose design from a yellowing issue of *The China Decorator*. The group included the organist at the Presbyterian Church, Agnes's next-door neighbor (a widow like herself), and Lizzie Duncan, a young woman new in town.

The scent of lavender oil hung in the air. While she liked the lavender, Agnes would have much preferred to open a window to let in the warm Lake Huron breeze. But she had to be careful about dust. As it was she'd removed the curtains and rugs from her small studio, a former bedroom, so there'd be fewer places for particles of lint and dirt to collect. Painted china took a while to dry, and the less dust settling on a piece before it was fired, the better the results.

Having finished her piece, Agnes turned away from the window and watched the others. Lizzie was painting the stem on her fifth rose. For having started only six weeks ago, she was quite adept. A long curl of auburn hair fell from its pin into Lizzie's line of vision and she blew it away, only to have it return. The young woman tucked the hair behind her ear with the end of her brush without lifting her gaze from the plate. How beautiful she was.

Lizzie glanced up from her work. Agnes averted her gaze.

"What color do I paint the shadows?" It was the organist.

Agnes, grateful for the diversion, said in her teacher voice, "That's a good question." As the most experienced she was the group's de facto leader. Though quiet by nature, when it came to china painting, she could talk the bark off a tree. "For shadow work I prefer the pearl grey, with a small amount of black mixed with it. You'll want to lay the color close to the flowers and leaves—copy the shadows in the design. Then you'll soften the edges. If you do it right it will be difficult to distinguish where the shadow ends and the white of the china begins."

An hour later, the women finished painting their plates and left them on the table. Agnes promised to have the china fired by the following week's session. She had her own kiln here in the cottage she shared with Maman. Shortly after Amos died there'd been an ad in the *Port Austin News* offering the kiln for next to nothing, the previous owner requiring only that the buyer be able to remove the beastly thing from his property. Agnes had enlisted the muscle of the local life-saving crew, who'd been more than willing to help a fellow surfman's widow.

The pale-yellow, two-story cottage where she and her mother lived was perched atop a small slope. The front door opened up into one largish room, which Maman called the parlor. Opposite the front door, along the parlor's far wall and at the center of the cottage, a black woodstove sat on a semicircular brick hearth. With the help of vents cut into the second-level floor, the woodstove heated the four upstairs bedrooms in winter. In the summer they rented the spare bedroom and the sleeping porch upstairs to vacationers visiting the lake.

The next-door neighbor and the organist donned their hats as Agnes walked them to the front door. When she'd closed the door behind them, she turned to Lizzie.

"To the skiff!" Lizzie said, her eyes sparkling.

Maman called from the kitchen, which occupied the back of the house on the main level. "You're going all the way to the station? You're still planning to help me refresh the feather pillows this afternoon, I hope?"

"Yes, Maman. Of course."

"It's a difficult job for one person," Maman said. "Cordelia always helped me with it. I think she rather liked doing it."

Agnes rolled her eyes and Lizzie stifled a giggle. Lizzie, only twenty-three, reminded Agnes how it felt to be youthful in a way that her own eighteen-year-old daughter Aimee somehow did not. "There'll be plenty of time before supper," Agnes said. Then, smiling at Lizzie and repeating her words, "To the skiff!"

Years ago Agnes and her husband had built the skiff so she could take Aimee fishing on summer weekends as well as access those hard-to-reach areas along the shore in her search for shipwreck treasure. Now it rested on a strip of sandy beach at the edge of the sparsely wooded backyard, the yard stretching two hundred feet from the kitchen door to the water's edge. Agnes pulled the small wooden boat into the shallowest water and Lizzie got in, holding Agnes's hand to steady herself. Agnes pushed the skiff a little further into the lake, wetting her boots past the ankle, and climbed in, deftly adjusting for its rocking under her large frame. She was tall for a woman, and strong. Her late husband Amos had called her, affectionately, his "sturdy gal."

Agnes handed Lizzie a cork life belt. Then, anticipating her objections, "We don't leave until we're both wearing one. You do know my father used to be the keeper?" Agnes's father had retired from the U.S. Life-Saving Service in 1906, months later dying of pneumonia during a grippe outbreak. The man who'd replaced him seven years ago had transferred to Grand Haven this past spring, prompting the Duncans' arrival.

"Yes," Lizzie said, teasing, "you do like to remind me." The young woman had arrived in town six months earlier with her mother and her brother Elzie, the new keeper of the Port Austin Life-Saving Station. Lizzie claimed her brother couldn't marry her off in Marquette and so he'd had to bring her along. The way Lizzie said this was not from a place of old maid shame, but pride, like she had avoided something dreadful. Lizzie's widowed mother, along with Lizzie, fulfilled the role of keeper's wife—namely, cooking for the bachelors among the eight-man crew and cleaning the main living quarters.

From Agnes's house to the life-saving station it was an easy trip by boat, less than two miles east along the shore, which, from Port Austin to the Pointe Aux Barques resort, was one long rock outcropping. The area was called Pointe Aux Barques, or "Point of little boats," by early French explorers either because the rocks resembled boats' prows or because large boats ought not to venture there, depending on whom you asked.

Agnes rowed her skiff through the water. Mere feet beneath the surface lay a tremendous reef, which extended more than a mile from the shore and came dangerously close to the surface. There were places where on calm days you could get out of your boat a mile from shore and stand on the reef and the water barely reached your knees.

A lighthouse marked the spot where the rocky reef ended, beyond which, ships could safely approach Saginaw Bay. The Port Austin Reef Lighthouse sat on a massive octagonal block of concrete that rose thirty feet from the water. It was a castle on its own island. Agnes loved that lighthouse, but even without it, she knew every bit of the reef.

"I couldn't live anywhere but near the water like this," Lizzie said. "When I go inland, it's like I can't breathe."

Lizzie had a way, Agnes had discovered these past weeks, of putting into words things she herself had long thought, but had never given voice to. Agnes had lived here by the lake all her life, and except for one week she'd spent in Detroit, taking classes from a china painting professional after Amos died, had never been anywhere else. As much as she'd loved the instruction, being away from Port Austin had dispirited her. At the time she'd chalked up her melancholy to missing her family, but maybe it was the water, too.

No matter how long Agnes looked at the lake she could never absorb all its beauty. Canada's shoreline was only sixty miles to the east, and Tawas City across the entrance to Saginaw Bay was twenty-five miles to the west, but from her kitchen window Lake Huron seemed to have the expanse of an ocean. *"La Mer Douce,"* or "The Sweetwater Sea," those French explorers had called it. Agnes's daughter wasn't similarly affected by its grandeur. Aimee couldn't leave Port Austin fast enough and had gone to Detroit months ago to attend secretarial school. Agnes missed her so much sometimes it hurt, as if a piece of Agnes's heart had been torn from her chest, leaving in its place a dull ache.

Lizzie was chattering about a surfman whom her brother had dismissed the day before, for drunkenness. It was hard finding qualified men for the service, Lizzie was saying. Agnes knew this all too well, remembering her father's lamentations. The work was dangerous, the pay small, a pension nonexistent. It wasn't ideal to be short a regular man. Volunteers and temporary men were often untrained and undisciplined. But you couldn't have a man who got drunk or who didn't respect the keeper's authority.

Lizzie talked and Agnes rowed and the warm breeze blew across the lake and through her hair. A wave of happiness washed over Agnes. She didn't want to reach the station, not ever. The lake, this breeze, Lizzie's company: this was everything. Lizzie's youthful enthusiasms had brought a new lightness to her days. Perhaps Agnes had been lonelier than she'd realized since her daughter moved away and Cordelia eloped to Cleveland.

"So what's next for Agnes Inby?" Lizzie grinned playfully at her.

Startled by the directness of the question, Agnes looked away. "What do you mean, next?"

"Your daughter is grown now and moved away, and as a widow you have freedom...I mean no disrespect to your late husband, of course."

Freedom? Agnes never thought of her life in that way. Lizzie was being almost impertinent. "I take care of my mother. I have my job at the store. And my china painting." What more did Lizzie want?

"Yes but what *else* do you want to do? What's your idea of heaven?" The way Lizzie smiled at her, it was like she dared Agnes to answer the question.

"My idea of...? I don't know, Lizzie. What a question!" Agnes said, a little irritated she didn't have a satisfactory answer. She had familial obligations, that's what she had. It's what she'd always had. Growing up there'd been little Cordelia to take care of, and then her husband Amos, and then her daughter, and now Maman. That she might have a dream she could simply think up and then go do, as simple as that sounded, had not occurred to her. "What's *your* idea of heaven?" Agnes countered, wanting the attention off her.

Lizzie gestured toward the open water, ready with an answer. "To sail the Great Lakes and write about everything I see and everyone I meet."

Agnes harrumphed. "You'll need a boat first."

Lizzie smiled. "All in good time. For now I can write about what I see from Port Austin."

Agnes quietly marveled about Lizzie's confidence as they approached Turnip Rock, which marked the entrance into Alaska Bay. The giant rock was wide at the top and narrow at the bottom where the waves had worn it thinner. Trees grew on its top like turnip greens. Agnes rowed past Turnip Rock and into Alaska Bay, around which was nestled the Pointe Aux Barques summer resort community. The Port Austin Life-Saving Station was situated within the small bay in part for its proximity to the resort's sunbathers, boat rowers, and rock-outcropping explorers, who from time to time required the lifesavers' assistance.

Whenever Agnes approached the station, with its cedar shingles and steeply pitched roof, it was like coming home again. For fourteen years she had lived here with Amos, her surfman husband, in one of the station's cottages, and before that she'd lived at the station at Burnt Cabin Point. Station life was all she'd known until Amos died three years ago, and it was strange to be removed from it.

There were two main buildings, several outbuildings, and a few cottages. Closest to the shore was the one-and-a-half-story boathouse. Two sets of large double doors opened to launching rails that ran from inside the boathouse down to the water. On the peak of the boathouse roof was a small open lookout deck where a surfman was always on duty.

Agnes rowed the skiff up to the pier that extended alongside the launching rails.

"Mrs. Inby," Keeper Duncan called from the boathouse. One set of double doors was open to reveal the *Stalwart*, the thirty-four-foot lifeboat. Like his crew, Keeper Duncan wore a blue flannel uniform shirt and trousers, and a cap with U.S. Life-Saving Service on the band. "It's good to see you on this beautiful day."

"Thank you, Keeper Duncan."

"Call me Elzie," he said, approaching them.

"I do cherish days like this in November," Agnes said as she tied the boat to the pier, using preoccupation with the line to avoid inviting Keeper Duncan to address her more informally. She liked Keeper Duncan, but in his attentions she sensed a question, a need, and despite Maman's prodding she hesitated to encourage the familiarity. "It's like getting extra days to your life."

"Well put." He extended a hand to help his sister from the skiff. "We're setting up for our breeches buoy drill. The men don't think they need practicing this late in the season, but it is Thursday and Thursdays we drill. I'm afraid the warm weather has put them in a summer mood and they'd rather be fishing."

"I can't fault them. There's nothing like fresh lake trout," Agnes said.

"Won't you stay and watch?" Keeper Duncan asked. "If you like, you could be our damsel in distress."

"Oh please, Elzie," Lizzie said, stepping onto the pier. "Agnes is no damsel in distress."

Agnes glanced from Lizzie to Keeper Duncan. It was a beautiful day, and suddenly she felt as expansive as this great lake, and despite cherishing her time alone she now wanted to be around people. Maman's feather-pillow refreshing could wait. "I'd be happy to help."

Agnes followed the Duncan siblings along the pier to the boathouse, beyond which, connected by a breezeway, was a two-story building with a kitchen and mess room, as well as living quarters for the keeper and the unmarried surfmen. Beyond that lay a grassy lawn where the surfmen were gathered, as well as a small crowd of onlookers. Lizzie and her mother lived in one of the cottages surrounding the lawn.

"Keeper Duncan could steer his way through a chicken coop without ruffling a feather," one of the younger surfmen was telling a bystander. Agnes smiled to herself. She'd heard the talk. In his short time at the station, Keeper Duncan had earned a reputation for his skill at the steering oar. Rowing was one thing, but to be able to read the waves, to steer around a cresting breaker or quickly maneuver to avoid debris—that took a unique talent.

Agnes counted six surfmen. There ought to be seven men practicing the drill; that plus the one in the watchtower would make a full crew of eight. It took eight oarsmen to row the lifeboat while the keeper steered. Someone was missing. What was it Lizzie had said? Keeper Duncan had dismissed a man for drunkenness. It was a bad time of year to be shorthanded.

The keeper ordered his crew to begin. A hundred yards away stood a raised platform attached to a tall pole, meant to replicate a ship's mast. Closer to her, the surfmen removed a rope from a box. They attached this to a projectile which they then put into the Lyle gun. A surfman shouted a warning, Agnes covered her ears, and then out blasted the projectile, which pulled the shot line all the way to the raised platform. A surfman attached the line to the pole at the center of the platform and motioned for Agnes to climb up. She hurried to the ladder as the other surfmen pulled on the line to make it taut.

In the summer months, Port Austin locals as well as vacationers from the resort would come and watch these drills. The surfmen often picked a pretty girl to play the shipwreck victim. Growing up, Agnes had never been allowed to participate. Maman said it was unladylike. And so Agnes had done it only once before, when she was newly married to Amos. She'd found it so invigorating, she was sorry she'd never ridden in the breeches buoy before.

Upon reaching the platform she climbed up and waited with the surfman. Along the line came the aptly named breeches buoy: a pair of trousers sewn to a life preserver.

Had she been wearing trousers herself, she would have put her legs into the breeches buoy trouser legs and held on to the preserver, which would have come up to her underarms. Wearing a skirt, however, she could not do this as it would expose her legs. So she sat on the preserver and put only her feet and calves through one of the trouser legs. This did reveal her ankles, but so be it. Lizzie waved to her, smiling. Agnes grabbed the rope that connected the life preserver to the cable above and waited. The surfmen on the ground pulled on the rope and she moved off the platform and out over the imaginary water. Even though all eyes were on her and she typically didn't like to be the center of attention, she couldn't help but smile and laugh as she rode the line to the imaginary shore. It was as fun as she remembered.

The breeches buoy came to the end of the line. Keeper Duncan held the life preserver steady while Agnes pulled one foot out of the trouser leg, then the other, and then swung both legs over the preserver. As Agnes found her footing, Lizzie put her hand gently under Agnes's arm to steady her. It had been years since anyone had touched her with such tenderness. Quite without warning the sensation brought tears to her eyes and she quickly wiped them away. How embarrassing, to be a lonely widow reduced to such sentimentality! When Lizzie asked if anything was the matter she mumbled something about sand.

Agnes was approaching her skiff to return home when quick footfalls sounded on the pier behind her. They weren't light enough to come from Lizzie, and as she turned around Keeper Duncan slowed his pace.

"Agnes," he said, catching his breath as he reached her. "I just had an idea. Why don't you come back tomorrow, for a fish fry? The weather's supposed to be good for one more day and I plan to let the men go fishing in the morning. I'm sure they'll catch enough to feed us all and then some."

Agnes considered the invitation. She did love a fish fry, and Lizzie would be there. On the other hand, this sounded almost like a date, and she did not want a date.

Perhaps sensing her hesitation, Keeper Duncan added quickly, "Bring your mother, too."

Maman's presence would surely quash any romantic overtones. Agnes's shift at Bisbee's, the dry goods and grocery in the village, ended at four. "Thank you for the invitation. We'll do our best to come."

Keeper Duncan smiled, a little too broadly for her liking, but she let him help her into her skiff all the same.

It was nearly half past three when Agnes arrived back at the cottage.

"I thought you'd forgotten about me." Maman sat at the kitchen table, sewing something onto the corner of an empty pillowcase.

"I didn't forget." Agnes sat across from her mother. On the table lay that day's newspaper, opened to an article on household hints (how to fix jam that had become hard and sugary; how to bake potatoes quickly; how to remove fruit stains from tablecloths). No doubt it was left there for Agnes's edification. "What are you sewing?"

"These are loops. What took you so long?"

"They needed my help."

"With what?" Maman asked without looking up.

"The breeches buoy drill." Agnes skimmed the newspaper article on domestic tips, then turned the page. There was an article about Niagara Falls. She'd long been fascinated by the falls, which was where lakes Superior, Michigan, Huron, and Erie all flowed, and made a note to read the paragraphs later. She turned to the local weather observer's forecast. "Maman, why are you sewing loops onto the corners of the pillowcases?"

"They could have found somebody else. I'm surprised they didn't have Lizzie do it. She's young and pretty. Fetch me the high chair from the cellar, would you please."

Warmer temperatures continue Friday. Snow or rain and colder, Saturday, with west to southwest winds. Sunday, unsettled. "First tell me what you're doing. We've been invited to a fish fry at the station tomorrow."

Now Maman looked up. "I knew Keeper Duncan had his eye on you. If you play your cards right you could be a keeper's wife yourself."

"I don't think—"

"Keep in mind, however, you don't want to appear desperate. He knows you were widowed years ago and men don't like feeling hunted. Maybe it's better we stay home."

"I'm not hunting anyone. And it was Keeper Duncan who asked for help with the drill. I didn't offer."

"Well that's good. Just don't be too quick to accept every invitation." Maman looked up from her sewing. "You're still a handsome woman. Although you are getting lines around your mouth. I guess it's to be expected at thirty-seven years."

"Thirty-six." Her birthday was two months away and there was no need to round up.

"I was about your age when I got those same lines. I may have been closer to forty, but you spend more time in the sun. You ought to wear a hat with a wider brim."

Agnes felt the skin at the sides of her mouth. "I'm sorry I was late. I can help you now. What do you need the high chair for?"

"I've figured out a way to manage this myself. I'll turn the chair upside down—this box here will steady it—and then I'll fasten these loops to the nails I'm going to drive into the bottom of the legs. That'll hold the pillowcases open."

"You don't need to do all that. I'm here now. I can hold the pillowcases open."

Maman ignored this. She set down her needle and lifted a sliver of soap. "I found this in the waste bin in the bathroom."

"It's too small to use."

Maman shook her head. "You can make a new cake of soap with it. Save these small pieces, put them in a cup. When the cup is full you add a little water and boil them for a few minutes. When it's cooled a little, you press it in your hands and you have a new cake of soap. I've taught you better."

Agnes's chest tightened, as it often did during these conversations. "You certainly have."

"Then you shouldn't be tossing these away. No sense wasting good soap. Sunday Marie wouldn't waste it, that's certain. Here. Find a cup for it." Maman was the only one who didn't call Sunny by her nickname. (Born on a Sunday, Sunny had almost been named *Dimanche*, their mother's pride in her

French heritage being what it was, but their father had put his foot down.)

Agnes took the sliver of soap from her mother's hands, found a cup, and dropped the tiny piece in. She inhaled deeply, filling her lungs with air to push out the tightness. No, it wasn't good to be wasteful, she acknowledged with a pang of guilt (another deep inhalation), and yet this was a lot of effort when she could get cakes of soap at a discount at Bisbee's. No matter how hard she tried to please Maman, to do what was expected of her, she so often missed the mark. Just once she'd like to hear her mother say Agnes was a good daughter. That she was loved and that she was *enough*.

FRIDAY & SATURDAY
November 7–8, 1913

Lake Erie

Sunny was by necessity an early riser. As second cook she was responsible not only for the salads, breads, and desserts served at dinner and supper, but also the entirety of breakfast. Friday morning she'd risen well before dawn to make the snap doodle bread. She'd mixed the wheat flour, sugar, baking powder and salt; added the milk and eggs; and then, after pouring it all into bread pans, sprinkled the tops with brown sugar and cinnamon and dotted them with pats of butter. The galley smelled of cinnamon as the loaves baked. In the officers' dining room an hour later, Captain Hànna had been duly appreciative. By the time he finished his eggs and bacon, Sunny had put the gingersnaps he'd requested into the oven. They'd be cooled and boxed well before the *Titus Brown* reached Detroit in the evening.

The breakfast dishes from the mess room and officers' dining room had been cleared and washed before the coal loading had begun, and for that Sunny was grateful. Once that loud and messy business started up, the air on deck filled with clouds of black dust. Even in the galley, you could wipe a plate clean only to have a fine layer of black dust coat it before you could put it away. It had taken several hours for nearly ten thousand tons of coal to fill the cargo hold, plus another three hundred tons in the bunker to fuel the engine.

Cleve was refilling the salt shakers—adding a pinch of cornstarch to prevent clumping—when Sunny poured herself a cup of coffee and went to the spar deck, as she liked to do when the *Titus Brown* left harbor. She sipped her coffee and prepared to watch the Ohio coast retreat once again. In her early years of sailing, there'd been a feeling Sunny would get, upon the sounding of the steam whistles and the moving away from shore, a feeling that earthly concerns could be left behind, that she was unreachable for a time from all those cares and struggles that burdened the people on land. It was almost impossible now to call up that feeling. She could only remember that she'd had it, once.

The straight deck freighter approached Lake Erie from the Black River. At the river's mouth they passed the Lorain Life-Saving Station, where storm signals had been raised. Evidently the weather observers were expecting a storm of marked violence, so said the square red flag with black center. The red triangular pennant indicated the winds would blow from the southwest.

A storm would make her work more difficult, but they rarely got through a November without some foul weather. It would mean several trying hours of preparing meals in a galley where horizontal surfaces refused to stay horizontal. The *Titus Brown* itself was a strong and sturdy ship, and Captain Hanna had made sure the vessel was prepared for foul weather. Coal was loaded flush to the hatch coamings so it wouldn't shift in heavy seas and tarpaulins protected the hatch covers, which were a weak point on straight deckers. There were so many hatches, and whether you had the old, heavy, wood covers or the newer metal telescoping ones, water could find a way into the hold if they weren't properly covered.

Sunny finished her coffee and returned to the galley. It was time to get the noonday dinner started. And if a storm was coming in the next twenty-four hours, she ought to get ahead of things.

It was late afternoon when the *Titus Brown* approached the mouth of the Detroit River at Lake Erie's western end. The galley windows were open to let in a breeze that, along with the bright blue sky, might have fooled the crew into thinking it was summertime. Sunny was preparing a celery, nut, and pepper salad. The crew would sup on their way up the river toward Detroit and Lake St. Clair. Ernie, the assistant engineer who'd gone ashore in Lorain, was probably home with his wife and children by now. Was his wife upset with him for leaving wages on the table? Or was she relieved to have him home early? The rest of the *Titus Brown's* crew would spend Thanksgiving on the lakes.

Sunny was chopping celery for the evening's salad when there was a great scraping sound and she lost her balance. She fell forward, catching herself on the edge of the counter as it pressed into her stomach. Her body tingled in a rush of alarm. Bits of celery had scattered and several stalks had rolled onto the deck. She'd nearly cut her finger with the knife. "What the blue blazes?" Out the galley window there was only calm Lake Erie and clear sky as far as she could see. There was no shouting, no distress whistle. Her heartbeat returned to normal. From the sound of it, they'd hit a sandbar, a highly unusual occurrence for Captain Hanna.

Cleve, who'd been coming from the pantry, had braced himself in the doorway. He picked up the celery she'd dropped and the two of them went onto the spar deck. To the north was the mouth of the Detroit River. Sunny could just make out Grosse Ile. Michigan lay to the west, Ontario to the east.

"I can't believe it," Sunny said. "How on earth did the Old Man hit a sandbar?"

"Probably a seiche," Cleve said after a minute.

Cleve knew everything about the lakes. The grandson of a stevedore who'd found work on the Ohio River after escaping slavery in Kentucky, Cleve was born in Cleveland, named after his birthplace, and raised on the docks. He'd spent all his twenty-two years around ships and the lakes and knew something about everything. First as a dockworker, then a deckhand, and now as a porter, he learned everything he could on the job, and during his time off could be found with a book in his hand, always something to do with the maritime business or Great Lakes history. If Captain Hanna were as smart and broad-minded as she suspected, he'd promote Cleve out of the galley and make him an officer. Though Cleve didn't talk to her about his aspirations, with his knowledge and temperament it wasn't hard to picture him as a mate or wheelsman.

"A seiche. You think so?" Sunny said, even though Cleve was certainly right.

"I'd bet on it. The Old Man knows these channels well. He wouldn't fetch up bottom at the mouth of the Detroit River if there wasn't something else going on."

"Why'd we stop?" The newest deckhand, a tall young man whom the bosun called Stilts (everyone else following suit) because of his height and his long, thin legs, had come out of the boilerhouse. He was a sweet young man who gave everyone the benefit of the doubt. When his cabin mate, an indolent boy related to the ship's owner and bound for college in the spring, showed up late to meals, the bosun always chided him. Stilts would come to the defense of his cabin mate, whom the bosun nicknamed Harvard (though he was to attend Ohio State). "Better late than never," Stilts would say cheerfully. Sunny admired Stilts's magnanimity. The bosun, unimpressed, would retort, "But better never late."

"A seiche, see? It's caused a temporary grounding," Cleve said now.

"A satiate?"

"Seiche," Cleve repeated. Then, when Stilts looked perplexed, "Picture Lake Erie like a giant bathtub. The southwesterly winds are blowing the water from this end of the lake all the way to the eastern end. Which means in Buffalo right about now they're dealing with some high water."

"But in a bathtub the water would slosh back and forth," Stilts said.

"It'll oscillate here, too. It just takes longer."

The second mate walked aft along the deck, stopping every so often to peer over the side. When he reached Sunny and Cleve, he echoed Cleve's speculation. When Sunny asked what Captain Hanna planned to do, the mate said they'd wait for the water to rebound to this end of the lake and lift them off the sandbar. It could take a few hours, he said. Captain Hanna wouldn't be happy about the delay, but at least there appeared to be no damage to the hull.

A bumboat pulled up alongside the *Titus Brown* as if it had been expecting them. Roughly the size of the supply ship where Sunny had gotten her cinnamon the day before, the bumboat drafted fewer feet and didn't get stuck in the lake's sandy bottom despite the low water level.

"Now that's good timing," said an oiler coming out of the boilerhouse, red-faced and sweaty. It was his job to ensure the engine ran properly, touching certain parts of the massive triple-expansion engine at regular intervals to check for overheating. He swung his leg over the side of the ship where a ladder had just been hung.

Stilts, who watched the oiler climb down to the bumboat, asked the second mate if there was anything he needed done.

"Go change light bulbs," the mate said.

"Which ones?"

The mate laughed.

"None of them," Cleve said.

Stilts gave them both a puzzled look.

"Go on down to the bumboat," Sunny said, feeling sorry for Stilts. He was too easy a target for the men to make such sport of it. "He's got nothing for you to do right now, and he wants you out of sight until he does."

Stilts looked to the mate, then back to Cleve, and then followed the oiler down the ladder to the bumboat.

Cleve returned to the galley while Sunny remained on the spar deck, the letter from Agnes tucked in her skirt pocket. A wild idea struck her. If she went down to the bumboat, she could hitch a ride to shore and take the train to Port Austin. She could make an offer on the restaurant, if not tonight, then in the morning.

She snickered at the ridiculous thought.

Back in the galley, Herb was breading yellow perch. Sunny resumed her celery chopping, halfheartedly. "Herb," she began. "I know we don't really believe in this sort of thing"—Herb was not the spiritual sort—"but what if this grounding happened for a reason? What if it's a sign?"

"A sign?" He was giving her that look. That look that said she was talking nonsense.

She would ignore it. "Well, first there was Ernie all of a sudden deciding it was time to go ashore. Now here we are, not far from Detroit—his hometown—and we've fetched up bottom."

"Could be it's a sign we've slowed down so that he can get back on the ship."

"You know that's not what I meant." Sunny ripped a celery rib from its stalk. "There's also the letter from Agnes—she wants me home. And the moon had a halo last night."

"Ah, I see. These signs are meant for you."

"Herb, what if I'm supposed to get off this ship? You know I never meant to do this for so long. Not for ten years!" Ernie's departure, the halo, the seiche; these were signs she should return to Port Austin immediately and start making her dream a reality. Especially now that the lakeside restaurant was up for sale.

"What if staying on the *Titus Brown* is exactly what you were meant to do?" Herb countered. "Maybe that's why we were never given children, so we could always sail the lakes together."

"Oh Herb, you have an answer for everything. It's a wonder you weren't a college boy."

Herb wiped his hands on his apron and pointed at her. "Sunday Marie, if you want to leave me and get off this boat so darn bad then why don't you go ahead and do it?"

Sunny set her knife on the counter. "All right then I will. You tell the Old Man for me."

"Tell him yourself."

She needed a moment away from Herb, given how annoyed she was with him right now. The man had an answer for everything! He knew she wasn't going to just walk off the *Titus Brown* and leave him there. A childish part of her wanted him to think she might. She marched out of the galley and along the exterior passageway to their cabin. As she opened the cabin door an idea struck her, sending a rush of excitement through her body. She found a piece of paper, wrote a note to Agnes, and took some money she kept in the locked box behind their life belts. She tucked both money and letter in an envelope. The bumboat captain could mail it.

Moving quickly, Sunny descended the ladder to the bumboat, which had a wide, flat stern and tall sides that reached up to cabin height. Portholes dotted the sides, letting in light to the floating store inside. A sign near the door said "Friendly Boyce, the Sailor's Choice!"

The oiler and Stilts were smoking cigarettes on the bumboat deck. The new assistant engineer, the one who'd replaced Ernie at the last minute, had followed her down the ladder and joined the other two.

"What's for dessert tonight, Mrs. Colvin?" Stilts asked. Then, before she could answer, "Say, you ever make butter tarts? I grew up in Lorain but my grandma's Canadian and she made the best butter tarts."

"I don't know, it's hard to compete with someone's grandmother. I suppose I could give them a try," she said, clasping the envelope in her hands. "Tonight it's Scotch shortbread."

The new assistant engineer took a drag of his cigarette. Then, after blowing the smoke out over the water, "My missus, she's Scottish, and she makes the best shortbread. Adds a little rosemary. You ever try that?"

Sunny glared at Ernie's replacement, this Not Ernie. He'd joined their crew only yesterday and he thought he'd give her baking advice? Did she come down to the engine room and advise him how to maintain the equipment? "No."

"Well if you want to try something new, rosemary's the thing."

Some people thought that because they could eat a cake, they could bake a cake. "I make shortbread the traditional way. If that doesn't suit, I hear there's a good café about twenty paces thataway," Sunny said, pointing down at the dark water.

Not Ernie just shrugged, unconcerned. The oiler laughed, shaking his head. "Ain't nobody like you, Mrs. Colvin. You know we'll gobble up anything you and the steward make."

"It's the truth," Stilts said. "This is my second month on the *Titus Brown* and already I gained five pounds."

"You could stand to gain five more," Sunny said, eyeing his lanky frame. "Which boat did you come from?"

"The *Schuck*. She was my first berth but I only went to sea this summer. I worked on the docks before that."

"The *Schuck*? Well then it's no wonder you're hungry for good food. Even the seagulls don't bother with that boat come mealtime."

The oiler chuckled and flicked his cigarette butt into the lake. He and Stilts climbed the ladder up the side of the *Titus Brown*. Not Ernie followed them.

Sunny opened the cabin door. Inside it was like a smaller version of the general store you'd find in any Middle West town. The bumboat captain had crammed as many goods as possible into the space. And although she didn't plan to buy anything, only wanted to ask him to mail the letter, she picked up a tin tube of carbolated Vaseline while summoning the nerve.

In the letter, she had asked Agnes to make an offer on the restaurant on her behalf, to use the enclosed money as a down payment and to tell the seller she'd be home at the end of the month with the rest. Once she mailed the letter, there was no turning back. She hadn't even told Herb yet! But she needed to make the owner an offer before someone else did. For years now she'd been waiting for the right time to act, and she was tired of living in her daydreams. The time was now. Like Ernie with his cupboard business, she had to choose the moment herself or it would never happen.

"Ma'am? Do you know what you want?"

Friendly Boyce the bumboat captain, about whom Sunny had momentarily forgotten, was giving her a strange look.

She had an awful pit in her stomach. Who was she fooling? She couldn't do this without first talking to Herb. They were a team. He hadn't given her his blessing and without it, she'd never feel right about making such a big decision, let alone spending money on a down payment.

Sunny tucked the envelope into her skirt pocket. "Only this." She placed the carbolated Vaseline on the counter.

A wave of relief coursed through her body. It felt almost like progress. And yet she knew it wasn't. As she climbed the ladder back to the *Titus Brown*, she made a promise to herself: before they reached the Soo Locks, she would tell Herb about her restaurant idea. Not only that, but she would also convince him of its merits. Then, at the Soo Locks she would mail this letter to Agnes with a clear conscience. Now all she had to do was to work up the nerve.

Lake Huron

Saturday morning a steam whistle sounded: one long blast, deep and loud. A couple seconds of silence and then another blast, this one half as long. Cordelia rolled over in the berth, not quite awake. What did the whistle mean? She'd ask Edmund in a minute, after a little more sleep...

Another long blast of the whistle. Now fully awake, she opened her eyes to the dimly lit cabin. Edmund had already gone. The steam whistle sounded again. She pulled on her robe, which hung on a hook by the berth, and slid the metal cover from one of the porthole windows. A thick fog pressed against the glass. Silence for nearly a minute and then another extended blast of the fog whistle, followed by a shorter one.

The *Marguerite* must be nearing Lake Huron's northern end. They'd sailed more than two hundred miles up the vast lake. Cordelia had tracked their progress on a map Edmund kept in his office. If her estimation was correct, the fog whistle came from De Tour Village, at the eastern tip of Michigan's Upper Peninsula. The De Tour Point Lighthouse marked the place where they would enter the St. Marys River on their way to Lake Superior.

Cordelia dressed and climbed the stairs to the wheelhouse, eager to see the Upper Peninsula for the first time. She also wanted to watch the wheelsman navigate the river. Edmund had told her that the St. Marys River was especially precarious, the river rocky and twisty, with a bedrock bottom and rock outcroppings. He clearly took pride in his wheelsman's skill. She would show an interest in what Edmund thought was important, all the better to demonstrate what a devoted wife she would be.

Edmund stood next to a chart table along the back of the D-shaped wheelhouse, holding a white coffee mug.

"Is the fog whistle from De Tour?" Cordelia asked softly, not wanting to disturb the wheelsman as he navigated the haze.

Edmund nodded, and replied in a low voice, "The second whistle means the river is clear."

Squeezed into the center of the small wheelhouse were a compass binnacle and steering wheel. Richard had been sitting on a stool in front of the large wheel, his hands on the spokes at the ten and two positions. Now he stood, and the second mate, recovered from his illness, removed the wheelsman's chair to a back corner. One never sat while steering in the St. Marys River, Edmund explained. Strong river currents required the wheelsman's utmost attention.

The lighthouse whistle repeated its signal. Through the windows wrapping the wheelhouse, Cordelia watched the fog ahead, mesmerized. All at once the land appeared through the mist. On the left bank stood the lighthouse, a white cylindrical shaft surrounded by four levels of iron braces. Next to the lighthouse was a large keeper's cottage with three chimneys.

"The signal flags, captain," Ollie said. Ollie was the first mate, though not much older than Cordelia, and had a charming spread of freckles across his cheeks.

Edmund wrote something in his log book. Cordelia asked about the flags, but all he said was that a storm was coming.

A storm. Cordelia's stomach swirled in anticipation. She'd seen plenty of November storms from the vantage of the Port Austin Life-Saving Station. Her father had rescued countless sailors whose vessels had been pushed by storm winds and waves onto the rocky reef lining the coast. What would a storm look like from the deck of a great steel freighter? She had every faith in Edmund's abilities to navigate treacherous conditions. He would not let them founder. And when she returned home to Marlowe Avenue she would have a story to tell.

Edmund grabbed the megaphone from a hook and stepped outside. Cordelia went below to the cabin for her woolen coat before joining him on the covered walkway outside the wheelhouse. Overnight the temperature had dropped to near freezing, a good thirty degrees cooler than when they'd left Cleveland two days earlier. Cordelia shivered inside her winter coat.

The lighthouse keeper emerged from his dwelling a short distance away from where the *Marguerite* approached the St. Marys River. Edmund called to the keeper through the megaphone, asking what he knew of the storm. The keeper answered through a megaphone of his own. The storm had hit Superior Friday night, he called out. Winds nearing seventy miles an hour. Rain turned to snow. All vessels had found shelter.

Seventy miles an hour! Cordelia felt a wave of apprehension, but Edmund's expression was impassive. He waved his thanks and opened the wheelhouse door for her. From the back of the room, she watched, rapt, as the wheelsman steered the massive ship through the mouth of the St. Marys River, leaving Lake Huron behind. The fog dissipated completely, just as the lighthouse whistle had said it would. She had a great appreciation for the wheelsman's skill, especially after her experience the day before.

Yesterday, when the *Marguerite* had passed Port Huron at the southern end of Lake Huron, the warm weather still held, although Edmund had predicted the temperature would drop by the end of the day. After breakfast Cordelia had taken her novel to the wheelhouse deck. She'd already finished *The Reef*, and although she was tempted to take a nap, for she'd gotten a poor night's sleep on the noisy freighter, she wanted to spend time with Edmund, and show him that she was interested in his work. So she went to where he almost always was: the wheelhouse. It was proving difficult to get to know him better under these conditions—with him always working, surrounded by his wheelsman and first mate and others—but she could at least show she was thinking of him. Edmund was spending more time in the wheelhouse than he normally might, he'd said, due to the second mate having taken ill. Once the man's health improved, there would be time for just the two of them.

From a stool at the back of the wheelhouse she studied his map: finding places familiar and unfamiliar, counting lighthouses, memorizing the names of islands and bays. She traced their course to Duluth, Minnesota, all the way at the far end of Lake Superior. The course they followed yesterday was a straight line up Lake Huron that bent to the northwest near the lake's northern end. She studied all this, for knowing his work would give them something to talk about, later.

After an hour or two, however, she'd begun to feel bored and somewhat invisible, sitting quietly at the back of the wheelhouse. Then she had a flash of inspiration. She approached Edmund, who was noting something in the log, and placed a hand on his shoulder.

"Edmund, do you think I could have a go at steering the ship?" she had asked him midmorning on Friday.

Richard sat in a tall armchair, his hands on the huge wooden wheel before him. He glanced at Edmund. Edmund leaned against the chart table, his arms folded across his chest. "It's not as easy as Richard makes it look."

"But you're just going straight, yes?" It was the wrong thing to say and she'd have reeled the words back in if she could.

Edmund smiled as one might to a child who'd said something precocious. "That's the idea, yes. The current and wind have other ideas."

"Of course." Cordelia reddened.

"Tell you what. Wait until we pass that freighter up ahead and you can give it a try."

The downbound freighter approached. Edmund placed his hand on a large bronze rod. She knew from her earlier tour of the wheelhouse that this was how he operated the ship's whistle. He pulled the bronze rod and there came a long blast from the whistle, followed by two short blasts. Captain's Salute.

A few minutes later the wheelsman stepped down from the platform at the center of the wheelhouse, and Cordelia took his place in the tall chair. The wheel was tremendous—as big as she. Without the platform and chair she'd never see over the top of it. She placed her hands on the smooth wooden spokes at the ten and two positions. These two handles were more worn than the others, the finish paler and duller.

It was a tremendous thrill, and not a little unnerving, to have the massive ship under her control. Her two hands had never before wielded so much power. It was a strange feeling and she felt every bit the impostor.

Edmund told her to turn the wheel a half turn to the right. Cordelia turned the wheel as he directed, but the ship kept going straight. Maybe she hadn't turned the wheel as much as she thought she had. She turned it a little more to the right.

"That's enough," Edmund said. "It takes a while for the ship to respond. You have to be patient and wait for it to grab hold or you'll end up turning her too much."

Cordelia waited. Still the *Marguerite* continued straight ahead. Had something gone wrong? What had Richard done that she hadn't? Finally, nearly a minute after she'd turned the wheel, the ship slowly turned leftward. The left! But she'd meant to turn right! What was happening?

"Cross chain steering," Edmund said. "Whichever direction the wheel is turned, the ship turns opposite."

He might have told her that in the first place. She had done it correctly, after all. Or had she? The *Marguerite* kept turning. And turning. This was all wrong. Cordelia looked to Edmund but his face registered only calm. Still the *Marguerite* turned to the left. A panic rose in her chest. It seemed as though the ship would never stop turning.

Enough with this. Cordelia turned the wheel back to the left, more than the half turn she'd initially gone to the right. She waited for the ship to stop turning to the left.

Still the ship turned.

How long were you supposed to wait for it to go the way you'd intended? Her hands felt clammy but she didn't dare remove them from the wheel to wipe them on her skirt. She glanced at the wheelsman. The wheelsman watched Edmund.

"Edmund?" Cordelia didn't want to fail at this.

"Hold steady," Edmund said. "You're doing fine."

At last the ship stopped turning to the left. Now it began turning right. When for a full minute the ship continued to turn right, Cordelia panicked. The massive freighter was out of control. It would zig and it would zag and heaven forbid another vessel appear on the horizon! A glance passed between Ollie and Richard. No one said anything; surely, though, it was time to give up. Flee this platform and let Richard take over.

Turning to Edmund, she was about to say she'd had enough when the expression on his face—serene, confident—stopped her from speaking. Her husband knew what he was doing. She inhaled slowly. He was patient, unflappable. Perhaps she could absorb some of that steadiness. And so she waited.

At last the ship stopped turning.

"Good," Edmund said, breaking the silence. "Now bring the wheel not quite a quarter turn to the right."

Cordelia turned the wheel. "Like this?"

"Perfect."

She breathed a sigh of relief. "That was fun," she said, smiling at him. He winked at her, like they were sharing a secret. "Thank you for indulging my whim. I think I'd better let your crew get back to it now." She stepped from the platform.

Without a word, the wheelsman resumed his place.

"Take her midships, Richard," Edmund said.

"Taking her midships, Captain."

Cordelia wiped her sweaty hands on her skirt. "Boy, it's a lot harder than it looks. I don't know how you steer this beast in a river."

Edmund lowered his voice so that only she could hear. "I love that you wanted to give it a try."

"You do?" She wanted to kiss him then, but given the other officers in the small room, she placed a hand on his arm instead, a gentle squeeze before turning to leave. Glancing over her shoulder she realized he was watching her go.

Buoyed by her success at the wheel, pleased by the steady patience she'd displayed, Cordelia wandered the forecastle without any particular destination, finally settling on the observation room forward of Edmund's quarters. She paced the empty room, circling the solid oak table and leather chairs. At the back of the room was a phonograph and a small collection of records, a selection of great composers. Edmund loved music—it was fitting that they'd met at a concert. She wasn't well-versed in classical music but played the Chopin anyway, a rather melancholy piece. Listening to it made her feel closer to him. She hadn't ever thought of Edmund as a romantic, given his reserve. But perhaps he was. It *would* take a romantic nature to propose to a woman you'd met only once. She smiled to herself. The inscrutable Edmund might best reveal himself through his possessions.

Now on the St. Marys River, Cordelia asked Edmund to join her for Saturday morning breakfast. When he said he had to stay in the wheelhouse to navigate this treacherous part of the river, it stung more than she cared to admit. She offered to bring something back for him and he asked only for a Danish and another cup of coffee. Edmund made it difficult for her to be the doting wife she was supposed to be, in large part because he didn't seem to *need* anything from her here. Trying to be of help all the same, she took his empty mug, and two more besides. Edmund asked the first mate to accompany Cordelia, and when she said that wasn't necessary, he urged her to be careful crossing the open deck.

"Keep a good hold of the lifeline," Edmund said. "We're more protected on the river, but the wind can come out of nowhere."

Cordelia promised to be careful. She left the wheelhouse and descended the exterior stairway to the deck, where with one gloved hand she held three empty mugs and with the other she grabbed the lifeline, a steel cable suspended above the gunwales the entire length of the deck.

Wilderness bordered the St. Marys River on both sides, the riverbanks and little islands thickly forested, dotted every so often with cottages that appeared empty. The sky was washed with gray. As she made her way aft her breath formed tiny clouds. The metal cable she grasped for safety chilled her fingers even through her gloves. If her stomach weren't growling she'd have skipped breakfast altogether to avoid the cold. Unfortunately, the only way to get from bow to stern was to cross the open deck. There was no passageway below. Beneath her it was all cargo hold, filled to the top with coal.

As she walked aft and the ship continued upriver, it was as if she were moving yet staying in one place at the same time. For a while she remained even with the same pine grove on shore, and the sensation of both moving and standing still at the same time made her dizzy.

The steward, a stocky, clean-shaven man in his forties, with buzz-short hair and graying temples, brought her a mug within seconds of her sitting down in the officers' dining room. She'd taken an immediate liking to him. He poured her coffee from the silver coffee service on the built-in sideboard. The sideboard's mirrored panels reflected the tipping coffee pot, the hot coffee flowing into the white china mug. Cordelia thanked him, and he asked what else he might get for her. She requested an egg over medium and some fruit.

A chandelier with glass shades hung above the white-cloth-covered table. From the chandelier extended chains that attached to the ceiling like spider legs.

"To hold it in place when there's pitching and rolling," the steward said when he noticed her staring at it. She hadn't needed the explanation but smiled at him anyway. He asked how she was enjoying her trip, and when she asked about him, he gave her his life story: how he'd grown up on his uncle's farm in De Pere, Wisconsin before moving to Milwaukee and getting a job as a deckhand; how he'd worked his way up to steward; how he'd met his wife at a Christmas party ten years ago, and how three years ago he'd lost her to illness, and that he'd never marry again because he still considered himself a married man. When he left the room, Cordelia leaned back in her chair, gazed through a window carved out of the oak paneling, and wondered who she'd know better by the trip's end: her husband or the steward.

When the *Marguerite* reached the Soo Locks at midday, Cordelia was in the observation room playing phonograph records and reading. There were two American locks, the eight-hundred-foot Poe lock and the five-hundred-fifteen-foot Weitzel lock. On the other side of the river, the Canadians operated a single lock nine hundred feet long. The *Marguerite* joined the Weitzel queue. There were at least five ships ahead of them waiting to lock up to Lake Superior. It would be several hours before it was their turn.

A ship approached them from the locks and Cordelia cried out at the sight. The ship, a freighter like theirs, was coated in ice, a layer of ice so thick it would require a sledgehammer to break through. The sailors inside must have encountered something terrible on Lake Superior.

The ghostly ship had just disappeared from view when Edmund appeared in the doorway and invited her to the dining room for the noonday meal. Cordelia lifted the needle on the phonograph and went with him, casting one more glance to the windows. She'd never forget that thick encasement of ice, and the terror it betrayed.

During the meal—codfish balls and scalloped tomatoes, sponge cake and cocoa—she did her best to be a good listener, keeping in mind Maman's admonition that she tended to chattiness. "When others are speaking, don't put in your oar every few sentences," her mother would say. "And besides, you're so pretty you don't need to be clever in order to shine." Despite this advice, well-intentioned and oft-repeated, Cordelia found it difficult to restrain herself when she had something to say. Her father had encouraged her loquaciousness, just as he'd encouraged her studies.

"Apologies for the weather, Mrs. Blythe," said the first mate, Ollie. "We went from Indian summer to Old Man Winter lickety-split. Looks like we're in for some snow."

"A little cold weather never bothered me," Cordelia said. "I grew up in Port Austin and we got our fair share. My father was the keeper of the life-saving station. Keeper Day. He died in '06, not long after retiring. To think it, all the dangerous rescues he'd led and then when his life was finally quiet and peaceful—"

She was doing it again. Talking too much. And of death! She would find a more pleasant topic. "Anyhow, I've lived at the water's edge all my life but I've never been this far out on the lakes. It's wondrous how at times we see nothing but water—we might as well be on the ocean for all we know!"

"The ocean, bah," Ollie said, swatting away as inconsequential that which covered most of the planet. "Captain Blythe could run rings around an ocean freighter. You wouldn't want a saltie piloting a Great Lakes freighter, I'll tell you that."

Edmund smiled.

"These lakes are more difficult, see?" Ollie went on. "We've got sandbars that shift with every storm, we've got reefs that come right to the edge of shipping channels. And our storms! They can whip up in no time. Our seas run short—the waves come at you fast. Not at all what the salties are used to. And the ice! Freshwater freezes much faster than saltwater, you know."

Edmund had spoken of salties before, of their arrogance when it came to comparisons of the oceans and the Great Lakes, as if the ocean's vastness required a likewise expanse of skill. Those salties wouldn't be so arrogant the first time they sailed the lakes in a gale, Edmund would say. You find yourself in a storm on the ocean, you might steer out of it, even if it meant taking your ship off course hundreds of miles. On the lakes you had no such luxury. There's nowhere to go. You're either in the thick of the deadly storm, or you're navigating your way around the hazardous shoals near shore.

"Yes," Cordelia said. "This afternoon I saw an iced-up ship headed downriver and—"

"And the ocean doesn't have our mysterious sea serpents," said the second mate, the one who'd been ill at the start of their journey. He had thick white hair and he looked right at Cordelia as if to see whether he'd succeeded in scaring her.

"Sea serpents?" Cordelia splayed her fingers over her chest, feigning horror.

"Sailors have seen 'em in all the Great Lakes," the second mate went on. "Most especially Lake Superior—the biggest and deepest. Twenty years back the captain of the S.S. Curry says he saw one off Whitefish Point. Neck fifteen feet long!"

"No!" Cordelia egged him on, enjoying herself.

Ollie nudged the second mate with his elbow. "And what about those boaters from Detroit, said they were attacked by a giant squid near Duluth? That was back in '97, '98 maybe."

No matter that squid were saltwater creatures; she wasn't about to ruin the fun.

The second mate pointed at Richard. "Don't you natives say there's creatures in these lakes?"

Richard glanced at Edmund, then said to the mate, "Mishipeshu, Great Lynx. It has the body of a giant panther, the horns of a bison, and the tail of a serpent. Mishipeshu can create tremendous waves and whirlpools with a whip of its tail. For safe passage the Ojibwe would appease it with an offering."

"An offering of what?" Cordelia asked.

"Tobacco or copper. My grandfather said its horns are made of copper, although some say it's the tail."

Ollie waved his hand. "Never mind the serpents and the lynxes. 'Tis the Three Sisters that sailors fear most." He leaned forward for effect. "During big storms, see, the waves hitting Superior's rocky coasts bounce back into the lake and collide with other swells and it makes for a messy confusion of waves. That's bad enough. But once in a while, the waves rebounding off the shore combine with the ones headed for it, and that's when you get the Three Sisters. Most ships survive the first sister—though she's half again as big as your typical storm wave. The second is bigger still, but a good captain and crew can withstand her. Now it's the third sister who's biggest and meanest: Three times the size of your ordinary storm wave, a good fifty feet tall, and she's the deadliest of all."

"That's enough, Ollie," Edmund said, pressing his mouth with a cloth napkin and folding it neatly. "You're going to scare my wife and she'll jump ship as we're locking up."

"Oh, they haven't frightened me," Cordelia said. "I'm all for an adventure. I do have to wonder, though, why the waves are called the Three Sisters and not the Three Brothers."

"Because women get so angry, of course!" Ollie said, laughing. He looked around the table as if to check for agreement.

The second mate leaned in. "I, for one, avoid my wife's anger by staying on the *Marguerite* nine months a year."

The men laughed and Ollie said he was sure that was true.

Cordelia asked Ollie lightly, "And you believe women are angrier than men?"

"I know they are!" he said, clearly on a roll now. "Take those suffragettes—there ain't nobody angrier than them."

"Well I'm sympathetic to their cause," Cordelia said. She chose her words carefully, not wanting to embarrass Edmund by venturing too far into political matters. "Some women, my neighbor for one, say women shouldn't get involved in politics, but I am for suffrage."

"If women get the vote, it'll be goodbye John Barleycorn!" Ollie said, waving his hand. "I wouldn't be opposed to suffrage, if only you ladies weren't going to take away my booze."

Edmund gave Ollie a look. "Might do you some good."

"Well," said Cordelia, liking Ollie less the more he spoke, "I suppose we all must take a stand for what we believe in, whether it's the freedom to drink whiskey or, say, the idea that our government is by the consent of the people, and half the population hasn't consented."

Ollie, for the first time during the meal, was silent.

She'd said too much. She glanced at Edmund to see if he was upset with her. On the contrary, he seemed pleased. Proud, even. "Cordelia had the highest marks of her class," he said, patting her hand. "She's far too smart for me."

"No," Cordelia said, downplaying her academic talent, for she didn't know him well enough yet to know if he truly was pleased or merely pretending to be. "I'm good at memorization, that's all."

At last it was the *Marguerite's* turn to pass through the lock. The second wheelsman steered the ship through the Weitzel lock's open wooden doors and into the canal. The ship stopped before reaching a second gate, this one closed. The water in the canal was low, and the ship's deck was even with the concrete pier on either side. Lock workers quickly secured the ship to mooring bollards.

Edmund stepped outside the wheelhouse. Though it was near freezing, Cordelia followed him, curious how everything worked.

"The *Sheadle* locked down earlier," a lock worker told Edmund when he asked of the storm. "Captain Lyons said he left Fort William Thursday evening. Outside Thunder Cape he found heavy seas running, and a strong breeze, too. He sought shelter overnight."

"At Pie Island?"

The worker nodded. "Anchored there until early this morning when the wind went north."

"Anyone have serious trouble?"

"Not so far as we know. Most of the ships headed for Duluth anchored at Isle Royale last night. Winds were too strong to attempt the harbor."

Just beyond the ship's stern, the doors of the first gate closed. Then, as if by magic, the water between the two closed gates slowly began to rise. Through openings in the floor, water from the higher-elevation Lake Superior flowed into the lock. The water level rose about a foot each minute until the ship was lifted a full twenty feet. It was like they were levitating above the ground they had just been even with. Once the water stopped rising, the lock workers freed the mooring lines, the doors in front of the *Marguerite* parted, and the ship moved out of the canal.

All that in less than forty-five minutes. It was nothing short of magical. Why had Sunny never told her how wondrous the locks were? As they sailed along the upper St. Marys River, it dawned on Cordelia that she'd been so impressed with the lock workings that she'd forgotten to mail her letter to Maman. Well it was too late now. The letter would have to wait until Duluth.

The sky was low and gray. Edmund said it'd be another fifteen miles until they reached Whitefish Bay, which was situated at the easternmost edge of Lake Superior. They were in the wheelhouse again when Cordelia expressed concern about what the lock worker had said and the ice-encrusted ships—for she'd seen more than just the one—coming from Lake Superior.

"The worst of these November gales lasts only a day or so." Edmund stood at the front of the wheelhouse. "Most storms blow themselves out in three days. I expect to find better weather on Superior tomorrow."

"Can you call someone to find out what the conditions are?"

"I could get out my megaphone but I don't think anyone will hear me."

"I mean the wireless telephone."

"We don't have one."

Cordelia didn't know how to respond. Why wouldn't the *Marguerite* have a wireless? Agnes's late husband, Amos, used to talk about how sailors could reduce the number of shipwrecks if only they had this wonder of the electrical age on board.

"We've got the telegraph," Edmund said, perhaps sensing her unease. "And there are storm signals posted at every lighthouse and life-saving station. I won't get a wireless telephone until the shipping bosses demand it. I get one of those things in here and I'll have the home office calling me every hour, wanting to know where I am and when I'll arrive, and who knows what else."

Cordelia opened her mouth to protest. Before any words came out, she thought better of speaking.

"If I want to know the weather conditions, I look outside and to the west." Edmund gestured to the window. "I can see now that it's starting to snow, and as it will be dark before long, we'll drop anchor when we get to Whitefish Bay. We'll stay at anchor overnight, until the storm passes."

SUNDAY
November 9, 1913

Lake Huron

It had been after dark Friday when the water sloshed back to the western end of the giant bathtub that was Lake Erie. The *Titus Brown* was lifted free of the sandbar and had sailed a few miles north, anchoring overnight near Grosse Ile, just past the mouth of the Detroit River, until the seiche was fully resolved. Saturday the straight deck freighter pushed its way up the Detroit and St. Clair rivers. The strong currents and winds, now coming out of the north, slowed their pace to four or five miles an hour.

And so it wasn't until early Sunday morning that the *Titus Brown* started its two-hundred-mile journey up Lake Huron. As Sunny carried a tray of pumpkin muffins to the officers' dining room, she mentally rehearsed the conversation with Herb that she promised herself would happen before they reached the Soo Locks: the restaurant she wanted, the ideal location now available, the money she'd saved. She imagined Herb's objections and what her counterarguments would be. All the while the deck hummed with vibrations emanating from the room below, where the triple-expansion engine gobbled up coal and turned it into steam. She'd gotten so used to the vibrations she rarely noticed them anymore, except on quiet early mornings or when there was a change in speed. She placed the tray on the sideboard in the dining room and glanced out the window. Across the lake's choppy surface thousands of pointed peaks rose and fell like so many Christmas trees.

As soon as breakfast was over, Sunny started on the soup for the noonday meal, taking the pounds of potatoes Cleve had peeled and putting them on the cook-stove to boil. Next she went about combining the ingredients for an apple tapioca pudding. The warm pudding would be just the thing in the dropping temperatures. When the potato soup was simmering and the pudding was finished, she turned her attention to the salad, making her dressing with the leftover vinegar from a pickle jar for extra flavor. Daylight faded throughout the morning as she worked, the galley skylight becoming a rectangle of overcast grayish white. The lake grew choppier, too. Now and again she reached for a rolling bar to steady herself. Fortunately she was not prone to seasickness.

When her preparations were complete Sunny took a short break in her cabin. From her cabin window she spied a white lighthouse sitting along a breakwater a good five hundred yards from shore. Harbor Beach. She held a fondness for Harbor Beach, the only safe harbor along Michigan's coast for fifty miles in either direction. The *Titus Brown* had never sought refuge there, but in the early and late weeks of the shipping season when the weather was most precarious, she was reassured by its presence. On a calm day the concrete breakwater at Harbor Beach rose ten feet above the lake's surface; the waves now crashing against it were just a couple feet shy of the top. If the weather worsened, they would have a heck of a time preparing and serving supper. She watched until the lighthouse grew smaller in the distance. When it was barely a white speck she returned to the galley to start serving the noonday dinner.

That afternoon waves continued to rock the *Titus Brown*, though not calamitously so. By three o'clock the Old Man still hadn't come aft for his meal. Normally Cleve might be the one to take something forward for the captain, but he was chopping vegetables for that evening's shepherd's pie. She would take care of it. After putting a couple of sandwiches, some pudding, and fruit in a basket, she went to tell Herb where she was going.

He was in the mess room, a spartan space with two long tables surrounded by stools, all bolted to the deck. Several crew members gathered at one table. Herb sat with his back to the doorway, drinking coffee and listening as the bosun spoke of the Duluth ore docks, and the idiosyncrasies of various captains when it came to loading iron ore.

"This time of year especially," the bosun was saying. "He prefers a bit more weight in the stern."

"Ah, I prefer a bit more weight in the stern, too," said the new assistant engineer, the one who'd replaced Ernie at the last minute. "Only I ain't talking about ships!"

Sunny rolled her eyes. This assistant engineer, this Not Ernie, rubbed her the wrong way. Not because he told a bawdy joke, but because he was a know-it-all. Rosemary in your shortbread, indeed. When the laughter died down Herb launched into a story about a youthful misadventure with his brothers. The man's nostalgia for his childhood knew no bounds. The five Colvin brothers had been inseparable, and then everything changed. One brother moved out west in search of sunny skies and dry air; one died falling off the top of a moving boxcar in the wee hours of the night; and one was killed in a shipyard accident. That left his youngest brother, who worked as a fisherman in Toledo and who used to come up for the holidays but had grown reclusive in recent years.

There was no need to interrupt his trip down memory lane. Carrying the basket of food, Sunny went out onto the spar deck. The sky had fully clouded over now, and appeared as if dusk, although it was barely three o'clock in the afternoon. The waves were as high as they'd been at Harbor Beach, maybe higher. The *Titus Brown* had about ten feet of freeboard, and with growing trepidation she watched the waves nearly spill over the starboard gunwales. She should have done this earlier. In any case, Captain Hanna needed to eat.

Despite the boat's rolling, her balance was good. Her heartbeat quickened as she clipped herself to the starboard lifeline. If a wave washed her over the side, heaven forbid, she would dangle from the cable until somebody hoisted her on deck and though she'd be terrified out of her wits, she wouldn't drown.

She squinted against the snow flurries and began to tread the long straight path toward the bow. She would have to cross more than a football field's length of flat deck before she reached the forecastle. The winds were coming strong and loud out of the northeast. A gust of arctic wind struck her face, so cold and fierce that, for a panicked second, she couldn't breathe.

With her right hand gripping the lifeline, she continued forward, shifting her weight as the boat rolled, watching the waves as they rose ever closer to deck level. She was halfway to the forecastle when a tremendous wave—twice the size of those nearly breaching the gunwales—reached up from the lake's surface and smashed into the wheelhouse on the starboard side. She inhaled sharply and watched, awestruck. Moments later the force of the blow reverberated in the metal deck beneath her feet.

Sunny knew the strength of water. An icy fear spread through her limbs, rooting her to the deck. She ought to retreat. Even if she did make it forward the captain wouldn't want to see her in the wheelhouse when he was dealing with rogue waves like that one. And he might not let her return aft if he deemed it too dangerous. Snowflakes whipped about her furiously. She shifted her weight to steady herself as the freighter rolled from starboard to port and back again. What had she been thinking, coming out in this?

"Mrs. Colvin! Get back here!"

The gravelly voice came from the boilerhouse behind her. It was the bosun.

"It's too dangerous!" the bosun shouted. "Get back now!"

The worry in his voice scared her more than anything. If the typically unflappable bosun was fearful, then she was in real danger. Yes, she would go back. Without another thought Sunny turned and started for the boilerhouse, more quickly now, all the while adjusting her weight to match the rolling of the ship and readying herself for a tremendous wave to crash over the deck as it had the wheelhouse. With a singleness of focus she watched the deck in front of her meet her feet, her vision obscured by the thick snowflakes whipping past.

In her peripheral vision a big wave approached. An awed terror surged in her chest. Even if she ran as fast as she could, it was going to hit before she reached the boilerhouse. Sunny planted her feet on the deck, bent her knees, and clung to the steel cable, her heart racing. In mere seconds the wave closed in. It broke several feet over the starboard gunwales. Freezing spray stung her face and thick water pushed hard against her. She held herself firm against the force of the water, and when it had finally rushed past her, she was still standing, holding her breath. She exhaled shakily and hurried on. Seas on the lakes were short—there would be little time before the next one.

The snow turned icy and stung her face. The boat rolled and she moved almost without seeing—had she gone so far forward? Her pulse rushing, her legs moving with new strength, deftly shifting her weight to avoid slipping—until at last she reached the boilerhouse. She would have to unclip herself from the lifeline and take a couple perilous steps to the galley door. She would time it with the rolling of the boat. She was hesitant to unclip herself, lest a sea wash over the boat at that exact moment.

The galley door opened.

"Sunny!" Herb extended a hand. Cleve and the bosun stood behind him.

She grabbed his arm at the wrist, and he had hers. With her free hand she unclipped herself from the lifeline and he yanked her into the galley. With the force of his pull Herb lost his balance and the two of them collapsed on the galley deck. The door slammed shut.

"What were you thinking?" Herb yelled, the fear in his voice unmistakable.

Sunny put her head on his chest and closed her eyes. She shivered uncontrollably as much from cold as from terror. Someone brought her a blanket. Herb held her to him and kissed the top of her head.

"You're soaking wet," Herb said, calming down. "What were you doing out there?"

"Taking the captain his meal." The wind howled so loudly it was as if it was inside the galley with them. The others left the galley so she was alone with Herb. "I thought I could make it forward. Things got bad real fast."

"That's how things change out here. Real fast. You know that."

It was true. You could be drifting along any of the lakes, the surface smooth as glass, and ten minutes later there'd come a gale bringing five to ten footers. Sunny pulled off her shoes and unbuttoned her coat in order to more easily remove her wet stockings.

They had just stood up when a wave slammed the boiler-house and sent them staggering. Sunny reached for a rolling bar. "This is bad. You should've seen the tremendous wave that hit the forecastle. It might've damaged the wheelhouse."

"If there's trouble the engine room would know." Herb was trying to sound reassuring. He took her wet stockings and hung them on a rolling bar near the stove to dry. "You're going to catch cold."

Sunny waved away his concern. She put her bare feet into her shoes, went to the pantry, and forced her thoughts to her work. It was no use worrying about the storm. There were supper preparations to see to. They'd make the usual amount of food, enough for twenty-five, although it was unlikely they'd see Captain Hanna or any of the officers aft until the storm had passed. It was hardly the first time she'd cooked a meal in rough weather. The galley was built with unsteady conditions in mind. There were rolling bars—half-inch pipes raised above the edges of the stove and counters—and there were latches on all the cupboards. Plates were stacked in vertical shelves, so that you had to reach in and lift each one up before you could pull it out. The shelves were beyond Sunny's reach, but Cleve usually got the plates anyway. At mealtime, wet towels on the tables would prevent the plates and glasses, forks and spoons from sliding off.

Herb was assembling five oblong pans of shepherd's pie. Sunny's yeast loaves, which she'd made with some of the warm potato water, had come out of the oven an hour ago and smelled divine. Dessert would be preserved peaches with cream. As she fetched the jars from the pantry the boat pitched suddenly, causing her to stumble, and the jars slipped from her hands. Broken glass and splattered preserves spread across the galley deck.

"Oh!" Sunny cried, grabbing a rolling bar for support. A wave of alarm washed through her body. She looked to Herb for his reaction. "That was a big one, wasn't it?" Her voice cracked a little. With shaking hands she started to clean up the mess.

Herb knelt beside her and helped. "We're in for some excitement tonight." He didn't seem worried. Then again, he hadn't seen the rogue wave she had. She reminded herself of how well-prepared the *Titus Brown* was, and how competent the captain and crew.

"Dessert's ruined," she said.

"There's plenty of iced cookies from yesterday. The men won't have much of an appetite in this weather anyway."

The broken glass and ruined preserves disposed of, Sunny went to a galley window. Heavy snow crowded the skies, and she caught only glimpses of the gray-green water through the galley windows. Icy pellets whizzed past, aggressively rapping on the glass. They were too far north of Harbor Beach to seek refuge there, even if Captain Hanna were willing to turn around in these seas. And that was dangerous in and of itself. A steamer turned broadside to the wind in a storm like this could get caught in the trough and turn turtle at any moment. Most likely, they would keep heading into the storm.

Sunny had no idea how far they were from Tawas Bay, which was fifty miles north of Harbor Beach and the next shelter. The seas were so strong they might not be making any headway at all.

The *Titus Brown's* whistle blew constantly now, warning any nearby ships of their presence. She listened for responding whistles, if they could even be heard over the crashing waves, howling wind, and the pounding of her own heart. During a brief break in the squall, she spotted a ghostly ship in the distance. A downbound freighter, similar in size and construction to the *Titus Brown*, encased in layers of ice. Every part of the freighter, from the forecastle to the boilerhouse, from the railings to the rigging, all were thick and white. It was unearthly. Exquisite. Whoever was trapped inside had been battling the storm for some time. If only the *Titus Brown* were downbound like that freighter, they could be racing ahead of the storm instead of straight into it.

As she checked on the shepherd's pies baking in the oven, the deck hummed reassuringly beneath her feet. The roar of the furnaces and thundering of the gigantic pistons below meant the boat was working as it should. From the sound of it, the engines were running at full speed.

Still, she couldn't put the image from her mind, that massive wave smashing into the wheelhouse. There may have been damage done. The chief engineer would know. She filled a mug of coffee for him and carried it carefully down the companionway to the engine room. She had a chill from her misadventure on deck, and the engine room would be warm.

Five years ago, the first time she'd seen the *Titus Brown's* engine room, it had overwhelmed her. "Room" was too small a word for the space, which spanned several deck levels. You could fit a three-story house inside. That is, if you took out the incomprehensible network of pipes and cranks, the massive pistons and cylinders of the triple-expansion engine.

Next to the engine room was the boiler room, where firemen fed the boiler's firebox with coal to keep the engine going. Two firemen were always on duty, shoving coal into the firebox twice a minute. On the blustery days of early spring and late fall, the boiler room was the one place on the boat the cold never reached.

How difficult a fireman's job was when the boat pitched back and forth like this! The best firemen didn't just hurl the coal any which way; they placed it within the firebox so that the fire burned evenly. An even fire kept the steam pressure constant. Too little steam would cause the boat to slow; too much steam meant wasteful excess. The chief engineer was able to hire good firemen because Captain Hanna didn't skimp when it came to coal. Lower quality coal meant more work, as more of it was needed to keep the fire burning. It also meant the firebox had to be cleaned twice as often. The best firemen knew which ships bought good coal, and stayed away from those that didn't.

Sunny found the chief engineer shouting at an oiler. She waited a short distance away. When he looked in her direction she held up the coffee. He came to her and took it with a nod of thanks. She asked about the wheelhouse. Its starboard windows had been broken by the rogue wave, the chief engineer said, and the Old Man and wheelsman were soaked but otherwise all right.

The officers must be freezing, Sunny thought. Her own chill now gone, she climbed the companionway back to the galley. Despite the boat's pitching she let herself be lulled by the din beneath her feet. The chief engineer had started the syphons and pumps to prepare for any flooding, and he'd put canvases over the dynamo to make sure nothing would stop those pumps from working, and as long as that noise below continued, they were all right.

The ship rolled heavily to and fro at supper and the aft crew picked at their shepherd's pie and talked of anything but the weather. The officers had stayed forward as she'd expected. It was too dangerous now to make the trek from bow to stern simply for a meal. The mood was subdued but no one was in a panic. With the exception of Stilts, they'd all been through a November storm before.

After supper Sunny tidied the galley while Cleve and Pug, the night cook, washed the dishes. The rest of the aft crew remained in the mess room, as their cabins were accessible only by the exterior passageway and no one wanted to go outside. When Sunny walked past the mess room on her way to the dining room, the bosun was telling a story about a girl he'd met the last time they were at port in Duluth and had gone "up the street." Most of it was baloney. Nevertheless the other men listened, rapt. Except for Stilts. He was staring out the window, watching the gray-green waves that now stretched up twenty feet from the lake surface. Sunny's chest tightened. She knew that longing look. He was searching for a break in the clouds, for an end to the storm.

With seas this rough, there was no work for the deckhands. Normally Stilts and the others might clean or do basic maintenance tasks while sailing up Lake Huron. In weather like this, however, they couldn't go on deck, and the boat was pitching too much to attempt interior painting or cleaning. And besides, today was Sunday, the deckhands' day off. Sunny felt for Stilts. When you were at sea and scared, it helped to have something useful to do. Taking on a project, however small, took your mind off your situation, and even reinforced the idea that the foul weather would pass and you would live to benefit from your labor.

She moved toward him, shifting her weight from one leg to the other as the boat rolled. "I was wondering if you could help me in the galley."

Stilts turned away from the window. His face was so pale. "Sure, Mrs. Colvin." He followed her to the galley, where she retrieved a cloth sack from the pantry.

"I had a mind to make some fudge, and I've got a whole mess of walnuts that need shelling. I could use your help. It's your choice, of course. Sometimes I find, in weather like this, it's best to keep my hands occupied."

When Stilts agreed to help, she handed him two pails and they made their way to the officers' dining room, which wouldn't be used anytime soon. They began their work and Stilts was mostly quiet, although after a time he asked if she ever felt uneasy in a storm.

"Oh, I used to, my first couple years," Sunny said, ignoring her current worry. "Until this one storm on Superior, where I spent hours in a state of panic, certain the Three Sisters were going to sink our boat at any moment. 'Well, after that storm I gave myself a good slap in the face. No, I really did! I said to myself, 'Sunny, the Old Man doesn't pay you to cower in the galley. He pays you to do a job. And no matter how bad the weather is, people are going to get hungry. And they're going to do their work better if they're well fed.' Ever since that storm I just focus on the task at hand and it keeps me steady."

"You're the bravest lady I ever met."

"Hogwash." Sunny felt herself redden. "I'm not saying it's always been easy. But I trust Captain Hanna. He knows what he's doing. If I didn't believe that, I wouldn't be here, and that's the truth."

Stilts dropped a walnut into a pail. "That's what I like about you, Mrs. Colvin. You're real clear about things. You know where you stand."

Honestly! Stilts said the darnedest things. "Oh, I'm just as muddled as the rest of them. Taking each day as it comes, vulnerable to the vagaries of fate, and rationalizing all my actions as a choice."

Stilts laughed. "I don't know what you just said, but something tells me that if there's something you want to do, you'll do it."

If only that were true. She hadn't been clear with everyone about where she stood. She'd never told Herb exactly why she wanted to leave the *Titus Brown*. All she'd ever done was complain about working another season on the lakes. She'd recounted time and again the things she didn't like about sailing: the monotony; the same people day after day; the lack of female companionship; the close quarters. She'd made noises about seeing more of her sisters and helping with their mother. But she hadn't found the words to tell him about her dream of opening a restaurant by the lake. And why hadn't she?

It dawned on her then that she was afraid. Afraid Herb would hate the idea. Or that he'd love it! If he loved her idea, then she would have no excuse not to give it a whirl, and what if she failed? What if she had no customers and had to close the restaurant and return to sailing? And what if Herb had given up his steward job in the meantime? He wouldn't be able to get it back, not with Captain Hanna, at least.

Sunny and Stilts shelled walnuts in companionable silence, the pail of shelled nuts and the pail of nutshells resting on damp towels to prevent them from sliding as the boat rolled. She said she could use some of the walnuts in the filling when she made the butter tarts Stilts had requested. The look on his face told her that that clearly wasn't how his grandmother made them. "Or just raisins?" she asked, and Stilts nodded, daring to suggest that he also preferred them with a runny center. She promised that's exactly how she would make them, after the storm.

Then it became too difficult to talk. Outside the wind blew stronger still, howling louder than Sunny had ever known it.

Ungodly, is what it was. The snow had stopped but the howling was getting so loud you had to shout to be heard above it and the breaking waves.

With a sickening swirling in her stomach, she glanced out the dining room window. It was too horrific to be real. All her experience with November gales was now irrelevant. For these waves, illuminated by the electric lights mounted outside, were taller and steeper than any she'd seen in her ten years at sea. Had Captain Hanna ever seen a storm like this?

She looked to Stilts to see if he'd registered her worried expression. He hadn't, thank goodness. She reminded herself to pay attention to the engine lest she work herself into a panic. Beneath her feet the deck hummed as it should. Please let that engine keep humming. Let the wheelsman keep us headed into the wind.

The boat lurched and the pail of walnut shells toppled over. Stilts, looking pale and tinged green and maybe about to be sick, asked if he could stop. Sunny said of course, and put an end to their task. It was getting increasingly difficult, ridiculous really, to be shelling nuts while outside the storm raged and the *Titus Brown* tilted to ever greater angles. With one hand against the bulkhead to steady herself, she carried the pail of shelled walnuts to the pantry. She would return to the dining room in a minute to clean up the spilled shells.

As she placed the pail inside a cupboard next to some canned tomatoes there came a tremendous crash and shudder. The boat pitched violently to port. She lost her balance and stumbled. Her ankle twisted and something hard knocked into her. A searing pain tore across the back of her skull.

Port Austin, Michigan

The sky glowed pink over Lake Huron as Agnes settled herself at the kitchen table with her coffee. Early Sunday morning was her favorite time of the week: Bisbee's was closed, the house was quiet—although today the cottage creaked and moaned in the freshening wind—and Maman always slept in. It was a brief yet precious respite.

In the pocket of Agnes's flannelette night robe was a brooch she'd painted with delicate blue and yellow flowers. She reached into her pocket and pressed her fingers against the smooth porcelain. She would wear the brooch to church today. Lizzie might admire it and if she did, then one day Agnes would give it to her. Agnes's daughter Aimee was utterly uninterested in china painting and while it saddened her that it hadn't been a hobby they could share, she reminded herself of the importance of letting Aimee choose her own way.

She warmed her hands on the coffee mug, one of her favorite pieces. Decorated with a simple daisy, this mug was the first piece of china she'd ever painted, a dozen years ago now, long before she became a widow. She'd taken up the hobby at the life-saving station. When her daughter was at school and Amos busy with work, Agnes and two other wives would often gather at one of their cottages to paint china and talk about life, their children, their husbands—long before Aimee was old enough to disdain Port Austin and the life-saving station and make it her mission to leave. Those were happy days.

Agnes was in a pensive mood as she looked out over the white-capped water and the trees swaying in the breeze. She was a product of this place, this beautiful place where the sun rose *and* set over the water, where the lighthouse was a castle on the lake, and where the waves shaped coastal stone into works of art. It struck her then that she owed her very existence both to the lake and to an exceptional variety of abrasive stone. She was alive because of water and stone.

In the 1830s a schooner captain had found safe harbor here during a gale. While ashore he'd discovered a large flat stone along the beach, and saw the potential for the stratum of rock from which it came. A grindstone quarry was opened, and then a second, and by 1850 the quarries sold thousands of dollars' worth of grindstones every year. Grindstones as small as whetstones and as large as three-ton stones were shipped all over the world. Scows carried the finished stones from the dock to steamers waiting on Lake Huron. Amid all this activity, a life-saving station went into operation at Grindstone City in the late 1870s, on a spit of land called Burnt Cabin Point.

Maman had come to the area as a young girl, her father having secured a management position at the quarry. Years later she met and married a surfman, a restless sort who always looked outward, at the lake. This was much to the consternation of Maman's parents, who'd hoped their daughter would marry a quarry boss. Maman's new husband kept his job with the life-saving service despite his father-in-law's offer to secure him a land-based, more remunerative, and safer line of work in quarry management.

And so Agnes was born at the life-saving station. Three years later, Sunny followed. They went to school in a white frame schoolhouse, one large room with two rows of seats on either side of a cordwood stove. Agnes was a middling student who found it hard to keep her attention where it ought to be. She much preferred to be outside, walking the shore, searching for shipwreck treasure.

At seventeen years of age she had married a surfman and moved from the main building (for by then her father had been promoted to keeper) to one of the cottages on the grounds. In the late nineties, when Agnes's daughter was a toddler, the station was moved two miles to the west, within the boundaries of the new Pointe Aux Barques resort community. The resort, with its grand summer homes on spacious lots, tree-lined winding roads, and large hotel, was easy to reach by train, and, important to its well-to-do guests and residents, inaccessible to the excursion crowds that swarmed places like the St. Clair Flats and Put-in-Bay.

Amos died in 1910. The circumstances of his death during a rescue gnawed at Agnes still, though she tried not to dwell on what could not be changed. With his passing she was, for the first time in her life, no longer attached by blood or marriage to a Port Austin surfman, and so she and her daughter had moved in with Maman. After Aimee had left for secretarial school in Detroit earlier this year, and Cordelia had eloped soon after, the days had taken on a new sameness.

Her days had brightened when she'd met Lizzie Duncan. The young woman's playfulness, her confidence, her welcoming of the world and what some might see as innocence—but which Agnes saw as a considered acceptance of what is—belied a steely determination not to ground her life in others' expectations.

But something Lizzie had asked a few days ago gnawed at her. *What else do you want to do?* It wasn't something Agnes had ever given thought to, and now that Lizzie had posed the question, it was all Agnes could think about. What else *did* Agnes want to do with her life? Up to this point she'd always done what was expected. By Lizzie's age Agnes had been a wife and mother, the same as all her school friends. And it had pleased Maman that Agnes was both married and still living on the station grounds. Maman had needed help with Cordelia, who was only a baby then. And now Maman wanted Agnes to marry Keeper Duncan, going so far as to suggest it would be selfish, should he propose, to say no. Married keepers ran their stations more smoothly, she insisted. Maman was getting ahead of herself. And yet Agnes already felt herself pulled toward this potential obligation. The knot in her stomach told her she couldn't let that happen.

When Lizzie spoke of sailing the Great Lakes and writing about her adventures, Agnes had felt a pang of envy. Maybe Agnes wanted to travel? See Niagara Falls? She was so used to letting other people decide the big things for her that deciding for herself felt incredibly strange—indulgent, even. Almost like she wasn't equal to the task of choosing. It wasn't fully clear where other people's desires ended and her own began. What, exactly, *did* she want?

Agnes stood at the kitchen window. A layer of snow covered the sparsely wooded backyard down to the lake and formed small white dunes at the shed that housed her kiln and skiff. The weather observer had been right about the snow on Saturday. She had spent the better part of yesterday morning bringing her skiff up to the shed to wash and store it for the winter. She'd finished just in time. By mid-afternoon the weather had turned cold and rainy. As the temperature dropped, the rain turned to sleet, and by evening, thick snowflakes blew past the cottage windows. That winter had come at last was something of a relief: there was no more anticipating it.

Now the fresh breeze stippled the water with whitecaps and shook the trees, stealing from them the last of their leaves. The steely gray lake churned thick and heavy, as if it had been mixed with molasses. Waves twice her height crashed near the shore. Though she worried for Sunny and Herb, she loved the lake on days like today. Lake Huron was angry, and the release of all that fury was immensely satisfying. An enchantment that never failed to calm her.

Upstairs, the floor creaked. Agnes finished her coffee and put her mug in the sink. She took two plates from the cupboard and set to making breakfast. She got the eggs and milk from the icebox, the bread from the cupboard. She was putting breakfast on the table when Maman appeared in the doorway, dressed and ready for church.

"You're still in your bedclothes," Maman said.

With a glance at her night robe—did it need washing?— Agnes set an egg and toast at Maman's place. Maman claimed she didn't need such a big breakfast, and when Agnes pointed out that it was only an egg and toast, said she would just have some tea. Agnes didn't mind, for in truth she was famished and she didn't like to see food wasted. So she added Maman's egg and toast to her own plate.

"You're hungry this morning," Maman said. "Careful or your skirt won't fit."

Though Maman rarely missed an opportunity to remind Agnes of her stout frame, Agnes was not self-conscious. She was strong, and her physique gave her strength. "I've been thinking of buying a new one anyway. This one's showing signs of wear. I could use a new blouse, too."

"When I was your age I would have mended it. Now my joints ache most days so I have to make do."

Agnes's stomach was pitting again. She ate the rest of her meal in silence. In her mind's eye she saw herself throw her plate against the wall. Without another word she washed the dishes and went upstairs to dress.

"You're gussied up this morning," Maman said when Agnes came back downstairs. "Would this be for Keeper Duncan's benefit?"

"Maman." Agnes was thirty-six years of age. She hated when Maman spoke as if they were conspiratorial sixteen-year-olds. It made fools of them both.

"It's just that I haven't seen you wear that brooch before. The pale blue matches your eyes."

"Thank you." Or was noting a similarity in color in fact a compliment? Surely it was close to one, anyway. "What do you think?" Agnes said suddenly, testing an idea, "about going on a trip next summer? I was thinking of Niagara Falls. I've always wanted to see it, and I just read an article—"

"Niagara Falls is for honeymooners," Maman said, shooing away the idea with her hand. "I never understood the excitement. It's all the same water we see out the window. Besides, I don't care for traveling. I've got all I need right here." She patted Agnes's cheek.

"Yes, of course. It was just a thought." Agnes's heart sank. Maybe it *was* a dumb idea. She put on her gray wool coat and her mittens lined in wool fleece, and then held the door open for Maman. The pewter skies promised more snow.

They walked several blocks into town, to the church on the corner of Arch and State. Upon entering the church Agnes scanned the worshippers moving toward the sanctuary. The Duncans weren't among them. Agnes and Maman sat in their usual pew. Agnes scooted from the end of the pew to allow room for Lizzie and her mother and brother when they came, as the Duncans often sat with them. But by the time the minister began the sermon, it was clear they weren't coming.

The light of Agnes's day dimmed. Now it was just her and Maman for the rest of the long, gray afternoon. Added to her disappointment was the fear that something was wrong. She sat through the service, sang the hymns, listened half-heartedly to the sermon. With her index finger she gently stroked the brooch at her breast. She should have gone to the fish fry at the station two nights ago. She could have seen Lizzie and it was certain to be the last good weather they'd have until spring. Instead she'd stayed home to tend to Maman, who had complained of a headache and dizziness and implored Agnes not to leave her at home alone.

After church Agnes started a fire in the parlor woodstove.

"Don't you think that's too many logs?" Maman said.

"The temperature is dropping and you saw how it was blowing on our way home. I think we're in for a big one."

"Then maybe we should ration our wood. I'd rather make it last longer than have a bright fire now and no fire at all later."

There was always a better way to do things, and Agnes consistently missed the mark. Her face and neck grew warm. "We have plenty of firewood. The entire Thumb is a forest." This part of Michigan, the tip of the Thumb, once had been a vast woodland. Pine and ash, beech and maple, cedar so thick patches of snow remained on the forest floor until midsummer. Quite a lot had been harvested, but much remained. "The pastor gave a nice sermon today," Agnes said, searching for a neutral topic, although in truth she hadn't paid much attention to the pastor's preaching.

"I wonder why Keeper Duncan wasn't there," Maman said.

"Maybe he was on duty."

"He's the keeper. He could choose to go to church if he wanted to. If it was important to him."

"He must be preparing for the storm." Agnes's thoughts again turned to Sunny and Herb and where on the lakes they might be in this weather. Through the kitchen window she cast a worried glance at the wild and snowy lake. Please let Captain Hanna have found safe harbor.

"That must be it. Although Keeper Duncan should've already had things prepared, seeing as how it's been snowing since yesterday. That's how your father ran the station. What he needs is a wife to help him run the place."

An urge to escape the house swept over Agnes, an urge to run far away and keep on running. She saw herself doing it, as if she were already out there in the snow, running.

Maman pointed. "You've gotten loose bark on the rug. Get those pieces before you grind them into the rug with your heel."

She ignored her mother's command. For only a second. Then she bent down to pick up the pieces of bark and toss them into the fire. Of course she did. That's who Agnes Inby was: an obedient daughter who sought to please Maman at every turn. Hounded enough she would probably even marry Keeper Duncan, were he to propose, even though she didn't love him.

"You missed two more. Over there."

Something inside Agnes twisted. She put her heel onto an errant piece of bark. She turned her heel back and forth, grinding the bark into the rug.

"What in heaven's name are you doing? Stop that at once!"

Agnes couldn't stop. Her mind spun, like egg whites whipped into a froth. She couldn't believe what she was doing but she also couldn't stop.

"You're ruining my rug!"

Yes, she was ruining the rug. And enjoying it! She would have more. Down went her heel on the other piece of bark, twisting and grinding it into the braided fibers. Agnes shouted words that came of their own volition—*And you're ruining my life!*—and that she wouldn't remember later; the words were let loose and without stopping to register Maman's reaction, she ran to the door, grabbed her coat and hat and mittens, and dashed outside.

And then she ran, pushed forward by an invisible fury. Even as the wind gusted and moaned and icy snow stung her face, she ran. She ran east along the shore of the raging lake, passing the forested cottages until they were few and far between and there was only woodland to her right and Lake Huron to her left, a thin strip of sand dividing them. Breakers dashed against the rock-strewn shore and she dodged them, and when the beach disappeared and the shoreline rose into a wave-cut cliff she followed the clifftop path trod by the beach patrol.

The wind off the lake had grown in strength and with some gusts Agnes lost her balance. Still she ran. It started to snow. Waves crashed on the shore with a growing rage. Atop a forested bluff she stopped, out of breath. She bent over and put her hands on her thighs and gasped for air. Angry waves pounded the rock below, as they had done for thousands of years, and would do for thousands more.

She continued on, putting more shoreline between her and Maman. More than a mile offshore and somewhere behind her, the fog signal sounded from the reef lighthouse.

Up ahead, a lone figure walked the coastline, looking toward the angry seas. He wore the storm suit and sou'wester of a surfman on beach patrol. She would duck into the woods...No, it was too late. He'd already seen her. She kept going, slower now, a more deliberate walk, as if she were out for a stroll.

"Agnes?" The man said when the distance between them closed. She knew this surfman well. Irvin. He'd been a good friend to Amos, and Agnes got on well with his wife, although she hadn't seen much of her since Amos died. Irvin carried a lantern, for though it was midday the storm made it dusk-like.

"What are you doing out in this weather?"

"I needed some fresh air."

"You should go home. It's likely to get dangerous out here."

"I'll be fine." Once she'd taken a few steps past Irvin she started running again, in the direction of the life-saving station. Let him think she was a simp. Maybe she was. Foolish, selfish. Out of her mind.

She ran faster. The waves were a crowd of wild spectators, spurring her on. She was a new woman now. She could do anything, say anything. She was strong, independent. Free!

In the near distance the watchtower rose from the roof of the life-saving station boathouse. Had she already run as far as that? She slowed to a walk, contemplating her next move. She was out of breath and thirsty. And the station always felt like home. Its stick-style construction and decorative wood bracketing symbolized family, a sense of belonging. Yet how would she explain her presence to the Duncans? What possible reason could she give? There was none, and she went into the main building without having settled on any.

Lizzie and her mother were in the kitchen. It was warm and smelled of roast chicken.

"Agnes?" Lizzie's eyes widened. "What are you doing here?"

"Just taking a stroll to enjoy the beautiful day." She touched her hair to gauge how much had fallen from her bun. Quite a lot, and it was all damp as the snowflakes caught there quickly melted.

Lizzie laughed. "You must be addled, coming out in this."

"Oh it's not that bad."

"Is that so? Spoken like a lifesaver's daughter." Lizzie opened a drawer. Her long fingers picked among the flatware with a casual gracefulness. She might have been a dancer or a harpist. "Stay and eat with us. You can set the table."

Dinner. Agnes hadn't prepared a meal for Maman after church. "Maman hasn't eaten," Agnes said, hanging her coat on a hook.

Lizzie shrugged. "There's food in your house, yes? She'll find something."

Agnes nodded, somewhat taken aback by her friend's lack of concern for Maman.

"She'll be *fine*," Lizzie said.

"I know, but it's our routine. We come home from church and I make dinner. She expects it of me. She'll be disappointed."

Lizzie pulled a pan of baked macaroni from the oven. "Oh Agnes," she said breezily, "you can't spare her from life's every disappointment."

"I'm not trying to—" Agnes stopped, lacking a response she could defend.

"And why would you want to, anyway?" Lizzie offered Agnes a handful of forks and knives and gestured, not unkindly, at the table.

If the mile-long run and furious waves had ameliorated Agnes's foul mood, her nearness to Lizzie mollified her completely. Lizzie's presence had often calmed her. The young woman was as serene as Lake Huron in midsummer—one of those days when the gentlest of waves lapped the shore, the water's surface so flat you could almost convince yourself it was frozen. How unlike Agnes, who was more like the lake as it was now, with all its churning.

"You will stay for dinner, then?" Lizzie said. "We'll be eating soon."

"I don't know. Maman and I fought. I should get back—"

"Do you want to telephone her?" the white-haired yet youthful Mrs. Duncan asked. It did not go unnoticed that the woman had avoided asking any probing questions about why Agnes had left her mother in the first place, nor, upon learning that Agnes and her mother had fought, pried as to the nature of the argument.

"We don't have a telephone. My mother doesn't believe in such modern conveniences."

"Let me guess," Lizzie said, smiling. "She says, 'If someone wants to talk to me they can knock on my door.'"

Agnes laughed. "That's precisely what she says!"

"All the same, why don't you stay?" Mrs. Duncan said. "You can take leftovers to your mother when the weather lets up."

Agnes relented. She was happy to stay in the warm, cozy kitchen while a storm brewed outside, to sit with Lizzie in the glow of the electric lights.

Finished with the place settings, Agnes took a seat at the table, and Lizzie brought her a glass of water and sat down beside her. As the liquid slid down her throat she was overcome with a profound contentment.

Keeper Duncan entered the kitchen and Agnes tensed a little. "Mrs. Inby, this is a pleasant surprise," he said, cheerful as ever.

Agnes said hello to the keeper. It could be, she thought then, that she only imagined Keeper Duncan's interest in her. She flattered herself! He was a handsome man in his middle thirties and he must think her too old. He would want a young wife. She felt the lines at her mouth. Yes, he thought her too old and that was fine with her.

"I think she's checking up on us," Lizzie told her brother while smiling at Agnes, "since we weren't at church."

"A-ha," Keeper Duncan said. "We stayed here on account of the weather. I've ordered everyone to remain on the grounds today. If a vessel gets into trouble I want to respond as quickly as possible."

Lizzie touched a finger to Agnes's brooch. "This is beautiful," she said. "Did you paint it yourself?"

Agnes felt herself blush at Lizzie's compliment. She'd forgotten all about the brooch. "Oh, this? I did paint it. Do you like it?" When Lizzie answered enthusiastically, praising her talent, Agnes beamed.

Four bachelor surfmen, three Duncans, and Agnes gathered at the table, the same table where Agnes had eaten most of her childhood meals. In running there that afternoon, she'd worked up a terrific appetite and was grateful for the food. As they ate roast chicken and baked macaroni, the conversation centered on the storm: how bad it would get, how long it might last, if and when they'd see a vessel in distress. Keeper Duncan reminded the surfmen that no one was to leave station grounds. They should all be prepared for a signal from beach patrol. While the surfman in the watchtower could see the coast well enough during the day, the beach patrol was an extra pair of eyes at night and during foul weather.

Nathaniel, a bachelor in his thirties who'd transferred to Port Austin last year, spoke of a storm during his early years at the Vermilion Station on Lake Superior. "It was November," Nathaniel said, "a day like this but colder 'cause it's the U.P. Now mind you it's called Shipwreck Coast for a reason. A godforsaken place. You'll find more broken hulls and masts half-buried in the sand than you'll find people. I'm making my four-mile patrol and the heavy seas are running up the beach. A hundred feet they're coming up. It's so cold that as soon as the seas retreat, the water on the beach freezes, and I'm slipping and falling. The only way I can make any progress is to crawl. There I am, crawling on my hands and knees trying to get to the halfway house."

"How awful!" Lizzie said. She hadn't looked anywhere but at Nathaniel since he'd begun his tale.

"The surfman from Crisp's Point had an even harder time," Nathaniel continued, referring to the life-saving station further west along Shipwreck Coast. Surfmen patrolling from the two stations would meet at a halfway house to exchange metallic checks, which were marked with the station and crewman number. "I was at the halfway house and almost gave up waiting. When he finally got there he looked miserable and was complaining of cramps. We exchanged checks and I told him to rest before heading back. I don't know if he listened, but later I found out he never made it to his station."

Lizzie covered her mouth. "No!"

"He'd collapsed in the snow and was beyond resuscitation by the time the next patrol found him," Nathaniel said, shaking his head.

A surfman dead on beach patrol? That had never happened in Port Austin. "What year was this?" Agnes asked.

"Boy, I'm not sure. Maybe '01, or '02."

Nathaniel, in Agnes's estimation, was a bit too pleased with himself and was probably embellishing for Lizzie's benefit. Agnes would look it up in the annual reports that were kept in the store room.

"Lizzie tells me your husband was a surfman," Mrs. Duncan said, looking at Agnes. "And your father had been the keeper?"

She gave them the broad outlines of her life: how she'd grown up at the station as the keeper's daughter and how she'd married a surfman at seventeen. How her father had succumbed to influenza after retiring and Amos died on the job three years ago. She rarely spoke of the night her husband died and might have ended her recounting at the mention of his death, but, there among a sympathetic group, found herself for the first time wanting to talk about what happened. No one here knew the story, as far as she knew, for none of the bachelor surfmen at the table had worked at the station the day Amos died. So she described how the lifeboat had broached and the surfmen all had tumbled out and Amos had been knocked unconscious, whether by the lifeboat itself or by an oar or floating debris no one was certain. When the crew brought him to shore they'd been unable to revive him. They had been a man short that day, and had filled the vacancy with a volunteer who, in Agnes's estimation, was a poor oarsman. It should have been her rowing instead. Her father used to say a single poor oarsman always hampers the boat. Agnes left out this detail, however, not wanting to lay blame.

Lizzie offered words of sympathy, and then asked, rather abruptly, "Do you think you'll marry again?"

Startled, Agnes caught Lizzie's conspiratorial glance at her brother.

"Lizzie, don't be impertinent," Mrs. Duncan said. Then, to Agnes, "Please ignore my daughter."

Agnes didn't answer. What would she say? That she didn't have a strong desire to marry again, although she felt others wishing it for her—Sunny and Maman and evidently Lizzie, too? And with Lizzie, it almost felt like a betrayal. Did Lizzie not know her at all? Agnes was content letting people assume her continued widowhood arose from an old-fashioned devotion to Amos's memory. Truth was she liked making day-to-day decisions without having to first check with someone else. A new husband would want to go one way when she wanted to go another. It was difficult enough with Maman. And if she married the keeper? Her days would be spent cooking and cleaning for a troop of bachelors and she'd have no time or energy for anything else. Maybe she was being selfish.

Agnes left the station at two o'clock. Keeper Duncan tried to persuade her to wait out the storm with them, and though it would have been more prudent, there was the pull of Maman's worry. Agnes accepted a basket of leftover chicken and macaroni, put on her wool coat and mittens, and set out for home.

She started along the water's edge, the most direct route and the way she'd come. But the strengthening storm made for difficult walking, and the wind pushed her inland. The bare trees and conifers bent away from the water. Snow rushed past her face, whipped into a frenzy by a wind that blew with a terrible ferocity. Her progress was slow and careful. One piece of driftwood in a gust could knock her from here to kingdom come.

Whitefish Bay, Lake Superior

Cordelia and the crew of the *Marguerite* had been waiting almost twenty-four hours since dropping anchor Saturday night. They were far from alone. The twenty-five-mile-wide Whitefish Bay was dotted with anchored ships, an argosy sandwiched between gray flannel sky and dark choppy water. The snow fell and the wind gusted near forty miles an hour, and because whatever lay beyond the Whitefish Point Lighthouse was surely worse, they had waited. Most storms blew themselves out in three days, and so by Sunday afternoon Edmund expected the weather to improve at any moment. He was intent on leaving the bay for the open water of Lake Superior before nightfall.

So that the officers would be ready as soon as there was a break in the weather he had requested an early supper. The steward served beef hash and creamed carrots in the officers' dining room. Edmund ate quickly, his mood soured. This trip had taken on an element of desperation; clearly he was anxious to avoid yet another late arrival. Cordelia had given up any pretense that this was a honeymoon, a chance to get to know her husband better. This was her husband's job. His work was difficult to begin with, and the storm made it immeasurably harder. Edmund, never effusive, had no time for long conversations with his new wife.

It was her fault. Despite never having set foot on a straight decker, she'd assumed Great Lakes sailing, even on a bulk freighter in early November, would be a romantic endeavor. The daughter of a life-saving station keeper ought to know better! She could imagine her father now, concerned about the weather yet also amused at her folly, the squinting wrinkles curling up like extra lashes at the corners of his eyes. They had always been close; her father had been her reading companion during quiet evenings at the station. He'd taught her how to swim. When she was very young he was the one she'd run to with a hurt finger or bruised feelings. He'd sit in his rocking chair, cradling her in his lap, and the sound of his voice never failed to soothe her.

When he died seven years ago, it was like she'd been set adrift. At thirteen years of age, she and her family were falling apart. Sunny was at sea nine months a year and Agnes lived at the station with her husband and daughter, leaving Cordelia and Maman alone in the pale-yellow cottage. It wasn't long after that that Lewis starting coming around, and she was grateful for his cheerful presence. There were other suitors, too, and though Lewis was a year younger than Cordelia, she ultimately chose him. Lewis was from a good family, well regarded in the small town of Port Austin, and together with his father ran a successful store. Even better, his sunny optimism made for good company. He made her laugh with his antics. He was daring, doing back flips off the side of his rowboat in summer and standing up on his sled as it sped downhill in winter. They had started talking of marriage just after his twentieth birthday. Weeks later he died in a wagon accident and Cordelia was set adrift again.

In an attempt to escape her grief, over the summer she'd fled to Detroit to visit her niece Aimee, who'd just moved there for secretarial school. Aimee, along with some fellow classmates, had taken Cordelia to Electric Park. The roller coasters and the Ferris wheel thrilled, momentarily holding her sadness at bay, but what truly made a difference was the Palais de Danse—the new ballroom that extended out over the Detroit River. It was at a concert there that Cordelia met Edmund

Blythe, the older brother of one of Aimee's new friends. What she hadn't realized at the time was that this was no chance encounter: Aimee had planned it all along.

Edmund Blythe was handsome, intelligent, and quiet. If he thought she talked too much he didn't say so. She told herself it was love and, not without some guilt over Lewis's memory, threw her attention to him. He proposed by letter a few weeks later. Cordelia imagined her father would be proud: she'd landed a Great Lakes captain. Although, in truth, it was Maman who'd always boasted about how well her youngest daughter would marry. For guidance, Cordelia wrote to Aimee, who replied that Lewis would have wanted her to be happy. That had to be true. Two days after their September elopement in his hometown of Cleveland, Edmund was back on the water. It had all happened so fast.

And now she found herself in a dark, vast bay at the eastern tip of the continent's largest body of freshwater, waiting for a storm to end. As they left the dining room at the ship's stern, Edmund looked to the sky. Somewhere beyond the heavy cloud cover the sun was setting. The snowfall had ceased at last, the winds lessened. The storm's worst had passed, he said, and it was time to leave Whitefish Bay. The snow had already put him a day behind schedule, and the owners wouldn't be happy about that.

Cordelia was eager to cross Lake Superior, too, if only to hasten the trip's end. She couldn't rid her mind of those iced-over ships locking down at the Soo in a ghostly procession. She shivered despite her overcoat and gloves, despite Edmund's arm around her as she held the lifeline. The gray sky darkened to charcoal, and the other waiting ships' lights grew more distinct, points of yellow-white scattered across the bay.

In watching that expanse of dark water stippled with whitecaps, it wasn't hard to imagine a fantastical sea creature like Mishipeshu rising up and thrashing ships with its gigantic tail. She'd read too many novels, as her mother would say, and they'd poisoned her mind. Be that as it may, Cordelia found a penny in her coat pocket and tossed it furtively into the water, an offering to the copper-loving Great Lynx.

After Edmund returned to the wheelhouse, she took a magazine to the observation room and chose a leather chair on the port side. There was a great shuddering as the windlass pulled up the anchor. The quaking would have scared her had she not known what it was. All the same she was glad when it stopped. The bay beyond the windows was black, save for the dots of light they were preparing to leave behind. How many other captains would follow Edmund's lead? She opened her magazine and tried to read a short story, but her gaze passed over the words, unseeing. She didn't want to be alone. After grabbing a sweater from Edmund's quarters, she went to the wheelhouse.

As she arrived, Edmund was approaching the engine room telegraph, or chadburn. It reminded Cordelia of a clock face, except instead of two hands and numbers, it had one hand and words: Full, Half, and Slow (Ahead); and Full, Half, and Slow (Astern); and Stop. When Edmund moved the pointer on the chadburn to Slow Speed Ahead, as he did just now, the pointer on the engine room's chadburn would move likewise.

It was a three-hundred-fifty-mile trip across Lake Superior. Once they reached Duluth, about thirty-six hours from now, the *Marguerite* would trade its cargo of coal for iron ore and return to Cleveland. Cordelia settled herself on a stool at the back of the wheelhouse to watch as the *Marguerite* maneuvered past the other anchored ships. Despite the freezing temperatures outside, she was comfortable thanks to her sweater and the wheelhouse's steam radiators.

To the west, off the port side, Edmund pointed out the Whitefish Point Lighthouse, which marked the spot where the bay ended and the open water of Lake Superior began. All she could see of it in the growing darkness was a white light with flashes of red every few seconds.

They were finally on their way again. But scarcely an hour after they passed the lighthouse, the lake changed. The seas swelled and came at them fast. The wind howled like it was alive and angry and intent on punishment. The wheelhouse windows rattled and moaned. Edmund had been tricked. He'd been lured from the safety of the bay with the promise of clearing weather only to find that out here, the storm hadn't subsided.

The wheelsman shifted his feet for leverage as he pushed against the large wooden spokes. Cordelia held her breath, watching the strain in his jaw as he worked to keep the ship's bow facing the oncoming waves. She found herself half-mimicking his movements, as if to help him steer.

There came a terrible gust of wind and the ship's bow swung to port. Edmund picked up the telephone to the engine room. They mustn't yield to the weather, he told the chief engineer at the stern. They must keep going, into the wind, full speed ahead. He hung up the phone and told the wheelsman to keep the *Marguerite* on course, that there was plenty of coal in the bunker to fight the wind and waves for as long as it took.

And so they forged ahead in the worsening weather, hour after interminable hour. Cordelia's head and neck ached from the constant tension. Sweat formed at her temples and her mouth was dry. This was madness, and she hated it. Anyone who did this more than once was addled.

The *Marguerite* was equipped with an electric searchlight, the hand control for which extended downward from the ceiling above Edmund. Now as he moved the searchlight's beam it illuminated a wave as tall as the ship itself.

Taller. Cordelia's mind raced with the ludicrous idea there might be somewhere to hide from this wall of water. She stepped off the stool but didn't know where to go next, so she just stood there, unable to move, unable to look away from the water. Unable to breathe.

The wheelsman struggled to head into it. Spray hit the wheelhouse as the monstrous wave lifted the bow, and as the deck slanted beneath her, she lost her footing. She stumbled, hitting her hip against the chart table. The *Marguerite* crested the wave and then slammed its bow down into the trough. The wheelhouse windows went black as water blocked out all light. Then came the spray flickering through the ship's searchlight.

"Brace yourself," Edmund said.

Cordelia moved to the back corner and put her hands on an aft and portside windowsill. Pressing against the windowsills, she readied herself.

The next wave came quickly. This time Cordelia held steady as the bow tilted up, crested the wave, and slammed with a tremendous crash into the trough, a momentary blackness followed by spray rising up all around. She felt almost giddy with terror. None of it seemed real.

Snow fell thickly now, as if they were trapped inside a giant snow globe. The wind roared against the deck and forecastle. The storm had gotten terribly loud: the screaming wind, the waves breaking all around that threatened to rip the steel hull. The only quiet thing was the snow, which now fell so heavily that, when she peered through the wheelhouse's rear windows, she could no longer see the electric light at the stern.

They were unreachable out here. Whatever happened, there was no one to help them. Cordelia thought she might be sick but couldn't bring herself to leave the wheelhouse and didn't dare say anything to Edmund. She wouldn't speak again until the storm was over. For once she was without words. Maman would have been pleased at her newfound quiet.

In the whiteout, the next wave wasn't visible, but she could hear it. Hear it rising, feel it pulling the ship up into its curve, into what must have been a giant wall of water. There was the sound of it cresting well above them. This monster wave was invisible to her but in her mind she saw it rise to insurmountable heights.

She braced herself against the windowsills. She should have gotten her life jacket, but it was down in their berth, and it was too late now, and anyway she was paralyzed in her fear. This was it. The invisible wave lifted the bow, unevenly, and the wheelsman struggled against the spokes. The bow kept rising, pushed up by the growing wave. They were going to flip, bow over stern.

The rising stopped and they began to fall, and Cordelia pushed against the windowsills with all her strength, and it seemed they would drop forever when the ship slammed into the valley bottom.

Cordelia lost her grip and the deck came up to meet her. A flash of pain in her jaw and she pressed her hands against the deck as it tilted one way and then the other. She tasted metal. Her knuckles were white. Still prostrate, she glanced up at Edmund's face, to gauge by his expression their chances of survival. But his features were stone. Neither Richard nor Ollie showed signs of panic. Again she looked to Edmund. Everyone appeared calm, as if this were nothing unusual. She was not soothed by their tranquil expressions; instead she felt more alone, as if only she saw things as they really were.

Silently she begged Edmund to turn the ship around. Go back to Whitefish Bay. It was folly to press on in this storm.

For interminable minutes Edmund said nothing. He watched the storm, his expression inscrutable. "We can't make any headway in this," he said at last, and gave orders to return to Whitefish Bay.

Richard responded no differently to this command than he had to all those preceding it, but Cordelia thought she saw a twitch of relief on his face, a momentary softening of his jaw. She glanced at Ollie, who bowed his head only for a second, perhaps thanking heaven they were retreating.

She lay her forehead on the cold tile. They were going back. This would be over soon.

She didn't see the next breaker, only heard its roar and felt the shuddering of the ship. There was a gust of wind and the *Marguerite* swung sharply.

"I can't get her to come around," Richard said, pushing hard against the spokes.

Edmund watched the compass. "We're pointed due south. Keep trying."

If they were pointed due south, then they were headed toward Lake Superior's treacherous southern coast. Shipwreck Coast, it was called. She watched Edmund's face. The waves were breaking over the stern now, pushing the *Marguerite* toward the rocky shallows. In this blizzard, even the watchman wouldn't see the coastline coming. Edmund ordered the engine room to put the ship in reverse.

Her husband knew what he was doing. He wouldn't let them founder. Edmund turned to her. Behind him, the wheelhouse windows showed only snow as it arced toward them out of the blackness, briefly illuminated by the ship's light just before hitting the glass. She became dizzy, almost hypnotized, by the never-ending flakes curving furiously into them.

But it was the way he looked at her now—a look she shouldn't have seen—that frightened her most. The flash of concern, of regret. He was wishing she hadn't come. He said nothing but he was thinking that her death would be his fault. But the blame lay only with Cordelia. She'd been so anxious for her life to begin. To get over losing Lewis. She'd wanted an adventure and here it was.

In an instant Edmund's stoicism returned but it was too late. She'd seen the truth. Her body tingled. Her fingers and toes went numb. The darkness seeped in from her peripheral vision and everything went black.

Lake Huron

The wave slamming the boilerhouse starboard sounded like the end of everything. The *Titus Brown* pitched heavily to port. Cold water rushed into the pantry where Sunny had fallen against the tilting bulkhead, icy water rising up and around her and soaking her skirt and legs. The boat leaned further, then further still.

She braced herself for the final tipping. Where was Herb now that they were all about to die?

The *Titus Brown* hung, mid-tilt. Suspended between air and water long enough for Sunny to change her mind half a dozen times about whether they would or would not tip all the way over.

Then the freighter pitched back to starboard and water sloshed in the opposite direction and Sunny slipped across the pantry with it. Grabbing the counter with one hand, she came to a stop and rubbed the back of her head where she'd hit a shelf. The boat rocked back and forth, though not as steeply as moments before, and with some effort she stood to escape the frigid water. Holding onto the doorway, she stepped gingerly through the water to the galley.

A galley window had been smashed right through. A prickling sensation swept up her arms. The storm was inside now, with them. Its roar filled the room.

Holding onto rolling bars as she went, Sunny moved closer to the exterior bulkhead near the broken window. Next to the galley was a companionway that led from a spar deck-level door down to the engine room.

The door was gone!

She peered down the companionway. With each big wave water rushed in through the breach, down the companionway and into the engine room below. Not every wave breached the gunwales, but those that did sent more water rushing through the boilerhouse's broken places and down below. If the pumps stopped working they wouldn't have long at all.

The steamer's whistle was up on the smokestack, which protruded from the top of the boilerhouse. Sunny listened for the abandon-ship signal—seven short blasts followed by one long one. The room spun and she struggled to organize her thoughts. She mustn't succumb to panic. She must stay calm. Remember her training. First, Herb. She had to find Herb. And get her money, and the letter to Agnes, and the rest of her savings. If they had to abandon ship, she must have that money with her. Then she would find Herb and they'd be ready for the lifeboat. If it came to that.

Moving from rolling bar to rolling bar, her legs shaking, she passed through the galley to the mess room. Men braced themselves between the tables and the bulkhead. The oiler stood beside the spar deck door. The ship took a sea over the stern, and water rushed in through the boilerhouse's broken windows and bulkheads and doors, carrying lima beans and spoons and what have you, and seconds later the oiler opened the door to let water and all it carried drain out of the mess room.

"Where's Herb?" Sunny shouted into the room.

Only shrugs.

She moved toward the door to the spar deck. Maybe Herb had gone to their cabin. Either way, she had to go there to get her money. Taking a deep breath to calm her quaking limbs, she waited for the right moment.

"No, Mrs. Colvin!" the oiler shouted when he realized what she was about to do. "You can't go out there!"

But when he opened the door to let the water flow out, she slipped past him.

The exterior passageway had iced over, and she clung to the slippery rolling bars hung at intervals. The boat pitched and the spray stung and if she wasn't quick another sea would slam the stern before she reached her cabin. She moved cautiously from bar to bar without stopping and made it around the corner to the port side. Now she was leeward, sheltered from the northeast wind's bluntest force. Pressing her body against the boilerhouse, she inched her way to her cabin and opened the door.

Anything they hadn't secured was being tossed around. The china mug where she kept her sea glass had fallen and china shards and sea glass scattered about like a broken kaleidoscope.

Herb wasn't there. She checked their washroom. Empty.

Panic rose up in her throat. The worst had happened. She envisioned the horrible scene: Herb on the exterior passageway. That giant sea washing him overboard. No one witnessing his last moments.

No. This was terrible thinking and she must stop.

The common washroom in the boilerhouse. She hadn't checked there.

Quickly, she climbed on their berth to reach the shelf where the life belts were stowed. She pulled them down and jammed her arms through the holes and tied it at the front. A canvas jacket filled with pieces of cork, the life belt was bulky and heavy and, like everyone else, she didn't like wearing it. Next she retrieved her saved wages and her letter to Agnes from the locked box on the shelf behind the life belts, and stashed them in the pocket of her pea coat.

In the drawer beneath her berth she found a woolen hat and put it on. How optimistic of her!

As she opened the door to the exterior passageway something whipped past in the near distance. A large piece of canvas. It flapped violently, as if there were a person inside struggling to get out. Then it was gone. The canvas reappeared in a flash, and Sunny recoiled in alarm. It wasn't the same canvas. Another had blown free. These were the tarpaulins that protected the hatch covers, which prevented water from leaking into the cargo hold. And without them—she didn't want to think about it. The second tarpaulin, flapping like a lunatic, became smaller and smaller until it disappeared behind a wave.

Sunny waited until the boat started to tip to starboard and then hurried out of the cabin. Unless they were called to abandon ship, this would be the last time she came out on deck. It was far too dangerous even now. She moved, rolling bar to rolling bar, straining her muscles to hold onto the rocking, tilting boat until she reached the mess room door. The door swung open as the oiler let out more water. She slipped inside, doubling over in relief. She'd made it.

Still no sign of her husband. "Herb!" She shouted as she made her way to the washroom, but her voice had no volume above the gale. The howling sounded less like wind, more like a wild beast racing across the water, charging at the *Titus Brown*.

Herb! He was coming out of the washroom at the end of the interior passageway. He slumped down, not seeing her. She rushed to him. He held his head, his eyes closed. When she put her hand on his shoulder he looked at her.

Her heart sank. He looked terrible. "Are you all right?" She shouted, inches from his face. He'd hit his head. Maybe he'd also been sick, although he said nothing. "What can I do?" The boat rocked ceaselessly and she braced herself in the narrow passageway.

Herb only shrugged.

She wanted to tell him about the washed-away door and the broken galley window, about the water pouring down into the engine room. She wanted to tell him she was scared. A shameful part of her wanted to tell him *I told you this would happen sooner or later*. Instead she helped him into his life belt without saying anything at all.

Dear, loving Herb. It was wrong to blame him for her being trapped in this storm. All he'd wanted was for them to be together. There were plenty of husbands who didn't care to have their wife around at all. She should be grateful she had a good man who loved her and wanted her near. If she had anyone to be angry with, it was herself. Angry at her own cowardice. For all her bravado, the real problem was her fear, wasn't it? She'd been afraid to tell Herb exactly *why* she wanted to go ashore. Afraid to put into words the dream that had sustained her for years. And because she'd waited so long, now none of it might matter.

Sunny helped her husband to the crew's sitting room off the galley. A small space, it had a table and four chairs, and a bookcase mounted on the wall. Like the galley and the pantry and the mess, it was a wet shambles. Water everywhere it shouldn't be. Sloshing about in the ankle-deep freshwater were paperbacks and envelopes and woolen socks. Playing cards and walnut shells. A banjo slapped repeatedly against the bulkhead.

Alone in a corner, his head in his hands, was Stilts. He looked at them, his face pale as white dough. The poor kid was terrified.

"You ok?" Sunny mouthed, moving closer. Her throat hurt from shouting. She sat Herb on a low table, which was bolted to the deck.

Stilts nodded, a vacant expression on his face. His life belt dangled from his lanky arm. "Mrs. Colvin?"

She moved closer to hear.

"My real name is Walter. My mama named me after my uncle."

Sunny put a hand on his shoulder. Then, with an enthusiasm she didn't feel, "Well, Walter, you'll have a story to tell when you get home!"

Stilts—it was too late, she'd always think of him as Stilts—smiled wanly. He put his arms through the life belt armholes and tied the front.

"Keep an eye on my husband, Walter. All right?"

The young man nodded and she left the sitting room. Bracing herself against the boat's pitching, she followed the narrow passageway to the mess room to see what anyone knew about their condition. The oiler stood next to the door, now closed, to the spar deck. Large waves were coming as fast as once a minute, and every third or fourth of those was greater still and washed over the boilerhouse. The ship took another sea over the stern, and the oiler opened the door to let water drain out.

The door was fully open when something moved in the darkness beyond. The electric light coming from within and above the boilerhouse illuminated a human figure flipped on its back, legs kicking up like a turned-over beetle. The man was tangled in the coils of the ship's towline. The hawser must have washed loose, but what on earth was someone doing out there to begin with? Sunny watched in horror as the man scrambled, slipping like a cat on a frozen pond. The man lunged at the doorway and the oiler pulled him in and closed the door.

It was one of the wheelsmen.

Without asking what in heaven's name he was doing all the way aft, Sunny ushered the shivering wheelsman toward the officers' dining room. On the way she asked Pug, who was in the mess room with the crew, to bring him a dry blanket if he could find one.

In the galley Sunny found Cleve standing in knee-deep water trying to salvage what he could from their stores, now floating freely about: broken china and pie tins, dinner rolls and potatoes. Dozens of apples. Though she admired his levelheadedness, she signaled for him to give up the task. He continued anyway.

The third mate appeared in the galley and for a moment Sunny thought she'd imagined him. It made no sense, another of the forward crew here in the boilerhouse! She gave him a quizzical look.

Shutters! The mate shouted above the storm, and Sunny understood that the Old Man had sent them aft to shutter the boilerhouse windows. The waves were too much, however, and the shutters had washed right out of their hands. They were lucky they hadn't gone overboard with them. She pointed in the direction of the dining room and shouted the wheelsman's name, and the mate nodded, clearly relieved, and left the galley.

By eight o'clock it was snowing so hard there was nothing but white beyond the mess room windows, cut through by angry sprays of water hitting the glass. Sunny forced herself to take deep breaths, to calm her nerves. Nothing in her memory compared to this. This was more than a November gale. This was a hurricane. The forecastle, several hundred feet forward and invisible in the whiteout, was now reachable only by the telephone between the captain and the chief engineer. For the crew aft, all the ship might as well be this boilerhouse.

It'd been maybe an hour since the seas destroyed the galley window and engine room door, and, mercifully, Sunny still felt the engine with its mighty pistons working beneath her feet. Hard as the engine must be working, it was impossible that the *Titus Brown* was staying its course. They were taking such a beating from the northeast wind and the waves on the starboard side. They should have been passing Alpena by now. Did Captain Hanna even know their location? As mighty as the 1600-horsepower steam engine was, this storm was pushing them toward the Michigan shore—that much had to be true.

Sunny collected several mugs and returned them to the galley sink, mostly out of habit. She shifted her weight to adjust for the pitching when a horrific sound came from overhead. Her initial reaction was that of wonder: Here was a sound that, in all her thirty-three years, was new to her ears. Her mind raced to categorize it. Not a benign sound. No, it was all wrong. The noise was malevolent. Disastrous. This was—

A rush of water knocked her to the ground and the frigid water rushed over her face. She held her breath.

Don't panic. Panicking helps no one.

The water slammed her against something hard and unforgiving and when the water receded she gasped for air and just as her lungs filled with oxygen a liquid wall slammed her down again.

This time the water was taking her with it.

This is the wave that sinks the boat.

The water carried her—where? Out onto the deck where she would go overboard. She reached out her arms that they might catch on something. This was the end of it. She kicked and screamed and somewhere outside her body watched herself get swept away: There went Sunny Colvin, washed to her doom. She was falling with the water. Her muscles tightened for the final submersion.

Something hard slammed into her torso. She was pinned against the hard thing and couldn't breathe for the force of the water against her chest and the water flooding her face.

This wasn't Lake Huron she'd fallen into. She hadn't gone overboard. This was somewhere inside the *Titus Brown*. Little that it mattered, for the water kept coming.

How long could she hold her breath? Five more seconds? Ten? Soon she would pass out, and then drown. Calm yourself, Sunny. Calm yourself, and you'll need less air.

Finally, mercifully, the rushing water stopped. She coughed and sputtered until she was breathing again. There was a noise—a rhythmic pulsing like a million flags flapping in unison. A grated metal landing lay beneath her. She lifted her head. The engine room. She'd fallen down the companionway to the engine room. The pulsing noise was the boat's steering mechanism.

The water that had nearly killed her had kept rushing past. It had washed through the grated landing and down another two stories to the lowest part of the engine room, the bottommost part of the boat.

Her right hip and shoulder throbbed. She brought herself to a crouching position, grabbed the metal railing, and peered down twenty feet. An oiler was tickling the pipes with one hand, his oilcan in the other, as always. He went about his work as if it were a normal day. This was good; nothing had overheated yet. With the engines running full steam for so long, overheating was a real danger.

The chief engineer appeared, gesturing wildly and shouting at the oiler. Sunny moved to put her feet underneath her to stand. She should get up to the galley and find Herb. Another sea rushed down the companionway, pressing her to the railing. She held her breath and waited for it to pass.

She forced herself to quiet the rising panic in her chest. The water would pass before she did. It would. Pinned to the railing, she closed her eyes.

When the rushing water stopped she opened them again. She looked at her hands and gasped. Her wedding band was gone! Her fingers must have shrunk with the cold, allowing the seas to wash the ring right off. This was a little death. She'd loved that gold band. To let the storm snatch it away was almost too much to bear. She could climb down into the engine room and search for it.

It was a ridiculous thought. She'd never find it.

She must move quickly. There wouldn't be much time before the next avalanche of water. Clasping the railing with both hands, she scrambled up the companionway to deck level. At the top she turned right, avoiding the opening where the door to the spar deck had washed away.

Her blood ran cold at the sight of the galley.

Half the galley roof had been smashed in. Broken planks splintered above her head. The skylight was destroyed. The exterior bulkhead had collapsed inward. Pieces of woodwork floated in the knee-deep water. She pulled herself along with the aid of the rolling bars, shivering wildly, moving through the water to the officers' dining room. The exterior bulkhead had crumpled there, too. The table, bolted to the deck, remained in place, surrounded by splintered chairs and broken salt shakers and forks and knives and spoons the seas had not yet taken.

What had become of the two lifeboats tied to the boat deck above the boilerhouse? The wave that had damaged the galley may also have washed away or destroyed at least one of them, if not both. Was there a way off the *Titus Brown*, if it came to that? She couldn't stop shivering. It was getting harder to walk, her feet were so cold. They'd been drenched in icy water for more than an hour.

Herb appeared in the dining room doorway, his face white with panic. He rushed to her and put his strong arms around her small frame. He squeezed her tight. Upon pulling away, he produced a blanket, opened it up and wrapped it around her body in one fluid motion. He was looking at her with an expression of deep concern.

She shrugged. *I'm fine*, was what she meant. She stumbled after Herb to the mess room where the others waited. The mate and wheelsman, who'd been in the officers' dining room when that monstrous wave hit, had moved to the mess room with the crew. So had Stilts. Only the mess room and crew's sitting room remained fully intact. The cabins too, maybe, but they were inaccessible as it was far too dangerous to go out on deck.

The storm was taking apart the *Titus Brown*, piece by piece. What about the wheelhouse and the Old Man? Were the forward officers all right? Had more windows broken? Sunny grabbed the edge of the table to steady herself as the boat rocked. They were all alone out there, in the middle of Lake Huron during the worst November gale in the history of the Great Lakes.

There were some positives: One, the boat was upright and, although it pitched and tossed, at times to terrifying degrees, it did not yet list. Two, the engine was still running. Three, there was no call to abandon ship. And four, they were facing the storm and waves head on. As long as the wheelsman could keep them head-to, they had a fighting chance.

How was it possible that the wind roared even louder? Had they not been surrounded by miles of water on all sides Sunny would have sworn a freight train was bearing down upon them.

There came a tremendous colliding sound and the ship swung violently. Water rushed in from everywhere and Sunny fell against the table as the deck rose up beneath her.

Port Austin, Michigan

The furious onshore winds and the threat of what objects they might whip in her direction convinced Agnes to trade the coastline for a more inland route to her cottage. There were several paths through the woods along which she might find her way to the road. The road would make for a longer journey, but it would be safer.

She searched for one of the trails she used to follow when her daughter was young and they'd traipse through the forest looking for fairies. Without too much trouble she found a path and followed it for a good amount of time. The howling wind off the lake was unnerving, but the dense forest protected her from its blunt force. Where the trail led out of the woods, she expected to find the main road into town. But the road instead was a different one, a side road leading to the life-saving station. She squinted, momentarily confused. It couldn't be. She'd made barely any progress at all! A moment of indecision and then she turned south, away from the lake. This would be a longer walk than she'd anticipated, made more difficult by the accumulating snow. The wind rushed at her back and she shrugged further into her coat.

She should have stayed at the station. That was her last thought before a tree limb flew through the falling snow and straight at her. She dove out of the way, and it was only the branch's twiggy ends that lashed at her legs as she hit the ground. Powdery snow pressing against her cheek, she lay flat on the side of the road. Her heart pounded in her ears. That branch could have killed her! The roast chicken lay several feet from her head in a nest of snow. The bowl of macaroni had landed upside down next to the empty basket, still hooked on her arm.

This was a fool's errand. Surely Maman would understand the danger.

Agnes stood up, brushed herself off, and returned the dish-towel and now-empty bowl to the basket. She turned north and followed the road back toward the station. More than once a strong gust of wind pushed her from her path. She would have to wait out the storm with the lifesavers. The very worst of these gales rarely lasted more than a few hours. And once the worst was over, sometime after supper most likely, she would walk home along the lake's edge and make her apologies to Maman. It would be dark by then, but if she timed it right, she could walk by the lantern of the surfman on beach patrol.

She returned to the station unharmed, but by seven o'clock that evening, the time Agnes had expected to start out for home, the roaring gusts were threatening to rip the station to shreds. Like everyone who lived along the Lake Huron shore, Agnes was no stranger to howling winds. Come January and February, when the northern winds raced unimpeded across a hundred miles of frozen or near-frozen lake, there came a howl you didn't soon forget. Some winters the unearthly moaning lasted for days. Many people found it unsettling. Agnes rather liked it. But nothing in her memory compared to this storm. She didn't dare leave the station.

"You'll have to stay here tonight," Mrs. Duncan said, handing Agnes the last plate to dry. "It's far too dangerous to go home. You can stay at the cottage with Lizzie and me."

Agnes felt a tremble of excitement. Suppressing a smile, she dried the plate and handed it to Lizzie, who stacked it in the cupboard. Mrs. Duncan dried her hands and took off her apron. "I'm going now. You both should come soon, before it gets much worse."

Agnes found herself unable to look directly at Lizzie for fear her cheeks had turned bright red. The prospect of spending more time with Lizzie, the more intimate evening hours, made Agnes feel thrillingly off balance. She found a chair and sat down.

Agnes had only just begun imagining the hours that lay ahead when Nathaniel sauntered into the kitchen. The way Lizzie looked at him made Agnes feel like a boat that had lost its rudder. Agnes knew what that look meant. Lizzie had fallen for this man from Vermilion who clearly thought very well of himself, and the young woman's friendship would be all but lost to her. Agnes went into a tunnel, Lizzie's and Nathaniel's voices becoming far away and indistinct. Without looking at either of them, she mumbled something about going to look at the boats. No one stopped her. As Agnes crossed the threshold Lizzie said something about being careful, a hint of worry in her voice that Agnes relished.

She'd come to the boathouse for a better view of the tempest—that was what she'd told herself, anyway. She really oughtn't to be bothered by Lizzie's affection for Nathaniel. Despite the young woman's protestations, she would marry sooner or later. It's what young people did. Lizzie would still be her friend, even if married to Nathaniel. Nothing would have to change between them. Agnes stood at the boathouse's north-facing window. Outside the station lights shone on a whiteout. Bursts of wind shook the boathouse walls. Waves crashed against the double doors and water seeped in under them. Agnes felt exposed out here, but less so than she had inside with Lizzie and Nathaniel. Had Lizzie seen the truth? For the truth of it was this: Agnes loved Lizzie. And not merely as a friend. Agnes was in love with her. It was difficult to comprehend how she got to this point. Agnes had loved her husband. Had loved him faithfully for nearly twenty years. And yet. The intensity of what she now felt for Lizzie, it made that love almost difficult to recall. Amos didn't deserve that. And he never would have understood this. Agnes felt terrible for it; her stomach twisted with guilt.

Icy spray pelted the boathouse windows like bird shot and she thought better of standing next to the glass. She moved to the center of the room, between the lifeboat and surfboat. She ran her hand along the lifeboat's cedar planking. These were some of the finest small craft ever built. That's what Amos used to say. Frames of white oak, planking from Pacific Northwest Port Orford cedar. Brass fittings. An image flashed before her: Agnes and Lizzie, together, happy. Blood rushed from her limbs; she needed to sit down.

Agnes climbed the stepladder into the lifeboat, careful not to disturb the meticulously packed equipment: an anchor, a funnel-shaped drogue, various lines and sheets, a life buoy, oars for eight men plus a steering oar, boat hooks, a lantern. She loved this boat, which had been put into service when her father was the keeper. He'd named it *Stalwart*. She sat on a thwart where Amos used to row. Her husband had been Surfman Number One, a position second only to the keeper.

Remorse and admiration swirled in her chest. This was where he had been sitting right before he died that terrible October day three years ago. With the crew a man short, Agnes had wanted to help row. She was an excellent oarswoman and Amos knew it. When he refused to let her volunteer, she'd threatened to ask the keeper directly. But what Amos countered was true: the keeper wouldn't allow what her own husband prohibited. And so instead they'd used a volunteer oarsman from the village. In Agnes's estimation they'd have been better off leaving the thwart empty. Even now she found herself wanting to change Amos's mind. To undo what had happened.

Dear Amos. She had loved her husband and their life by the sea. To now have these feelings for Lizzie, it felt like a betrayal of his memory, of everything they had shared. Agnes swallowed hard, forcing down the lump of conflicting emotions lodged there. Couldn't one thing be true, and then another, totally different thing, also be true?

There came a tremendous roar and Agnes dropped to the footings. A crash, a shattering. Her hands tingled. Several long seconds later she peered over the gunwales. The north-facing window, the one where she'd stood only minutes before, was gone.

The howling came fiercer now that the boathouse had been breached. Waves pounded on the double doors like a wild bull trying to get in. Water splashed through the broken window. Her heartbeat raced in her chest. She should get back to the main building, further from the water, but she didn't want to leave the security of the lifeboat. She felt like a hunted animal.

"Agnes! What are you doing out here?"

Keeper Duncan's voice came from somewhere behind her. She turned her head just as the electric lights went out. Now the sole light came from the main building behind Keeper Duncan, putting him in silhouette.

"Come back to the kitchen," he said, approaching the lifeboat. "It's a hurricane out there."

"What about the watchman?" Agnes asked. The watchtower sat atop the boathouse, and if it wasn't safe in the boathouse, it certainly wasn't safe above it.

"He's got a job to do."

Agnes climbed down from the *Stalwart* and followed Keeper Duncan through the breezeway to the main building. They'd only just crossed into the kitchen when there was a horrific sound. She'd once heard lightning strike a tree in her backyard. The cracking sound had been so loud she'd half expected the roof to cave in. This sound now was louder, fiercer; instinctively she crouched and covered her head.

When she turned around the breezeway was gone.

Keeper Duncan hurried her to the kitchen, which was the first-floor room furthest from the water's edge. The cottages were further still from the shore, including the one where Lizzie and her mother lived, but to get to them you had to go outside.

Nathaniel wasn't there in the kitchen. Agnes sat at the table next to Lizzie, who, for the first time in the months since they'd met, appeared frightened. Lizzie suddenly seemed so young. She was a decade younger than Agnes, of course. But the woman's usual self-possession was gone.

Lizzie clutched Agnes's arm. Agnes stared at Lizzie's hand, and even after the young woman had let go Agnes could feel Lizzie's grip on her skin. "You know the good thing about this storm?" Agnes said, trying to think of something to soothe her.

Lizzie looked at her.

"It'll churn up all sorts of treasures, treasures that have been resting on the lake bottom for years."

"From shipwrecks, you mean? Cripes, Agnes, that's morbid."

This new rejection stung. Even as an adult, it excited Agnes to spot a piece of shipwreck debris along the coast. How could Lizzie not understand? Over the years Agnes had found a broken oar still in its oarlock, bits of cabin, a personal diary, a lifeboat rudder, several wood-caulking mallets, a chair, crates, a hatch cover. One of her most interesting, and saddest, finds was a jar that had washed up days after a terrible autumn storm. There was a note inside: "Engines are lost. There is no hope. We are drifting in trough. Goodbye Josephine, I love you. Baines." Agnes had shown the jar and note to her father, and the mementos were sent to Baines's widow. Most of what Agnes found, however, was of little value to anyone but a curious collector like herself.

Nathaniel returned to the kitchen. When he glanced at Agnes she realized she'd taken his seat next to Lizzie. Agnes stayed where she was—a small act of defiance. She oughtn't to begrudge Lizzie her station romance. It was how she herself had met Amos, after all. It was hard not to idolize these men who risked their lives to save others in conditions that would scare most people away. Agnes was only jealous, which was silly. Had she really thought Lizzie had romantic feelings for her? Maybe Lizzie was more interested in conventional marriage than she'd let on.

Nathaniel wore his black sou'wester hat and rubberized cloth storm suit. That and the lantern in his hand meant he was going on beach patrol. He put his left hand on Lizzie's shoulder, who covered it with her own.

Agnes felt a pang of jealousy, despite herself. She looked down at the table, rubbed her finger in a gouge made years ago by a knife.

"Be careful," Lizzie said.

From the corner of her eye Agnes caught Nathaniel's gentle, intimate squeeze of Lizzie's shoulder. And then he was gone. A rush of frigid air filled the kitchen before the gale slammed the door shut behind him. It would be hours before he'd return. Nathaniel would have to walk three miles along the coast and back, watching for Coston signals and listening for distress whistles. A terrible part of Agnes hoped he wouldn't return at all. No, that wasn't fair. If she truly loved Lizzie, then she should want her to be happy.

Lizzie chewed on a fingernail and responded to Agnes's attempts at conversation with one-word, distracted answers. But when Keeper Duncan passed through the kitchen minutes later Lizzie didn't make a fuss to her brother, didn't ask if Nathaniel must go on beach patrol in weather as terrible as this. She must have known as well as Agnes did that Nathaniel had to patrol *because* the weather was as terrible as this.

Lake Superior

For hours after she fainted, Cordelia crouched at the back of the wheelhouse, fighting off seasickness. She felt like she'd swallowed a gallon of lake water and it swirled high in her stomach. Edmund could not bring the boat around to face the wind and waves. Monstrous seas broke over the stern, each one pushing the *Marguerite* closer to Lake Superior's southern shore.

Cordelia was exhausted. Her jaw ached where she'd hit the deck. Her muscles were strained from clinging to the stanchion at the top of the stairs to Edmund's quarters as the bow plummeted in a valley or pitched to port. Fighting her nausea left her little energy for fear and worry. The storm had been going on for so long now she was certain they'd ride it out this way, miserable as it was.

She had no idea where they were. An icy glaze covered all but two wheelhouse windows. Radiator steam had been plumbed against one window forward and one aft to keep them at least partially clear of ice. The watchman stood at the forward window, wiping the steam away with a towel and peering out into the blizzard. Ollie, the mate, wiped the steam from the window near her.

It was late into the night when Edmund checked his compass and ordered a sounding. Ollie operated the mechanical sounding machine that dropped a length of wire, lead at the end of it, into the depths of Lake Superior.

Fifty fathoms was what he hollered to Edmund.

This news pierced the fog of Cordelia's nausea. Fifty fathoms was three hundred feet. How much time did three hundred feet give them? Lake Superior at its deepest was more than a thousand.

They might hit the rocks. This new fear heightened her seasickness. She didn't want to move, but couldn't allow herself to vomit here. Easing down the stairway as the ship pitched, she clutched the railing and focused on a bit of tile at the bottom of the stairs. If she stared hard enough at the pattern of quatrefoils, she might will herself not to be sick. She made it to the washroom just in time to vomit into the toilet bowl and then collapsed on the black-and-white checkered tile. The cold squares against her cheek soothed her aching head and jaw.

Rising to her knees, she vomited into the bowl again.

Cordelia sprawled on the cool tile floor, bracing herself against the porcelain bowl as the ship tilted this way and that. She would stay here awhile. Her insides were at peace for the moment, and any change of position could stir unrest. And she was awfully tired. It was as if someone had pulled a stopper from her toe and all the strength she might have used to lift her limbs had seeped out. She lay across the tile, in the pool of her drained energy, and closed her eyes.

Cordelia roused—had she slept?—not knowing how much time had passed. It could be midnight or three in the morning. The *Marguerite* still pitched and tossed. It was really something, how she'd gotten used to it. She waited for her sickness to return, and when it didn't, she felt hopeful. She was feeling better and certainly they'd made progress upstairs. She went up to the wheelhouse.

Edmund was staring at the compass binnacle. He gave orders to the wheelsman, then asked the watchman what he could hear in the whiteout. The watchman had his ear to the window to listen for breakers slamming into a rocky coastline.

But there was nothing he could hear, he told Edmund, above the roaring wind and crashing seas.

Edmund ordered another sounding. Now the depth was one hundred fifty feet. Cordelia's stomach dropped. One hundred fifty feet was not much at all. They were getting too close.

Edmund appeared to deliberate something, then told the first mate to have the anchors ready. Ollie hesitated only a second before repeating the order and going below to the windlass room.

A minute later Edmund removed the cover from a tube and spoke into it. "All right, Ollie," he shouted. "Throw out the anchor."

The wheelhouse shuddered and Cordelia clung to the stanchion. The violent quaking felt like the ship was breaking apart. Her veins constricted and her heartbeat quickened. Once glance at Edmund, however, and she was reassured: It was just the anchor being released. The storm hadn't rent the ship to pieces. Nevertheless, when the quaking finally stopped, Cordelia had to rub her hands together until the blood returned.

Ollie reappeared from below. They'd released two hundred feet of chain, he said. Edmund, his face unreadable, gripped the stanchion near the front of the wheelhouse. He watched the forward windows. What could he possibly see? Even with the one window partially de-iced, nothing was visible in the blizzard. The *Marguerite* was heading bow first toward the coast with its anchor trailing beneath its spinning propeller.

If the chain caught in the propeller...

If the anchor didn't catch...

Cordelia held her breath and stared at the de-iced window and braced for something terrible. A collision with offshore rocks. A fracturing of the ship. She imagined it happening and her imaginings felt so real she clenched her jaw and tensed her body and thought she might go mad from the anticipation of it.

"She's not holding," Edmund said after a time. The anchors hadn't caught. He ordered oil poured down the anchor hawse pipes.

Cordelia covered her ears but couldn't escape the terrible roar of the breakers. The lake had an endless supply of fury, relentlessly pitching them up and down, always threatening to send them under. It was terrible to be so helpless. She shouted to Edmund: Was there anything she could do to help? He told her to stay put.

The wind roared louder and there was the sound of breaking glass. Cordelia screamed and dropped to the deck, covering her head with her hands. When she looked up she saw blood on the wheelsman's hands and wrists. He remained at the wheel, steady, even as the blood dripped down his arms.

Cordelia staggered to Edmund in the pitching ship. She offered to bandage Richard's hands, but Edmund pushed her away. There was no time for that.

How could a man steer a ship if he passed out from loss of blood? But she said nothing. Spray blew through the two broken wheelhouse windows. She wiped her face. Lake Superior got in her mouth, and it tasted of cold. The gale blew into the wheelhouse, stealing away what warmth it had managed.

Then the motion of the ship changed.

What did it mean? She looked to Edmund, but it was the wheelsman who spoke first.

"She's holding, Captain," Richard shouted.

Though she couldn't hear him above the storm, Edmund appeared to repeat the wheelsman's words, *She's holding*, with something like reverence. Then, louder, "Bring her head-to."

Cordelia cried out in relief. They would be all right.

Richard turned the wheel, hard. A wave hit on the port side. The *Marguerite* rolled to starboard and Cordelia slid across the wheelhouse deck. Fear jumping in her throat, she scurried to the stanchion at the top of the stairs leading down to Edmund's quarters. She wrapped her arms around the brass pole, now wet and slippery, and held on for dear life. The ship tilted to such an angle that she hung from the pole, nearly parallel with the deck. She held her breath and tried to make herself light. Light as the air in her lungs. The ship hung there an interminable moment before rolling to port, and she swung around to the other side of the stanchion.

Richard strained at the wheel and the *Marguerite* was hit broadside again. Again the ship pitched starboard to a terrifying degree. Edmund held onto a rolling bar between windows; his legs swung out from beneath him. They were going to die. There was no way to survive this. It was impossible for a ship to tilt this much and not tip over.

Richard worked the giant wheel and the ship— miraculously—righted, only to be slammed again, and again Cordelia dangled from the stanchion as if she were in mid-air. This was madness. She was all terror.

An eternity later, the extreme rolling ceased. A wave of relief coursed through her body. She laughed at her earlier fear, at her certainty of death. Richard had done it! He'd put the bow facing the wind and waves coming out of the north. Remembering her small attempt at steering the *Marguerite*, she now watched him, awestruck. This man's skill was beyond anything she'd ever witnessed.

"Bring her full speed ahead," Edmund shouted, and Ollie moved the handle on the chadburn's dial.

Cordelia, wet and shivering, was suspended in time. This was a never-ending night in a never-ending storm. But they had a chance, now. The anchor had caught. The ship was head to the wind, breasting the waves. They'd escaped the trough. Still the seas were high enough to crash over the ship and make it pitch—and with mere seconds between. After her earlier nausea she'd gone numb to the sickening sensation of rising and falling. Maybe the worst was over. They just had to stay like this until the storm subsided.

She was aware once again of her head aching with fatigue, her jaw throbbing from where she'd hit the deck. She was of no use in the cold, breached wheelhouse, and a new exhaustion overwhelmed her. She would try to get some rest, and if she were fortunate enough to fall asleep, then when she awoke maybe the storm would be over.

Without saying anything to Edmund she went down to his quarters. She opened the cover to a porthole window so she'd know when daylight came. Curled up on the berth, Cordelia closed her eyes. She would never sleep. She rolled from one side of the berth to the other in the pitching ship. She told herself not to worry. Things always seemed worse at night. If they made it until morning, they would be all right.

Lake Huron

With the force of that monster wave and the violent lurch it delivered, Herb had been flung against the mess room bulkhead. There was a nasty gash on his forehead and a broken electric light above him. Sunny, from across the room and in what little light remained, could see the blood drip down his face. A fear struck her heart that he might bleed to death, or if not that, then he might pass out from blood loss and drown right here in the boilerhouse. She had to help him, quickly.

She moved across the mess room toward her husband, a considerably more difficult task than it had been an hour ago. The boat rolled from starboard to port and back again, to such degrees it made the waves of just a half hour ago seem like ripples on a pond. No one had to say what was clear enough: The *Titus Brown* had fallen into a trough.

Icy water sloshed at her knees, flinging at her legs all sorts of debris—a coffee mug, an empty can, a splintered piece of wood paneling. She was dimly aware of others around her but focused only on her husband, collapsed in a corner. Water washed over him with each pitching of the boat. She touched a sticky area on his forehead and he cried out. Putting her arms under his shoulders, she helped him to his feet. The boat rolled and they fell against the bulkhead, which tilted to almost forty-five degrees. Then the boat rolled in the opposite direction and they stumbled against a table. To steady themselves, Herb pressed his hand to the bulkhead and Sunny pressed hers to the bolted-down table. The deck crew and the porters and the bosun, as well as the two officers, all were doing the same.

A preternatural calmness had come over the room. No expressions of fear or panic, despite the extreme rolling from the waves hitting them broadside. The danger was that their cargo—nine thousand tons of coal—would shift in the hold. If it shifted too far one way or the other, the boat would heel over to one side. And if that happened, the next big wave could roll them right over and there'd be no time for lifeboats. If they still had them.

Forget what might happen. Herb needed help now. He needed a bandage. And where was that carbolated Vaseline? The pantry, last she'd seen it.

Cleve came over to check on Herb's injury, but Herb waved him away. He liked to act tough, to never admit pain. It was hardly sensible. What would he do right now if Sunny weren't around? Bleed to death, most likely. Stubborn Herb. If they survived this night, he wouldn't even think twice about sailing next year. Most people would say to hell with sailing after a storm like this. Not her optimistic husband. On the contrary: He'd say it was a great time to sail. She could hear him now. He'd say, of course I'll keep sailing. What are the chances I'd ever see another storm as bad as that one?

She motioned for Cleve to help keep Herb braced between the bulkhead and table. Then she went to the passageway leading to the galley. A few deckhands, including Stilts, had moved from the mess room into the passageway. Its narrowness made it a good place to hold yourself steady. As she moved by Stilts, she barely had to duck to pass under his arm. She put her hand on his shoulder, and he responded with a weak smile.

Sunny continued to the galley, where the water splashed at her knees. With the boilerhouse roof partially collapsed and the starboard bulkhead of the galley and officers' dining room smashed in, more water rushed in with each tremendous wave. The desperate scene made her want to cry. She fought off panic by focusing on her task. On Herb.

But how to find a small tin tube of carbolated Vaseline in the soggy confusion that was now the pantry? She felt around in the icy water, reaching into splashing corners, her hands searching among waterlogged table linens and cans and the detritus of shipboard life. After a few minutes she gave up. The Vaseline and liniment were gone.

When she returned to the mess room the mate and wheelsman weren't there. Cleve nodded toward the engine room—they must have gone below to see how the engine was faring. Cleve was tending to Herb, pressing on the gash with a towel—a wet towel. Everything was wet.

The boat rolled severely again and Sunny fell against the bulkhead. The ship hung at port, as if it might stay there this time. Nearly prostrate, she felt water rush under her. The water wanted to overtake the *Titus Brown*.

The boat hung at an angle, perched between life and death.

"Goodbye, kiddos." It was the bosun. He lay next to her on the slanting bulkhead or she'd never have heard him. Not that he was talking to her. He had two children, a boy and a girl, seven and five. He was thinking of them.

She wouldn't give up, not yet. But what could she do, as they hung there between life and death? She might try moving to the other side of the mess room. If she climbed onto the table her weight might help the boat shift... Nonsense! Of course it wouldn't help! One hundred pounds wouldn't make the difference! And she'd likely stumble and fall anyway. The bosun was right. This was hopeless...She squeezed her eyes shut and held her breath. Agnes was going to be devastated. Who would make the chestnut stuffing for Christmas dinner?

And dear Agnes couldn't bake a good spiced gingerbread to save her soul. And now Sunny would never get the chance to run her own restaurant. She'd never know if she'd have succeeded or not.

Sunny slid off the bulkhead and onto the deck. Water sloshed all around.

She hadn't drowned! The *Titus Brown* had righted itself!

A second miracle: the little tin tube. It had washed into a corner of the mess room. She snatched it up. Of all things, here was something she could do. She could apply this ointment to Herb's wound.

Amid the relentless rolling and the waves of frigid water that splashed up to her waist as she braced between table and bulkhead, Sunny opened the tin tube. It took several tries as she struggled to maintain her balance but finally she applied the ointment to Herb's forehead.

Then the vibrations changed.

The boat tumbled and shook violently. Sunny's stomach lurched. The ship's propeller wheel had come out of the water. It would be impossible for the wheelsman to steer. They would never get out of this trough. The wind and the waves pressed in on them, holding them like a vise.

Waves slammed the stern. The metal groaned as the hull's plates pushed and pulled at the seams. The boat's construction allowed for some twisting and bending in the five-hundred-foot hull. A freighter this long riding seas this short needed some give. Exactly how much it could take was anyone's guess.

The first mate came into the mess room to fetch one of the oilers, to give the one working below a break. It was a dangerous job on a good day, and now the critical bearings were in constant danger of overheating.

The bosun asked about the steering gear and propelling power. Sunny, holding her breath, strained to listen.

"They're holding," the first mate shouted.

Sunny exhaled. That was as much as you could hope for. If either failed there was no chance of getting out of the trough.

The seas were coming even more quickly now. The gale rushed at them from the northeast, the winds having raced across a hundred miles of open lake. A one-two punch of waves slammed them starboard and they heeled even further than before.

A caving-in feeling lodged in Sunny's chest. They couldn't keep this up. They were losing the fight.

Focus. Next steps. She and Herb were assigned to lifeboat number two. She strained to hear an abandon-ship whistle above the freight-train winds and thrashing waves. As soon as it sounded she would grab Herb and they would go out the mess room door and along the exterior passageway and up the ladder to the boilerhouse roof. They would find their place on the thwart and hold on. Someone would untie the lifeboat and climb in and when the *Titus Brown* rolled they would launch.

What if there was no lifeboat for them? One of the boats must have been destroyed when that tremendous wave hit the galley and dining room. Even if they could all cram into one lifeboat, what chance would they have out on those mountainous seas?

A cold clamminess came over her. Her head ached. Nausea swirled in her gut. She needed to get away from the others, whose presence only made it worse. She left Herb and Cleve and sloshed her way through the passageway to the galley and then into the pantry.

The pantry porthole window was only partially covered in ice. It was in the boilerhouse's lee and somewhat protected by the small overhang of the roof, or else it might have been iced over entirely. Looking outside, she saw only whiteout illuminated by the *Titus Brown's* exterior electric lights. There was no horizon to steady her. She covered her mouth and pushed down the bile rising in her throat.

Clumped in a corner was a washcloth. Maman had knitted it for her ages ago. She picked it up, wrung it out, and pressed the cloth against her forehead. That felt a little better.

Water sloshed in and out of the pantry and with it came a tan booklet. *Hovey's Handbook of the Mammoth Cave of Kentucky.* She bent down to reach for it. Her fingers had nearly touched the soggy cover when the boat rolled and the handbook washed out of the pantry. Sunny let out a small cry—there went her memories washing out the door. Memories of Herb and their tenth anniversary vacation and their life together. The little booklet slid through the doorway and into the galley where it would probably wash out to sea. She would never see it again. She rested her head against the cupboards and closed her eyes. Bile rose up in her throat again. Again she kept it down.

Minutes later there was a break in the squall. She peered out the porthole window. The ship's lights illuminated waves like walls of water. Sunny drew back in horror. The thick coating of ice on the *Titus Brown's* deck caused them to ride lower, closing them in.

The boat rose up on a cresting wave and a light shone in the distance. It blinked out, returning seconds later. She stared at the light. Counted the seconds.

In her ten years of sailing up and down the lakes, Sunny had learned the lighthouse and lightship signals along Lake

Huron's Michigan coastline. Each one flashed a distinct pattern of light. The Tawas light, at the entrance to Tawas Bay, was twenty-five seconds of white light and then a five-second eclipse. The Pointe Aux Barques lighthouse, near the tip of Michigan's Thumb, was two white flashes every twenty seconds.

The *Titus Brown* rose up on a wave. Sunny watched for the light. A flash and Sunny counted one-one-thousand, two-one-thousand, three-one-thousand—and the boat dropped into the valley between waves and there was nothing but water. When they rose again on a cresting wave the light flashed and she counted until it flashed again.

Her stomach dropped. It was possible she hadn't counted right.

The boat fell into the trough and was hit with one wave and then another and she fell against the counter. She scrambled back to the window and—thank heaven—the boat righted. A wave passed under the *Titus Brown*, lifting them in the air and she found the flash of light and counted. She'd been right the first time: six seconds between flashes.

They hadn't reached Oscoda, where a red light flashed every three seconds.

They hadn't even gotten as far as Tawas Bay, with its twenty-five seconds of white light.

In fact they'd made no progress at all since the storm hit. Worse yet, they'd been pushed back to where they'd been early that afternoon. The blood drained from her face. Her knees went weak and she grasped a rolling bar to steady herself.

The light that flashed once every six seconds was the one she knew best, and it was the one she least wanted to see right now. The Port Austin Reef Light. The offshore lighthouse that marked a dangerously shallow and rocky reef. A reef that jutted from the tip of Michigan's Thumb, extending from shore to lighthouse like a trap waiting to ensnare vessel hulls and pull them under.

Port Austin, Michigan

The Port Austin Life-Saving Station waited. Hours past nightfall, when the fury outside only strengthened, Keeper Duncan and his crew waited for a signal. The signal might come from the surfman in the watchtower, or the one patrolling the beach, or from a neighboring station that needed backup.

It was terrible of her, given the danger, but a part of Agnes didn't want the storm to end. Sitting in the kitchen with Lizzie, the station windows covered with wood planks giving the room a cozy, cave-like quality, she had everything she needed. Almost. Lizzie was still fretting over Nathaniel, who was late to return from patrolling the beach. She was unusually quiet. When her mother had gone to their cottage for the night, Lizzie had refused to go, wanting to wait until Nathaniel returned from patrol. Agnes wondered why she'd never noticed Lizzie's affection for him before.

Then there was Maman. She must be terrified at home all alone. But it was already past eight o'clock, and with the storm showing no sign of letting up, Agnes would have to spend the night at the station. Maman hated to be alone on a pleasant day. After this storm she would no doubt punish Agnes for days with moody silence punctuated by multifarious demands.

Agnes was not eager for normal life to resume. Her feelings for Lizzie also made her realize she'd been treading water for too long now. Her world had suddenly expanded and she could not allow it to return to its old dimensions: work at Bisbee's, household chores, Maman. She was thirty-six years of age: not young, but not old yet, either. What did she want to do with the rest of her life? Besides spend as much time with Lizzie as she could.

Figuring out her own options was difficult enough, and then there was Maman to consider. If only her mother were more independent, then Agnes could more easily make a change. Maman needed to get out of the house and expand her social circle. Agnes had suggested the ladies club at the church and the quilting club run by a neighbor. And there was a group of widows who ate brunch every week at a café in town, the one newly up for sale and which Agnes thought Sunny ought to buy. "The food's terrible," was all Maman would say.

On the few occasions Agnes pushed back against Maman's demands, Maman would get upset, give Agnes the silent treatment, or start talking about her poor health. Agnes would feel so guilty that she'd drop the subject. Instead, she would seethe for weeks. And then, just as she did today, she'd explode. It was a great release, but the feeling was short-lived. She'd soon regret her outburst and the cycle would begin again.

At least Agnes wouldn't do that to Aimee. Though she had hated to see Aimee go, she supported her daughter's decision to attend secretarial school in Detroit. Agnes hadn't wanted her to stay in Port Austin out of a sense of guilt. She was proud and not a little envious at the freedom Aimee enjoyed, living in a different city, learning a career. It all sounded rather exciting. Maybe that's what Agnes wanted to do: see a new city, learn a career. Was she too old for that?

A tremendous thud on the station's north side. The building quivered.

Agnes startled. A chill ran through her veins. What had hit them? A large branch slamming into the station? A wagon wheel? It was impossible to tell. Keeper Duncan seemed calm, at least. Agnes exhaled slowly. Maybe he had seen storms like this in Marquette.

There were footsteps on the stairs and two of the surfmen who lived upstairs came into the kitchen. Safer on the first floor, they said. They joined Agnes and Lizzie and Keeper Duncan at the table. No one spoke. The wind had gotten so loud you'd have to shout to be heard.

The surfmen were fully dressed in matching uniforms, as usual, and ready to pounce at a word from the keeper. Would they really go out in this? The lifeboat and surfboat, as dependable as they were, hadn't seen such tremendous seas, not that Agnes had ever witnessed. Not in all her years at the station.

At nine o'clock the storm still raged. Agnes stared at the boarded-up kitchen window. She worried anew for the *Titus Brown* and hoped it was docked somewhere. No doubt even the harbors along Lake Huron's coast were taking a beating tonight, but at least in a harbor Sunny and Herb would be safe. Agnes listened for distress whistles, in the vain hope one could be heard above the screaming wind.

There was a high-pitched roar and then what sounded like a thousand axes striking wood all at once. Agnes grabbed Lizzie's arm and pulled her under the table. Was it the boathouse? Were they next? Agnes tensed every muscle in her body and covered her head with her hands. The invaders surrounded them and she braced herself for the assault.

Lizzie huddled close to Agnes. Feeling a need to protect her, Agnes put her arm around Lizzie, covering the back of her neck. Seconds passed. Agnes listened for the sound of splintering wood. The electric lights flickered and went out but the station walls held. Another minute passed. Someone lit a kerosene lamp and the room glowed yellow. Lizzie turned her face to Agnes, and for a terrifying, thrilling moment Agnes thought Lizzie might kiss her. Agnes's head went light as a balloon and she decided she would kiss Lizzie back. Just as she'd decided this, Keeper Duncan's blue flannel-panted legs stopped in front of the table. His legs bent and then he was peering at the two of them. Agnes was glad it was dark so he couldn't see what she was feeling.

"Stay put, girls," Keeper Duncan said before standing again. The door opened and shut and he and another surfman were gone, taking the lighted lamp and leaving a rush of cold air and darkness in their wake.

The spell was broken. Lizzie had already moved away from her. Agnes was relieved and crushed all at once. Lizzie crawled out from under the table and lit another lamp. Agnes followed, pacing the kitchen. She had to put Lizzie out of her mind.

When Keeper Duncan and the surfman returned, the latter was carrying a surfman whose head was bleeding and whose leg had an unnatural bend near the ankle. Agnes inhaled sharply—it was Irvin, the close friend of her late husband.

"Get the medicine chest," Keeper Duncan ordered the first surfman. He and the surfman placed their wounded crew member on the table. Lizzie stood and moved the lamp out of the way. The boathouse was gone, Keeper Duncan said. It had crumpled like an eggshell beneath Irvin, who'd been on watchtower duty.

Irvin's foot lay limp at the end of his swollen leg. He cried out when Keeper Duncan touched his leg near the ankle. Someone would have to make a splint. It would be impossible to fetch a surgeon in this weather.

"I can help." Agnes spoke loudly, over the storm. "I can make a splint." Truth was, she didn't know all that much about fractured bones. She'd never done a leg, but she had set Amos's arm once when the surgeon wasn't available. She'd learned how to do it from a newspaper article Maman had clipped and put in a folder with other "how-to" articles. You never knew when you'd need to know how to do something, Maman would say. Agnes didn't like admitting that the articles had sometimes proved useful.

"Please," Keeper Duncan said.

Grateful to be of use, Agnes asked for thin pieces of board, longer than Irvin's leg bones and at least as wide. The first surfman offered to go to the shed where they kept extra wood alongside blocks of ice, packed in sawdust, cut from the lake in the winter. But Keeper Duncan wouldn't let anyone go outside now.

Agnes considered possible substitutes. "Umbrellas. Do you have two umbrellas?"

Lizzie nodded and left the room, returning moments later with the umbrellas. Agnes would need something to pad them with, to prevent putting too much pressure on Irvin's leg. She suggested pillows for the padding, and again Lizzie left the kitchen.

In the medicine chest Agnes found strips of cotton cloth. She could use these to secure the splint. Lizzie returned with the pillows, and Agnes placed one on either side of Irvin's leg. Lizzie held the pillows in place while Agnes placed an umbrella on either side of the injured leg, securing the pillows and umbrellas with the cloth strips, careful not to squeeze too tight. The two women worked together as one, efficient and capable, without even speaking. The umbrellas and pillows looked a bit ridiculous but they would keep Irvin's leg steady until a surgeon could see him.

Keeper Duncan moved the injured surfman from the kitchen table to a cot brought down to the main floor. Irvin, who lived in one of the cottages, would sleep in the kitchen tonight.

When Agnes asked Keeper Duncan about the boats, he said both were in position and relatively unharmed, at least as far as he could tell from a passing glance. That was a relief. But the storm wasn't abating, and without the boathouse for protection the watercrafts were vulnerable. And they were down two surfmen—the one who'd been dismissed and now Irvin. Even though the lifeboat had a motor, it required eight surfmen for the same reason it had eight oars. Just in case. Agnes thought of Amos. If the lifesavers went on a rescue tonight, with two surfmen short, there was a greater chance that what happened to Amos would happen to one of these men.

If it came to that, Agnes would volunteer to row. She wouldn't take no for an answer this time. Having decided this, she sat at the kitchen table with Lizzie.

The young woman sighed. "I'm so worried about Natty."

Natty? Agnes tamped down a flicker of irritation. "You two are close, then?" Fearing she'd sounded disapproving, she put her hand on Lizzie's and said, "I'm sure he'll be fine. He seems very capable, by his own account." Oh, she'd done it again. She couldn't help herself!

Lizzie looked straight at her. "You don't like him much."

Agnes removed her hand from Lizzie's. "I like Nathaniel fine." She didn't sound sincere even to her own ears, so she added, "Perhaps he can be a bit boastful." And overbearing. Arrogant.

"He's confident. He knows what he's good at and he knows what he likes. He wants to captain his own boat one day." A pause and then, "He says I could join him." Lizzie looked at her directly again, as if to register Agnes's response. Lizzie looked away before saying, "He's not afraid to say what he wants. Even if he knows other people won't approve."

A lump formed in Agnes's throat. She was certain Lizzie had seen through her words and straight into her heart. She wanted to speak but didn't have the slightest idea what to say.

Keeper Duncan rushed into the kitchen, much to Agnes's relief. He ordered another surfman to patrol the beach in the opposite direction, to the east. Now that the watchtower was destroyed, patrol duty was more important than ever. A half hour later Keeper Duncan sent out another surfman to search for Nathaniel.

All the while the storm rampaged and the waves pounded and Agnes sat quiet with Lizzie at the kitchen table. A cold fear had entered Agnes's heart. She wasn't worried about the storm, not for her own sake, at least. What terrified her most was that Lizzie had seen who she was and what she wanted. Agnes's secrets were no longer her own.

Lake Huron

Caught in the trough, the *Titus Brown* was helpless against the northeast wind that pushed them ever closer to the reef. For Sunny, nothing existed but the Port Austin Reef Light, an indistinct yet persistent flash beyond the pantry porthole. The steel freighter, heavier now with its thick coating of ice, dipped low into the valley between waves. A wall of water blocked the lighthouse. When the boat again rose on a cresting wave, Sunny caught sight of the flashing light.

She shook her head. No, this wasn't happening. She backed away from the porthole.

The light was brighter now.

She had to tell Herb. Her heart racing, she lumbered through the sloshing water to the mess room. At the opposite end of the room, Herb stood at the door to the spar deck, wounded head and all. He opened the door to let the water rush out. Sunny cried out. Stop! Her husband had gone mad. In his weakened state he was likely to wash right out the door with the water, onto the fantail and over the stern.

"Herb!" Sunny shouted, moving closer, past the men bracing themselves against the tables and bulkhead. The ship heeled to starboard. Sunny—falling against the bulkhead, frigid water swamping her waist—pointed to port. "The Port Austin light!"

Herb opened the door once more, releasing the water. She motioned for him to come with her. He shut the door and made his way toward Sunny, holding onto the table as the boat pitched, and followed her to the pantry.

"Every six seconds!" Sunny shouted as Herb looked out the partially iced-over porthole. The realization spread over

Herb's face. The storm was too much. The Old Man couldn't get the *Titus Brown* head-to. They were nearing the Port Austin Reef Light.

They would hit the reef.

Herb leaned against the counter and rubbed his head. Sunny clung to a rolling bar mounted on the counter's edge. She didn't want to see it and yet couldn't take her eyes off the light. Even when the *Titus Brown* dipped in the trough, she watched and waited for the light to reappear, that she might gauge their proximity to the reef by its brightness.

She stumbled. A shiver of panic went through her. The motion of the boat had changed, but why? What was it? The *Titus Brown* seemed to come around a little. The anchors must have been dropped. Captain Hanna had seen the lighthouse and was trying to prevent them hitting the reef. The anchors were their only hope.

She watched the light. Please don't let it get brighter. She waited. The boat turned a little, but they were still drifting toward the light. The anchors weren't catching.

"I'm never sailing again after this!" Sunny shouted, her voice lost in the din. "I swear to it!"

The Port Austin Reef Light flashed. The anchors still hadn't caught on the lake bottom. Without looking in Herb's direction she blurted, "I'm opening a restaurant."

The light disappeared as the boat fell deep into the valley between waves. She shouldn't have waited so long to tell him her dream. "We could do it together!"

The boat crested again, and the light flashed brighter still. "Why aren't the anchors holding?" she cried.

Herb didn't answer. She looked to him now: He had put his arms on the counter and lay his head on top, face down. He hadn't heard a word she'd said.

Sunny turned back to the porthole. She watched in awed silence, the *Titus Brown's* doom laid out before them, the crew unable to do anything but watch it come. Rising on a cresting wave Sunny again counted six seconds between flashes.

The light grew closer. Time stretched.

Of all the places to founder!

Here I come, Agnes. Are you watching?

How strange it was to see your death coming, to know it before it happens. You live your whole life never knowing when you might breathe your last. But now, here it was. This was her time. She wanted to live and yet the knowledge of her death came not without a buzzing excitement, a mystery revealed. This moment was for her: She'd been chosen.

The light flashed brighter still. The reef was close now. She wanted to run to the other side of the boat, as if putting that distance between herself and the reef would prevent what was now inevitable.

A wave slammed them broadside and the boat heeled to port. Clutching the rolling bar, Sunny braced herself. It was all happening so fast. Images flashed in her mind: Water rushing in from everywhere at once, the *Titus Brown* sinking, she and Herb flailing in the water, gasping for air.

"Herb!"

Her husband lifted his head.

Rising and falling, she watched for the reef. As if she could see it! On a calm day it lay just below the surface. Now it was hidden further, beneath dark and furious waves.

She tightened her grip on the rolling bar. There wasn't much time left for the anchors to save them. When the *Titus Brown* hit she would try for the lifeboat. Would she even be able to move? She was frozen, rooted to this spot in the pantry. A dizziness overtook her, the room spinning endlessly...

Long ago, in the kitchen with Herb, teenagers they'd been, frying perch he'd caught with his brothers. By the lake with Agnes on a cloudy day, finding beautiful, smooth sea glass. In the water with her father; he was teaching her how to swim.

A terrible bang and an endless, violent scraping. An all-over shuddering. The cupboards slammed into her. She screamed against the chaos and curled into a ball. The ship was going to collapse around her. The water would rush in as they sank.

A momentary stillness. Then the boat lurched and the deck tilted underneath her. Herb fell against her. Another crash of water and more terrible scraping below, like the *Titus Brown* screaming in pain.

Stillness again. She held her breath, waited. She exchanged a look with Herb; he knew no better than she what would happen next. There was no more rising and falling with the cresting waves but the boat shuddered as the combers kept coming, pounding the *Titus Brown* starboard against the reef.

The pantry went dark. The deck beneath them went silent. Shivering uncontrollably, Sunny sat up and leaned against the cupboards. The boat had settled at an angle, so that in leaning against the cupboards she reclined somewhat. She looked at Herb, half amazed that they were above water and wondering how long until they sank.

Voices below grew louder, men coming up the companionway from the engine room.

There was a groan of twisting metal above her, then a thundering crash. Sunny covered her eyes and pressed herself against Herb's chest. The boilerhouse shook. The roof was caving in. Her heart pounding, she waited for the crash.

The roof hadn't caved in. It was the smokestack. The smokestack had collapsed onto the roof.

Sunny waited a few moments, and, certain the boilerhouse roof was holding, for now at least, she got up and crept—at an incline, slipping on the wet, slanted deck—to the porthole window. She looked toward the forecastle, where Captain Hanna and the officers were. It had gone dark, too. Everything was dark but the Port Austin Reef Light. She couldn't see the shore, but it must have been more than a mile away, given their proximity to the light, which itself was that distance from shore, and then some.

The wind roared and the waves pounded them into the reef. The *Titus Brown* was silent. The world spun. Nothing was real. It was as if gravity had been turned off. She floated above it all. Overcome by a terrible churning in her stomach, she slipped out of the pantry and into the mess room. She wouldn't be able to stop it this time. From far away Herb's voice called her name.

"Open the door!" Sunny shouted at the oiler standing there.

"Mrs. Colvin! Don't—"

She pushed past him and, gripping the rolling bar next to the open doorway, she vomited onto the fantail. She clung to the rolling bar and vomited again.

"Mrs. Colvin!" A hand pressed on her shoulder. The oiler had followed her.

Sunny wiped her mouth with the back of her hand. "I'm all right." The waves had already washed her sick away. She let the oiler lead her back into the boilerhouse, to the pantry with Herb.

The *Titus Brown* had stopped but the storm showed no sign of abating. The waves would keep coming. They would pound at the boat and claw it away, piece by piece, until one wave, hitting with just the right force and at just the right angle, snatched the *Titus Brown* off the reef, into the water.

With the engine no longer running the boat had gone cold. She couldn't stop shivering. Near the top of a pantry cupboard she found a wool blanket—still dry—and wrapped it around her body. That was better. It was a miracle they were still above water, but for how long? She couldn't just sit in the pantry with Herb, awaiting their fate. She would find the mate and see how she might be of help. If anyone had been injured she would tend to them. If the freighter was in imminent danger of slipping off the reef, someone would be going up on the roof to prepare the lifeboats. Best to find out what was needed of her.

The only light to guide her through the boilerhouse was the one that came every six seconds, a white flash that seeped through the broken windows and doorways and the missing parts of the roof. The crew gathered in the mess room, twenty of them including herself and Herb, where the roof still held. The mess room windows received little light from the lighthouse, however, and the room was dark. Shadowy figures sat on stools, still secured to the deck at intervals around two long bolted-down tables.

The first mate ordered the men to find whatever lamps they could and light them. The mate himself ventured out to search the cabins for dry blankets and towels. He brought them to the mess room and had the men put them around their shoulders. Lamps were lit. The smell of kerosene filled the room and the men's faces glowed eerily in the lamplight. Someone found a pail and bailed water from the room's lower corners. Sunny lit a fire in the cook-stove firebox and tended to several cuts and scrapes. There were no serious injuries. The mate advised everyone to huddle together for warmth, for they could do nothing now but wait. Tomorrow Captain Hanna would surely light a flare, if he hadn't done so already, and display the ensign at half-mast. But help was unlikely to come tonight.

The wind howled and some gusts were so strong Sunny was sure they'd tear apart the damaged boilerhouse. Every few minutes a wave larger than the *Titus Brown* itself slammed into the steel freighter, and icy water rushed in through all its broken places.

Sunny returned to the pantry to await their rescue alongside Herb. It must have been after midnight now. She wasn't sure she'd ever fall asleep. Only by staying awake could she be certain the straight deck freighter remained on the reef.

Herb's eyes were closed but he was awake. His head hurt, he said. Sunny huddled close to him and pulled the wool blanket over them both. She was glad to be with him. She tried to calm nagging thoughts of what would happen to the boat overnight. They would be fine, she told herself. The storm would abate. The freighter would remain on the reef until help came. She repeated these words in her mind until they became the truth. But when she closed her eyes she still felt as if the boat were rocking, even though its only movement now was the shuddering that followed each pounding wave. The *Titus Brown* was pressed fast to the rocks by the breakers, helpless to defend itself from the beating.

Home was so close. Agnes was just a couple miles away. If it were daylight, Sunny might be able to see Turnip Rock, where she and Agnes had picnicked on a beautiful summer day a lifetime ago.

MONDAY
November 10, 1913

Lake Superior

Her eyes still closed, Cordelia reached across the berth for Edmund, but found only the sheet and wool blanket. He must have risen early. No, he'd never come to bed at all. He'd stayed in the wheelhouse all night, keeping the *Marguerite* afloat. She pulled the thick blanket to her chin.

The porthole glowed a dim grayish white. What a relief it was to see daylight, even if it wasn't exactly as she had imagined, because the wind still wailed and the ship pitched to and fro. She'd spent the night's darkest hours slipping in and out of consciousness. Despite the howling wind and the waves breaking all around she'd somehow fallen asleep, although time and again she'd been roused to wakefulness by a wave slamming the side of the ship or a fierce gust of wind pushing against the hull. And now that it was morning, the storm had scarcely lessened, if it had lessened at all. But they'd made it to morning, and that was cause for hope. The storm couldn't last much longer. And she trusted in Edmund's steady competence. Despite the deteriorating weather the day before, Edmund's unflinching resolve had radiated throughout the wheelhouse, and had been reflected in the officers' faces.

Her stomach growled. Her head ached from a lack of caffeine. There would be no Danish and coffee this morning, no food at all until the storm subsided. Until then it was too treacherous to cross the ship's long deck to reach the galley.

The cabin dipped one way and then the other as she rose from the berth, wearing the same silk stockings, woolen skirt, and shirtwaist she'd worn the day before. She would put on fresh clothes later, when things calmed down. She did, however, hold onto the washbowl with one hand to steady herself so that she could brush her teeth with some tooth powder. When she was finished she regarded her reflection in the mirror. Her hair was a mess and there were dark circles under her eyes, but she hadn't the energy to care. And it's not like Edmund would notice.

Cold air rushed down the steps from the wheelhouse, and she went back for her coat. She clung to the railing as she climbed the steps. At the sight of the wheelhouse, a sudden heaviness came over her. Everything was as she'd left it the night before: a broken window at the rear of the wheelhouse; a wheelsman braced at the wheel; a watchman at a forward window. The de-icing rig hadn't kept up with the freshwater freezing to the windows, so now the watchman pressed his ear to the cold glass, listening instead of watching for the shore. She'd hoped to return to the wheelhouse to good news, but the *Marguerite* had made no progress in the hours she'd spent in the cabin.

A tremendous sea crashed over the bow—as everything tilted forward she held the stanchion at the top of the stairway to steady herself. The ice-covered windows went black, and then a bluish gray, and then, once the water washed away, white with snow again. Lake Superior's waves were as mountainous as they'd been yesterday. Since when had a storm lasted this long? Cordelia wanted to cry.

She tentatively approached her husband, nodding at the wheelsman as she passed—not Richard, someone else—and the wheelsman barely glanced at her, focused as he was on the wheel. Cordelia placed a hand on Edmund's shoulder. He started, and she yanked her hand away as if she'd been scalded.

"Has the storm lessened at all?" she asked doubtfully.

Edmund shrugged. "We just have to ride this out. We're head to the waves. The anchor's holding and there's enough coal in the bunker to keep the engine running full steam ahead for some time."

"How much longer, do you think?" Cordelia asked.

"Difficult to say." Edmund turned and said something to the wheelsman. Then he went silent again and stared out the window.

This reassured her and, not wanting to disturb him further, she went down to the observation room forward of Edmund's quarters, holding tight to the railing in the pitching ship. She chose one of the leather couches and watched the windows even though they revealed nothing. She felt confined as if in a bird cage covered in a white sheet, with no idea what would come next. It was something all right, how you could make a series of decisions that culminated in your being trapped in a blizzard at sea in a ship whose captain was your husband and whom you hadn't known this time last year.

She had no regrets about marrying Edmund. What had drawn her to him that first evening at the Palais de Danse charmed her still—his quiet intelligence and steadiness, the mystique of being a lake captain. The way he sometimes looked at her, like she was about to say something important and he didn't want to miss it. Observing him on this ship, and during this storm, she was becoming more certain that there were qualities in Edmund compatible with her own, that they could build a harmonious life together. She just needed to demonstrate a little of his patience. Once the storm was over, there would be time to learn all they needed to know about each other.

The snow abated that afternoon, which would have given Cordelia hope if only the wind weren't gusting so violently that it felt like they were still under attack. And still the seas came high and quick. Cordelia had returned to the wheel-house. As it had for many hours now, the *Marguerite* rose and fell with each cresting wave, and the windows momentarily went dark whenever a wave broke over the bow. Constant fear had formed a tautness in her chest that would not loosen.

Now she was looking aft, through the broken wheelhouse window. The sun hadn't set but the storm had darkened the sky to twilight. The break in the squall allowed her to see the ship stretched out behind them, several hundred feet all the way to the stern, where the fat smokestack poured out black smoke and swung in a wide arc. All twenty-four hatches, lined up from fore to aft like railroad ties, had lost their tarpaulins to the wind. Between the third and fourth hatches a life raft was tied to the deck. The raft was like a giant sandwich: two massive rectangles of wood planks atop and beneath a layer of steel oil drums.

The hatches did something strange, then. Those closer to her leaned one way, while the ones further aft leaned the other. Her stomach lurched. Her eyes must have deceived her. She squinted. There—it happened again. As the aft half of the ship tilted in one direction, the forward half tilted in the other.

The *Marguerite*, a ship made of steel, was twisting in the waves.

"Edmund," she said, trying to speak calmly. "There's something wrong." When he came to where she stood looking aft, she pointed.

Edmund, strange as it was, wasn't concerned. "The *Marguerite* is flexible," he said. "The hull's made of steel plates bolted together. It can twist when seas come quick."

Cordelia accepted his explanation and sat down, holding the stanchion for balance. She hadn't been sitting for long when something hit the floor with a sharp pinging sound. Instinctively she curled into a ball, covering her head, then scanned the floor for the projectile. No sooner had she spotted the small object than it rolled toward her as the bow rose on a wave. The object was gray. Steel. She picked it up. Her head spun. She knew what this was.

A rivet, a full inch in diameter.

She looked at Edmund, who was standing next to the wheelsman. He glanced at the broken window, then at Cordelia. She held up the rivet.

He appeared so unconcerned she assumed he hadn't seen it. She took the rivet to him.

"The ship is... coming apart?"

Edmund said matter-of-factly, "The *Marguerite* has thousands of rivets. She can spare a few." Then he went to write something in his logbook.

Cordelia took the rivet to the back of the wheelhouse. Who was this man she had married? Who in their right mind could be so calm as to witness such twisting of a steel ship—and rivets popping!—only to go and write in a logbook. Why bother, when that logbook was going to end up at the bottom of a Great Lake?

She put the rivet in her pocket and gripped the window frame until her knuckles ached. How could a storm last this long? It had begun on Lake Superior on Friday, they'd sailed into it Sunday evening, and now it was Monday afternoon and showed no sign of lessening. The seas were so high they washed over the deck from both sides. Not only were the seas high, but the *Marguerite* was low. Ice had built up everywhere on the ship's exterior, the freshwater that washed over the hull freezing to the hatches and the rigging, weighing them down. The lifeline she'd held while crossing the ship's deck two days ago was now covered in ice as thick as a man's leg!

It was getting dark again and they seemed no closer to safety than they'd been the night before. Cordelia's nerves were raw. She imagined jumping into the water just to rid herself of the uncertainty of their fate. She would be awake all night, watching for the moment when this was all over. Somehow the men in the wheelhouse retained their composure, acting like this was nothing they couldn't handle. She tried to let their calmness convince her they were safe. They'd lasted this long, after all. She would remain in the wheelhouse, surrounded by the stoic officers, and she wouldn't sleep until this was over.

"Captain." It was the watchman, standing with his ear to a forward window. Something in his tone made Cordelia bolt upright.

"Brace yourself," Edmund said to her, or to everyone.

She crouched at the stanchion, wrapping her arms tightly around it.

Edmund moved the pointer on the chadburn and shouted an order to the wheelsman.

Then came the tremendous, violent crashing, worse by far than any that had preceded it, and a liquid mountain engulfed them. The wheelhouse windows went dark. Water rushed in from somewhere behind her. The deck jolted and the ship lurched backwards and then everything changed.

"The anchor, Captain!" shouted the mate, who was clinging to the compass binnacle.

Edmund cursed—something Cordelia had never heard him do—and ordered the wheelsman to bring the ship head-to. The ship pitched wildly and she tumbled across the wheelhouse.

"She won't answer the rudder!" the wheelsman shouted.

Edmund picked up the phone to the engine room.

Cordelia clawed her way to the wheelhouse's broken aft window. She screamed but no sound came out. It was sickening, grotesque: the *Marguerite's* long, straight deck twisting to an improbable degree. She watched the middle hatches, where the ship tilted neither to port nor to starboard, but connected the two oppositely tilting halves. If it was going to happen, it would happen there.

Her attention was wrested from the ship's middle by the mountain rolling toward them, advancing upon the *Marguerite* from beyond the stern. The dark wall of water gathered height, swelling monstrously as it bore down upon the starboard side of the stern. There was no chance of it missing them.

Time slowed and stretched. The wall of water reached the *Marguerite* and lifted the stern, and the stern rose higher than the bow, and freshwater rushed onto the long, straight expanse of deck, along all the hatches, over the tied-down life raft and straight for Cordelia. She ducked and held her breath and a second later water gushed through the broken window and shattered other windows along with it.

She checked her hands to see if she was bleeding. She lost her footing, then, and slipped on the slick wood. She slid into the binnacle.

There was a horrendous thump and everything started to quake.

Her thoughts raced—where was safety? What should she do? Possibilities flashed in her mind and she had no ability to weigh one against the other: the lifeboat, the life raft, the life belt. Edmund's hand was in front of her face. She grabbed it and he pulled her to her feet.

"Get your life belt," he said.

Edmund's words meant there was no turning back: the situation would get worse, not better. And the awful, ceaseless shuddering! It wasn't the anchor this time.

"Your life belt!" Edmund shouted.

Life belt. Yes. Do what Edmund says. She groped her way to the stairs down to his office. She found the cork-filled life belt and put it on, with shaking hands tying the cloth strings at the front. Then her coat, her hat, her mittens. The ship wouldn't stop quaking. She swallowed back tears and hurried up to the wheelhouse.

Edmund stood at the aft windows, staring. She followed his gaze.

She tried to blink away the sight but there it was. A crack. The crack had formed between two hatches in the middle of the deck. It started on the starboard side, and reached about halfway to the port side.

She looked to Edmund. He was no longer there.

He was at the telephone. A call to the engine room. An order to abandon ship.

Then he was at her side again, an arm around her waist. Without a word he was leading her down the wheelhouse steps to his quarters. In his other hand he held an axe. When the door wouldn't open, he hacked at the iced-over seams until it gave way. He led her onto the ice-covered deck and pointed to the life raft.

Cordelia clung to the freezing railing. She couldn't do this. Not the icy steps on the shaking, shifting ship. Not with her feet that wouldn't move. She would stay put and hope for the best. Edmund turned to her and said she must get on the life raft. Now.

She was ashamed at her own fear. These men wouldn't let her stay, and if she hesitated she would risk everyone's survival. Powered by her shame, she let Edmund lead her down the steps to the life raft—the two wooden platforms lashed above and below a row of empty oil drums. The ship shook violently under her feet and she struggled to mount the raft. A lifeline was festooned along the side, and she used it to climb up the massive steel barrel. She placed her foot on a small ledge at the barrel's outermost part. Grabbing the edge of the wooden platform on top, she pulled herself up and over. There were no handles on the platform, only two planks on either side, perpendicular to the others, to which oars were tied. With shaking hands she held on. Richard and two watchmen climbed on behind her. When she looked back, Edmund was gone.

Her heart raced. This could not be happening. She looked to the stern, where the aft crew scrambled up from the engine room and out from the galley. There was a lifeboat above the boilerhouse.

At the ship's middle, metal plates were tearing apart. Sparks flying. The split between the *Marguerite's* fore and aft halves was racing across the ship's width.

Her entire body trembled and she used all her strength to hold onto the side of the raft. They could go at any moment. Where was Edmund? There was a shifting in the waves and a great wrenching sound and the forecastle lights went dark. The stern section was still lit; it had split from their half almost completely. Now the ship's two halves were connected only along the port side. The waves pushed the stern and forward sections so that the *Marguerite* bent into an L-shape.

Richard and the watchmen were working to untie the raft. Cordelia grabbed the wooden planks, wedging her fingers between them for a better grip.

The crew at the stern had climbed atop the boilerhouse. They were working to free a lifeboat. One man stood apart from the rest. She recognized his stocky frame. The steward. He stood motionless by the smokestack. He stared out at the seas as if taking in a sunset. What was he thinking, standing so still? Get on the lifeboat!

The bow listed to port and Cordelia's body tingled and she clung harder to the raft as it slid to the deck's edge and slammed into the lifeline. It would have been easier without mittens but she wouldn't dare lift her hands to remove them now. Some of the forward crew, barely visible in the darkening skies and absence of forward lights, had climbed to the highest part of the ship, the starboard side of the wheelhouse. There was a burst of light and the shadowy figures were briefly illuminated by the signal flare shooting high and bright into the charcoal sky. Edmund!

Edmund was still with the men on the wheelhouse when the next wave came.

This is it, a man next to her said. Cordelia did not want to die. She tightened her grip on the wood planks and the rope strung along the side. The tremendous wave rolled the bow all the way to port and the raft dropped through the air. When it struck the water she lost her hold.

She was in the air, flying. She hit water and went under.

A terrible shock of cold sent her into a panic and she was upside down, and once the violent churning was past she kicked her legs. She was going to run out of air. Everything was black and she kicked harder. She moved her arms to lift herself up. Her head broke the surface and she gasped for air. Her arms moved in wild strokes, and with her water-blurred vision she saw nothing in the fading light. With the fourth stroke she hit something.

A steel barrel.

Cordelia cried out in relief. Her hands—now bare—felt for the rope and just as she found it there was a grip on her arm. Someone was helping her onto the life raft. Richard. He pulled her up.

"Where's Edmund?" She glanced beyond Richard to the rest of the raft. It was empty but for the two of them. "Edmund!" she cried into the waves. "Edmund!"

Richard yelled into the darkness with her. Some light yet came from the *Marguerite's* stern, but it was already a distance away and Cordelia could see only as far as the next wave.

"Ollie! Over here!" Richard was shouting. Cordelia turned. Ollie swam toward them. Richard helped him up. Then one of the watchmen climbed onto the raft. There was no sign of the other watchman who'd been on the raft just before it slid into the seas.

There were other hollering voices. They seemed to come from everywhere and nowhere at once. A wave crested and Edmund appeared at the top. Cordelia screamed for him. He'd have to swim to them. They'd lost their oars. With everything she had she screamed for her husband, but the howling wind muted her voice. From twenty or thirty feet away, he started to swim in their direction. Edmund! Cordelia felt a rush of relief. But, no, it wasn't her husband. It was the third mate, Mack. He'd been with Edmund on the wheelhouse when the flare was lit. A new hope: if Mack could make it, then so could Edmund.

Another wave was rolling toward them, a ten-footer.

"Hurry!" Ollie shouted.

Mack moved quickly through the water. As he approached, Ollie and Richard leaned over the side and helped him onto the raft.

The ten-foot wave crested near them.

"Get low!" Ollie shouted.

Cordelia curled into a fetal position and grabbed onto the wooden planks. She wedged her fingers into the spaces between them. Shivering violently, she waited. The raft lifted up on one side and rocked with the wave but it didn't flip.

Cordelia looked back at the *Marguerite*. Could her husband still be on board? The freighter was two completely separate pieces now, split right across the middle. Maybe he'd somehow made it to the stern, where the boilerhouse crew had been working to launch the lifeboat. If they hadn't launched it by now... The stern half of the ship, still lit and powered by the engine, collided with the bow half again and again, as if trying to push it to safety, not knowing both of them were already lost.

The bow sank first. It slipped under the surface like there was nothing to it. The stern did not go so quietly. When it exploded, an orange ball of light briefly illuminated the dark water before a cresting wave blocked the stern from view. It would have been beautiful were it not so terrible. Cordelia put her head against the wood and tightened every muscle and clung to the raft as the wave crashed, stinging her with icy spray. When she looked up again the stern was going down, broken end first, the propeller high up in the air. She watched, disbelieving, and then it, too, was gone.

She stared at the spot where the ship had been. It seemed impossible that the massive steel freighter that had brought her hundreds of miles from home was gone. Impossible that the *Marguerite* had sunk for good—that it wasn't coming back up, that it wouldn't carry her home.

It was almost completely dark now. She scanned the water for the lifeboat the aft crew had been working to launch. For Edmund. But there was nothing, no one. Only the storm. The waves had swallowed everything else. She refused to give up hope. She would find him, later.

She lay back down, Richard and Mack on either side of her. She would never stop shivering. She was no longer scared, only cold. She couldn't see past the cold. The relentless cold. And the waves that kept coming. She turned her head in the direction the wind and waves were pushing them. They were miles from shore—how many, it was impossible to tell.

Port Austin Reef, Lake Huron

When the *Titus Brown* fetched up broadside on the reef the night before, the engine room flooded and the fires went out. The steel freighter had grounded not five hundred feet from the Port Austin Reef Light. All the heat had quickly left the *Titus Brown's* lifeless body. Sunny had put wood on the fire in the cook-stove and huddled under a blanket in the pantry with Herb, while the rest of the crew aft collected in the mess room. In the hours after their midnight stranding, Sunny drifted in and out of sleep, rising every so often to check on the fire, while outside the wind howled and the waves pounded the broken-down ship.

A faint bluish light now seeped into the pantry when Sunny awoke, shivering. Her breath formed tiny clouds. The fire in the cook-stove must have gone out. With some reluctance she removed the wool blanket from her body. Her life belt was still tied around her chest. She unbuttoned her pea coat in order to remove the cumbersome thing, and had some trouble manipulating the buttons, her hands stiff with cold. She noticed anew that her wedding band was gone, and she touched the empty place on her finger where the ring had been.

She could replace the gold band but it wouldn't be the same. It wouldn't be the band that had traveled with them on their honeymoon, or had sailed with them for ten years. And now she would have to leave her lost ring behind as she went ashore... This thought reminded her of her savings, and she reached into the pocket of her pea coat to make sure it was still there. The pocket was empty: no money, no letter to Agnes. She pulled her hand out of the pocket and put it in again. Spread her fingers to the seams of the lining. Still nothing.

The other coat pocket: also empty. No, no, no! She doubled over as if someone had punched her in the stomach. This wasn't happening. How could she have lost it all? *When* had she lost it? In the chaos of the night before had she put the money somewhere else and forgotten? Without it, her aspirations amounted to nothing. There would be no restaurant. No life ashore with Herb. Sure enough she'd find herself on another laker come spring.

Her body ached with cold. She'd have to look for the money later. First she had to keep everyone alive and that meant feeding them. She moved to wake Herb, to suggest they attempt a breakfast for the crew. But he looked flushed and when she put a hand to his injured forehead it was too warm. She filled with love for him, then. It was wrong to have gotten so angry. Herb wasn't a possessive man; he just cherished their life together. She ought to be mad at herself, if anyone. Wasn't she a woman who could make her own choices? No one forced her to be on this boat. She ought to take responsibility for that.

Herb needed sleep. Quietly, so as not to wake him, she doubled the blanket over him and left the pantry. Even in the dim light of pre-dawn she could see that the partially flooded galley was a wreck, all broken china and wet provisions. The wind whipped and waves splashed through the breaches in the buckled exterior bulkhead. The roof, damaged by a heavy sea, crumpled where it met the boilerhouse's battered starboard side.

The *Titus Brown* had settled on the rocks with a terrible starboard list. Water covered half the galley deck as the room dipped toward the lake. At the galley's outermost edge the partially frozen water, more like an icy sludge, was more than two feet deep. The exterior passageway was completely submerged. The water rose and fell, surging up to the cook-stove as each large wave hit the broken freighter.

The positives: One, the stove was in working order and presently out of reach of the water, even when it surged. Two, now that it was daylight, she could search the galley and pantry and dining room for whatever provisions hadn't washed overboard. Three, the latches on the huge refrigerator had remained secure.

The first thing to do was relight the stove. If she could heat up water and make coffee, it would do wonders for everyone's spirits. Without thinking she tried the tap. The faucet offered no water, of course, as there was no power to pump water up from the tanks below deck. A potful of Lake Huron, then.

After cleaning out the ashes from the firebox and adding more coal, she got a match from the refrigerator, which, despite its jumbled contents, had kept the matches dry. A strike of the match and there was fire again. The immediate heat was a salvation. When she put the pot of water on, it slid to starboard, and would have slid right off the cook-stove were it not for the rolling bar. Sunny found two soup tureens and placed them between the pot of water and the rolling bar. Now the pot stayed where she wanted it.

While she waited for the icy water to come to a boil, Sunny went to the pantry for the coffee pot, beans, and grinder. Several pantry cupboards had come unlatched during the violent pitching the night before, and their contents had collected in the pantry corners, those items that had not been swept out of the small room and off the boat entirely. Mercifully, the cupboard with the coffee and grinder was solidly latched, even if the contents inside were a mess.

Back in the galley, Sunny found Cleve warming his hands over the stove. He apologized for letting the fire go out and she told him not to worry. Truth was it'd been Pug's job, seeing as how he was the night cook, but Pug seemed to have lost all sense of time. She stood beside Cleve in the warmth of the stove, trying to warm away her aches and her constant shivering. In the summertime, the cook-stove's heat made the kitchen unbearable. In July and August Sunny would swear it was hotter in the galley than inside the stove itself. Now she hoped the heat would be enough to keep them alive until the lifesavers came.

Cleve went on a search for coffee mugs. The mugs had been stored on wooden shelves in the pantry, and while the shelves were intact, the boat had rolled so much in the storm that the mugs had leapt over the shelf's railings and scattered throughout the galley and boilerhouse.

After some searching, Cleve found eleven mugs in varying states of disrepair. A chipped rim, a missing handle. If it could hold coffee, they would use it. Sunny ground the coffee and added it to the copper-bottomed pot on the stove. She poured the boiling water through the filter. The smell of coffee reassured her that they could survive this ordeal.

She poured three mugs and, treading carefully on the slick, sloping deck, crossed the galley toward the mess room. A muted daylight lit the men's faces. The crew was a solemn bunch that morning, grimly quiet, too cold to speak. It was not without pride that Sunny entered the mess room with the coffee.

"Who wants a cup o' joe?" She asked this as if it were a regular Monday morning, as if they were not in a broken-down steamer fetched up on a reef more than a mile from shore. Though the wind still blew it was not as monstrously loud as the night before, and she didn't have to shout.

They looked at her like she had walked on water to bring them the coffee from Port Austin. Their spirits brightened at once. Coffee could do that.

"Mrs. Colvin, you're an angel!" the bosun said in his gravelly voice, a rare display of sentiment.

"I'm nothing of the kind. Only the ship's cook." She suppressed a smile so they wouldn't see how pleased she was. Because the first mate was not a coffee drinker, she handed the first mugs to the wheelsman and chief engineer and bosun. "You'll have to take turns, as we've only got eleven mugs."

"Make that twelve," a deckhand said, picking up a mug that lay without its handle in a corner of the mess room.

The mug without a handle was passed to Sunny, who promised to fill it just for him. Cleve had followed her into the mess room with four mugs of coffee, quickly served them, and returned to the galley for more.

"No cream and sugar?" the bosun said drily.

"Of course there is," Sunny said. She pointed astern. "It went thataway. You just put on your life belt and make sure you bring some back for the rest of us, all right?"

There was a snicker or two among the crew and the bosun cracked a smile.

"Did someone ask for milk?" Cleve was holding a can of evaporated milk. He poured some into the bosun's mug. Several other men raised theirs.

"And this here is how the Old Man gets the best crew," said the deckhand who'd found the twelfth mug.

"Then what are you doing here?" his buddy quipped.

There were no spoons for stirring the milk. Most of their utensils were long gone, sprinkled along the bottom of Lake Huron along with innumerable white china mugs, those lost in the storm as well as those tossed overboard in fairer weather by sailors avoiding a trip to the galley. Nevertheless, she'd done well, given the circumstances. She'd cheered up the solemn crew, and all it had taken was a bit of coffee.

Just then a tremendous wave pounded the ship, sending a violent shudder across the stern. Panic shot through Sunny's limbs and she grabbed the doorway for support. The moment of levity evaporated. Stilts and another deckhand exchanged a worried glance. No one knew how precariously they sat on the reef, or which wave might pull them off it.

"Drink up. When you're done Cleve and I will fill them up for the rest of you." Sunny let go of the doorway and addressed the room matter-of-factly, in an attempt to divert the crew's attention—and her own—from that awful pounding. "Now, about breakfast."

The men looked at her expectantly. Sunny held up her hand. "Don't get too excited. There's not a single uncracked egg in the pantry, so omelets aren't on the menu. Truth is I'm not sure what we can serve. Herb's not well, but I've got Cleve to help me—"

Pug started to stand, somewhat unsteadily.

"You just sit. It's not the night shift yet," Sunny said, immediately wishing she hadn't suggested they might spend another night on the reef. "Anyhow we'll be ashore before it comes time for that."

"We better be," said Harvard, the college-bound cabin mate of Stilts's, the one who was always late to meals. "A steel hull can only take so much pounding. Another of the Three Sisters comes, it'll take us under with it."

The bosun glared at him. "You shut your mouth!"

Sunny came over to Harvard and sat next to him. He may have been new to sailing, but a smart boy like him should've known better than to talk like that. Panic was getting the better of him.

Sunny placed her hand on his arm. "Let me tell you something. My father and brother-in-law were surfmen for the Port Austin Life-Saving Station. Those men are the best at what they do. And they train on this very reef, week in, week out. There's hardly a better place to be stranded! Now that it's daylight they'll see our distress signal and they'll come for us."

"Yes, Mrs. Colvin." The deckhand clasped a potato in his chapped hands as if it were a talisman.

Potatoes. She could fry up potatoes for breakfast. The potato bag had spilled about the pantry, but if she sliced them up...

Sunny left the men with their coffee and went to the refrigerator, grateful to have a job to do. Inside the refrigerator was a terrible mess: toppled cans of milk, soggy vegetables and fruits, broken jars of olives and relishes. It would take a while to clean it up and find what was still edible. The butter would be all right—by some miracle, the lid had stayed on the crock.

While Cleve cleaned out the refrigerator and served the rest of the coffee, Sunny found a frying pan and set to work on the potatoes. It was surreal, to be making breakfast on a shipwreck while outside the wind moaned and waves lashed the steel boat. But she went about her business and tried not to dwell on their circumstances. Fortunately, the stove was toward the interior of the galley where the water didn't reach, only lapped at her ankles from time to time. The warmth from the stove had melted the ice on some parts of the deck. Where it wasn't icy it was still wet and slippery, and because the soles of her shoes had worn smooth long ago, she removed them for better traction.

As she cooked the potatoes another breaker crashed on the boilerhouse roof, momentarily flooding the galley and swelling the water up to her knees. She gasped at the extreme cold and quickly stepped closer to the cook-stove's firebox.

The icy water retreated, yet remained nearly two feet deep in almost half the galley. With one hand on the frying pan so that it didn't slide away, she checked the firebox. The fire still burned. Despite her proximity to the fire, however, she couldn't fully warm herself. She needed to get off this boat. Where was the life-saving service? They ought to have come by now. Or at least to have acknowledged their presence with a signal. Any minute now she would hear the watchman say he spotted a signal flare. Be patient, Sunny. They'll come.

Periodically she poked at the coals so they lay flat and burned evenly, keeping the stove at an even temperature. The potatoes sizzled and crisped and she inhaled the earthy, buttery aroma. Despite the dreadfulness of their situation, a momentary lightness filled her chest, borne of her success with the coffee and potatoes. She could do anything. She would survive and go ashore and live the rest of her life how she wanted.

An indistinct sadness overcame her then. She followed the ominous feeling to its source, and remembered: The money was gone.

She finished the first batch of fried potatoes and lifted the pan to dump them into a large aluminum kettle Cleve had recovered. There were no unbroken plates, but he did find a couple of forks, and they would pass the bowl around, allowing the men to take turns spearing a stack of sliced potatoes.

Seconds after she'd dumped the potatoes from the frying pan into the bowl Cleve held, another horrible sea lashed the boilerhouse astern. She lost her balance and dropped the empty frying pan. Reflexively her hand reached for the cook-stove's rolling bar but missed. Cleve grabbed her wrist, preventing her fall. The boat shuddered and there was the sound of cracking wood.

Sunny covered her head with her free hand, fearing the roof would cave in. Her heart pounded in her chest. She held her breath. The wave retreated. She looked at Cleve but neither of them said anything. He must be thinking the same as she: this is the one that would pull them off the reef.

Seconds passed and the *Titus Brown* remained stranded. Most of it. A portion of the boilerhouse roof had just been swept away. The frying pan had slid into the slushy water at the galley's outer edge, where the bulkhead had collapsed and had disappeared under the surface.

"I can get it," Cleve said.

"No, I'll do it," Sunny said.

"Let me hold your hand, then. I'll hold onto the rolling bar."

Water flowed in and out through the doorless opening that led down to the engine room. Spray blew in through the broken galley window as water seeped through the cracks of the crushed exterior bulkhead. She wouldn't slide right out onto the spar deck, would she? Her limbs shaking, she reached for Cleve's hand and stepped into the water. The cold stung her legs. The pan was hidden in the murkiness. She'd have to feel for it. Crouching near the damaged bulkhead, careful of splintering wood, she reached under the frigid water until her fingers touched the pan's cast-iron handle.

"Got it!" Sunny said, clasping the handle. Seconds later a wave of freshwater smacked her in the face. For a moment Sunny worried she'd let go of the frying pan, but there it was, still in her left hand when she stood. Cleve held her right hand, and as she sputtered out the water, he pulled her back to the cook-stove.

She held up the pan. "Told you I could do it."

"Mrs. Colvin, I'm pretty sure you can do anything."

"You take the potatoes to the crew and I'll get the second batch going."

"But you're soaked. I can make the potatoes while you—"

"I'm fine, I'm fine." Sunny repressed a shiver. "We've got to think about getting something to Captain Hanna and the officers once the weather moderates and it's safe to go forward. They've had nothing to eat since yesterday noon."

In the forecastle, hundreds of feet forward, there was a similar, if smaller, cook-stove to warm the captain, mates, and wheelsmen—but no provisions to feed them. The last person to have contact with the captain, just before the *Titus Brown* hit the reef, was the chief engineer, a large Scotsman with a quiet manner. There had been no injuries among the officers, not then at least. Contact with the wheelhouse was cut off in their stranding, when the telephone between the stern and bow was rendered useless.

By the time the aft crew had finished their coffee and potatoes, several more big seas had crashed into the boilerhouse. Sunny left the galley and passed through the mess room to the door that opened onto the fantail. There the watchman stood, staring at the shore. He'd chipped away the ice from the door's window for a better view. A heavy snowfall had started up again.

"Anything?" Sunny asked.

The second watchman said there'd been no signal, that the life-saving service likely couldn't see them because of the snow. Or perhaps they were helping another vessel in distress. It might be that the lifesavers had run into trouble themselves.

Growing up Sunny had witnessed a storm that had damaged the life-saving station's boathouse doors and destroyed the dock. She'd been eleven or twelve and at the time it was the most savage gale she'd ever seen. And this storm was worse. There were many reasons their rescue might be delayed and with the contemplation of each one Sunny became more uneasy. Sailors who attempted to rescue themselves were much more likely to perish. Growing up at a life-saving station, she'd seen that for herself.

"Then I'd better figure out what to feed the men. I'd like Cleve to take provisions forward to the officers. Do you think it's safe?"

The watchman shook his head. "The deck is covered in ice and the lifeline is unusable. And the waves are still crashing over the hatches."

In the event of a stranding, Captain Hanna had always instructed them to stay put—so long as they were sheltered and safe—and await rescue. It made sense that the officers, sheltered in the forecastle, remained forward, while the crew remained aft. There was no reason for the officers to come aft unless they were in immediate danger themselves.

"But they must be starving," Sunny said.

The watchman thought about this for a moment, then nodded. "I'll talk to the mate."

Sunny left him to his post. She brought coffee to the pantry, where Herb huddled in a corner with his eyes closed. At the look of him her blood ran cold.

"Herb!" She rushed to him. His face was too pale, too still. Careful not to spill the hot coffee, she leaned in close. There was the faintest puff of breath on her cheek. "Oh thank heaven!" She kissed his cheek—it was so cold! Sleep was dangerous now. "Herb, wake up!" When his eyes finally fluttered open, she felt a wave of relief.

"Are you ok? How are you feeling?" Sunny asked.

"Better," Herb said groggily. "I can help with breakfast."

"Already done. You just rest. Drink." She lifted the coffee, and with considerable effort he straightened himself to drink.

"Is everyone all right?" Herb asked.

"Nothing serious, just some cuts and bruises. I've treated them like I did your forehead, with the carbolated Vaseline. We've been lucky, considering."

He sipped the coffee and said weakly, "Guess we won't be on the *Titus Brown* next year."

"No, we won't," she agreed, though not entirely sure of his meaning. Maybe he was being morose, insinuating they were all doomed. But that wasn't like Herb. He could be implying they'd be on a different boat next season, that they'd follow Captain Hanna to his next berth. Or maybe, just maybe, this was about what she'd revealed to him last night, her most precious dream, and this was his way of telling her that he'd decided to join her in going ashore after all. She'd confided in him at the darkest hour, when she was certain they were about to die. She'd thought he hadn't heard her but now there was a glimmer of hope that he had. It had taken the surety of imminent death for her to finally reveal her dream. That she wouldn't have to do it again was a relief.

Sunny dared to ask, "Where do you suppose we'll be then?"

Herb swallowed. "Wherever the Old Man ends up."

Her heart sank. She had wanted his blessing. To know that he would've supported her would give her the strength she needed to get through this ordeal. But it was like she'd never spoken of her dream at all. "What about what I told you last night, my plans for going ashore?"

"Plans? I'm sorry, love. I don't remember." He looked at her questioningly.

Not that it mattered anymore, with her money gone. A heavy weight perched in her chest. "Never mind."

She salvaged what she could from the pantry so that the crew would have something to eat when they got hungry again. There was ham in the refrigerator, as well as a bag of apples. It was a spartan noonday meal, but it would keep them alive. Her conversation with Herb had dispirited her. Not only was her money gone, but Herb already had a mind to sign up for another year on the lakes. He hadn't heard her—or was he pretending not to have heard?—when she'd spoken of her plans for a life ashore. She slid some fried potatoes into a covered bowl, and was putting the bowl and some apples in a basket for the forward crew when the first mate appeared at the galley door.

The mate has chosen the third engineer to take the food to the officers. Sunny went to the pantry to watch, through the porthole window's clear patch, the engineer's progress across the several hundred feet of straight deck to the forecastle. He stayed to port, which, due to the tilt of the boat to starboard, put him further from the waves that still broke over the boat at regular intervals. The lifeline was useless, coated as it was with ice as thick as a man's torso.

When the engineer was about midway across the deck, he slowed. He appeared to be studying something on the deck, near one of the hatches. What was he looking at? At last he started moving again, his dark figure retreating further from the boilerhouse. She watched until he made it to the forecastle and she was certain Captain Hanna and the officers would eat for the first time in twenty-four hours.

If the engineer had crossed more quickly, or if she hadn't watched his full progress, she wouldn't have been standing at the porthole to see, there along the shore, a small burst of red light. Sunny gasped. A signal flare! It lasted only seconds and then it was gone. Usually the Costons burned longer and brighter, and shot higher in the sky, but she was certain of what she'd seen. What else could it have been, but the life-saving service telling them they'd spotted the vessel and would be coming soon?

Her heart pounding, she hurried through the slippery galley to where the watchman stood in the mess room, at the door to the fantail. She told him about the Coston signal. He said he hadn't seen it. She was pleased with herself for having witnessed what the watchman missed, until she realized he was looking at her strangely. He squinted at her as if she might be lying, or hallucinating, even.

Sunny couldn't have been imagining it. She'd seen what she'd seen. The watchman was only disappointed he hadn't seen it himself, when it was his job to do so.

There were mumblings from the crew huddled in the mess room, wrapped in blankets and towels, hungry and cold. They'd heard what she'd told the watchman. Sunny exchanged a glance with Stilts, nodding once to assure him that what she said was true. Rescue was imminent. He and the other men believed her well enough; their collective relief was palpable.

"It's about time," the bosun said.

Stilts smiled, weakly, at Sunny. She was proud of him for not letting his fear get the better of him. Even in these awful circumstances, he'd lost neither his magnanimity nor his sense of humor. She knew what he was going to say before he said it: "Better late than never."

Port Austin, Michigan

Monday morning the wind outside the station was a constant moan, punctuated by great gusts. Combers broke against giant rocks near the shore, sending freshwater spray soaring into the frigid air. How much Agnes had actually slept was hard to say, for when she dreamed her dreams were of deafening winds and roaring breakers, and she awoke to the same, and one seemed as real as the other.

Now she found herself alone in the small room off the kitchen where she and Lizzie had slept on pallets. Keeper Duncan had refused to let them go to Lizzie and Mrs. Duncan's cottage the night before, worried as he was about debris flying around in the gale.

Agnes rubbed her neck. Last night Lizzie had curled up behind her, at one point placing her hand on Agnes's shoulder. Agnes had thrilled to the touch. And now she had the memory of it, a memory she could return to again and again. Was the memory all she would ever have, or was it possible that Lizzie had feelings for her, too? Maybe Agnes should tell Lizzie how she felt. No, she wasn't ready for that. And what about Nathaniel? Agnes's mind swirled with so many questions, questions she had no answers for. All she knew for certain was that she wanted Lizzie in her life, that everything was better when Lizzie was around.

Voices came from the kitchen. Agnes rose quickly, having slept in her clothes, and went to help with breakfast. Someone had removed the boards from the kitchen windows and a muted light shone in, the light filtered through snowflakes falling at an angle, blown by winds no longer hurricane force but strong all the same. The snow was thick enough to block the view of anything beyond the breakers that crashed onto the beach.

Lizzie stood at the cook-stove, frying eggs. Her slender fingers gently gripped the spatula, every movement graceful enough to make cooking eggs into poetry. "Morning, Sunshine," Lizzie said. She smiled and winked at Agnes.

Agnes's cheeks warmed. She cleared her throat. "Good morning," she replied in as normal a voice as she could manage. Acutely aware of Lizzie's proximity, but trying not to watch her too intently, Agnes helped serve the eggs and bacon. The crew came inside and ate quickly before resuming the enormous task of cleaning up debris and recovering blown-about equipment.

"Are you headed home?" Mrs. Duncan asked after the dishes were washed and put away.

"I might check on Irvin first," Agnes said, trying to forestall her departure.

"He's doing well. No sign of infection, and I gave him some laudanum for the pain. His wife is with him now."

"Oh," Agnes said. "Good, then." She did not want to go home, for several reasons. Thinking of Amos, she wanted to help the shorthanded crew with any rescues they may undertake. And she was not at all eager to face Maman after her outburst yesterday. Mostly, though, she didn't want to leave Lizzie. At the station with Lizzie, Agnes felt the happiest, the most alive she had in years and could not bear to have it end.

"You could stay and help with the cleanup," Lizzie said, putting on her coat. "We can always use another pair of hands."

"If I could be of help, then," Agnes said quickly. Her stomach fluttered. Maybe Lizzie didn't want her to leave, either. Lizzie had said very little about Nathaniel that morning.

Greatly encouraged, Agnes donned her coat and gloves and followed her outside.

Little remained of the boathouse. Wood planks were strewn around the beach and station grounds, a concentration of them where the boathouse had been. Bits of decorative wood bracketing lay here and there. Shingles had blown across the sand like bits of paper. Only the massive lifeboat stood, huge and resolute, at the terminus of the launching rails. Debris from the shattered boathouse surrounded it. A layer of ice encrusted everything.

As for the pier, it was nothing but isolated piles of wood planks, visible now and again in the raging surf. The surfboat, lighter and smaller than the lifeboat, had been thrown by the wind and waves from its perch and was all but buried in the sand, coated in ice from the surf that washed over it and froze almost immediately.

Clad in their oilskins and boots, the crew had been working in the heavy snowfall to remove debris from the launching rails. They'd nearly finished the job. Agnes and Lizzie joined in and once they'd cleared the rails, they went about the tedious work of finding the myriad pieces of equipment that had been blown from the boathouse.

Keeper Duncan asked them to place the equipment on the lee side of the station. Blinking snowflakes from her lashes, Agnes searched through the rubble. After an hour she'd collected a fair amount. As she walked from the shore to the station and back, salvaging signal flags or water pails or spare oars, time and again she would cross paths with Lizzie. Sometimes Agnes would look at her and smile. Sometimes, trying not to be obvious, Agnes would pretend to be absorbed in her task and not notice her. But whether she acknowledged it or not, Agnes was always acutely aware of the young woman's presence.

Some of the equipment Agnes found belonged in the lifeboat. Having been a keen observer of her husband's and her father's work, she could have packed the lifeboat all by herself. But she hadn't lived at the station in three years and, turnover being what it was, many of these surfmen didn't know her well, so she simply brought the equipment to them and let them stow it. The surfmen coiled the lines and placed them beneath the thwarts, clear from the foot boards. The masts were lashed amidships. Lines were righted. As she was returning an oar she overheard one of the surfmen say the lifeboat's motor had been severely damaged.

As for the surfboat, filled with sand at the water's edge, all that could be done at the moment was to collect the equipment that belonged in it. They would store the equipment in one of the outbuildings until the storm and waves had subsided enough that the surfboat could be dug out.

After Lizzie went inside to warm up, Agnes walked a distance from the remains of the boathouse to see what else she might find. Visibility was poor. The snowy haze hid everything more than a few yards ahead of her. At last the pine trees atop Turnip Rock came into view. She'd reached the end of the bay. Shivering and wet with sea spray, she decided she was unlikely to find anything else. It would be wise to warm up inside for a bit. Not just because Lizzie had gone inside, too, she reasoned to an imaginary referee, but because she, Agnes, was cold. She was about to turn around and head back when something in the sand a few feet ahead caught her attention. A megaphone, the one from the watchtower. It was remarkable, how far some things had blown. She picked it up and when she looked out at the vastness of the lake, spaces suddenly appeared between snowflakes, and these empty spaces expanded until all at once she could see beyond the beach. A break in the blizzard at last!

Squinting, she watched for vessels to materialize from the haze. The lighthouse appeared first. And then, the horizon. Agnes scanned the rough seas. A distance from shore, a mile or two, there was what at first appeared to be an iceberg. Her breath caught. As the shape came more into focus it looked like a ghost ship, white with snow and ice. The vessel's distress signal was clear.

"A vessel!" Agnes cried out, pointing at the ship wrapped in ice like a shroud. She turned back toward the station. No one was close enough to have heard her. She ran with renewed energy, lifting the icy megaphone to her mouth and calling out to the lifesavers as she closed the distance between them.

When she reached the men, they looked up from their work. Keeper Duncan, who'd been removing a half-frozen tarpaulin from the side of the woodshed it'd blown up against, dropped the canvas and ran along the coast toward her, and then past her. A couple of the crew followed. Breathless, Agnes stopped and turned to follow them but they didn't need her to point it out. They were already pointing; everyone saw the ghost ship.

After a moment Keeper Duncan ran back along the beach, to where the surfboat lay swamped with sand. Agnes and the crew gathered around him as he stared at the surfboat. The surf washed over it with each breaking wave.

She guessed at his thoughts: surfboat or lifeboat? Though the surfboat held fewer people, it would be preferable because of the way it darted across cresting waves and maneuvered around whatever logs and barrels and other debris might surround the stranded vessel. The heavy lifeboat, on the other hand, battered like a ram through the combers. But digging the twenty-five-foot surfboat out of the wet sand would take at least an hour. Likely longer, given that the waves would be washing over them the entire time.

Keeper Duncan would surely choose the lifeboat—even though its motor was broken, which meant they had to row, and they were two oarsmen short. The lifeboat could be readied the quickest. And who knew how long those sailors had been stranded? This break in the blizzard had provided the only real view of the lake since yesterday afternoon. The sailors could be half frozen by now.

The surfman on beach patrol sprinted up the beach. "There's a vessel stranded on the reef, sir," he said, panting.

"We saw it," Keeper Duncan said. "Do you have a Coston?"

"They were all blown from the boathouse, sir. A few washed up on the beach but they're badly damaged."

"Then let's waste no time getting out there," Keeper Duncan said. "Prepare the lifeboat."

The lifesavers moved swiftly and with purpose. Agnes's stomach pitted. It was time to ask the keeper. He was going to say no, but she had to ask. For Amos.

"Keeper Duncan," she said, shoring up her courage. "I'm an able oarswoman." Then, when he didn't respond, "I'm stronger than you might think."

The keeper shook his head without even considering her offer. "The surf's too dangerous," he said. "It's even worse than it looks from here, I assure you." He was different, now, in an emergency. Not unfriendly, but not solicitous either. The change came as a relief and Agnes felt a twinge of excitement.

She took a step closer. "I know it's bad. That's why I want to help." These men must not go out shorthanded. She could help prevent someone's wife from becoming a widow.

"There is something you can do," Keeper Duncan said. "Patrol the beach. If you see another wreck, run to the station and tell Lizzie. I'm putting her on the hunt for Costons."

Agnes raised her voice, pleading. "But you don't have enough—"

"Head that way," Keeper Duncan pointed east. "Toward Burnt Cabin Point. When you get to the telephone you can turn around. That's the limit—"

"I know where patrol ends," Agnes said, looking away in order to hide her frustration. How incompetent did he think she was? For goodness' sake she'd lived at the station nearly all her life!

"Right. Well the phones are out, so don't worry about checking in."

Agnes started along the beach, her stomach knotting with worry for the crew. Periodically she glanced over her shoulder to check on their progress. The six surfmen and Keeper Duncan climbed into the *Stalwart* and took their positions. They lifted their long oars as the lifeboat slid down the launching rails and into the water. The thirty-four-foot boat, so grand up close and mounted on its carriage, was immediately dwarfed by the tremendous surf.

With an impressive harmony, as if all the oars were connected by an invisible string, the crew lowered their oars into the water to try to get the boat under way before the waves could push the *Stalwart* back to the beach. They had to be fast if they were going to get through the breakers. Between the waves and the strong onshore wind it would take all their strength to make headway. Agnes scanned the horizon for other distressed vessels as she walked east toward Burnt Cabin Point. She worried for the *Stalwart* and for the stranded ship. Any of these breakers might force the lifeboat to broach and capsize.

She was pausing to check on the *Stalwart* when a heavy wave struck the boat. She winced but the crew rode it out safely. No sooner had they beaten the first breaker when a second hit. Agnes held her breath—this, too, they rode through without incident. In quick succession a third huge breaker struck.

The third wave was too much and they broached. Broadside to the waves, the lifesavers struggled to bring the lifeboat head-to. Moments later they capsized and the entire crew was dumped into the surf. Agnes cried out. The lifeboat righted itself, as it was built to do, only to have a huge comber knock it end over end. She watched the churning surf, afraid the boat might have hit one of the men. The lifeboat righted once again, and in the tumult of waves, only two lifesavers made it back aboard.

Where were the others? Fear rose up in her throat until she spotted five other heads bobbing in the surf. They made it back into the lifeboat with the other two, only to have the surging waves roll them again. This was too much! Someone was going to get killed. Then, as if putting the *Stalwart* out of its misery, a comber flung the two-thousand-pound vessel back upon the beach as if it were a piece of driftwood. The empty lifeboat landed not far from where the surfboat lay half-buried.

As she ran back toward the station to help, Agnes watched the pounding surf for the surfmen and Keeper Duncan. If the keeper had let her row, too, they might have made it past the breakers. No, she had to admit, it was more likely she'd have been tossed about in the waves like the rest of them. The surf was just too wild. She caught sight of one man emerging from the roaring surf and then another. Four, five. She hurried along the beach to where the lifeboat had come to rest. The sixth and seventh men staggered from the water. They were all standing on their own. She sighed with relief.

The lifeboat, however, had filled with sand and water. Now it weighed considerably more than its two thousand pounds. Keeper Duncan was pulling an oar from the surf. The lifesavers were drenched and freezing but, miraculously, no one was badly hurt. She asked what she could do to help.

"We've no boats left to attempt a rescue and our telephone is dead," the keeper said. "I need you to get to Port Austin as quick as you can and call the Pointe Aux Barques station. Ask if they can send assistance. If they can't help then call Harbor Beach."

Agnes looked inland. Further from the shore, massive snowdrifts had formed in front of the cottages and the smokehouse and the woodshed. The road to town would be buried in two feet of snow at the least. She would take the coastline, and scan the seas for more stranded vessels as she went.

Running with the weight of those shipwrecked lives on her shoulders, she scrambled over barricades of driftwood and treaded carefully over large flat rocks coated in ice. Her fingertips ached with cold despite her gloves. She glanced over her shoulder, searching for the stranded vessel, but the falling snow had obscured it again. Pray the sailors would stay put. Because the surfmen hadn't fired a Coston signal, the stranded sailors wouldn't know they had been spotted by the lifesaving service. And if the sailors thought help was not on the way, they might attempt their own rescue. And if they were to leave their steamer in a lifeboat on these seas, they were likelier to perish than if they waited for help a little longer.

Agnes stopped to catch her breath when she reached her cottage on the outskirts of town. Giant snowdrifts reached high up the first-floor windows, but at least the pale-yellow cottage was all in one piece. She would check on Maman after calling for help. She continued on and, a little further along the coast, she cut away from the shore.

It was harder going, now, through snow that reached past her knees and drifted much higher in places. She trudged her way south until she came upon Bird Creek, and then followed the tributary until she arrived at the bridge into the village. No one else was about in this weather. The buildings were hushed and covered in a thick layer of white: the tailor shop and the hotel, the jeweler and the furniture dealer. And Bisbee's, where on a typical Monday she'd already be at work, was as silent as the rest of the village. Wind whipped down the street leading to the harbor, momentarily taking away her breath. She turned her back to the lake and ducked her head into her coat. The wind off the lake rushed at her, pushing her the last block to the post office.

Thank goodness for the postal service: the door was open and the postman inside.

"Mrs. Inby," the postman said, alarmed. "What are you doing out in this weather? Are you all right? Is it your mother?"

"Are the phones working?" Agnes said, panting, one hand on the counter to steady herself. It took her a moment to catch her breath. Though her nose was numb with cold, the long run had overheated her, and she unbuttoned her coat and removed her gloves as she explained to the postman what had happened.

The postman led her to the telephone, pleased to be of use on this day where there would be no mail. She called the Pointe Aux Barques Life-Saving Station, which was about nine miles away in Huron City. When the station keeper's wife got on the line, she said their crew couldn't help them. Agnes slumped into a chair as she listened to the reasons why. Pointe Aux Barques couldn't help anyone, the woman said. Their boathouse and launching rails had been destroyed in the storm, and the lifeboat and carriage were thrown completely off track. Even their concrete breakwater was gone. What was worse, there was a vessel two miles off shore and they were helpless to assist it until they could clean up the rubble and launch a boat.

Agnes thanked her and then called the station further down the coast in Harbor Beach, a good twenty miles away. Their response was grimmer still. They had four vessels in trouble: a straight deck freighter and a steamer towing two barges.

"The destruction, it's incredible," said the Harbor Beach station keeper's wife. "It's like nothing I've ever seen."

Agnes pressed her fingers to her temples where a growing ache pulsed. Help wasn't coming.

"The resort's in terrible shape," the woman went on. "The casino's gone. So are the bowling alley and the billiard hall and the bath house. The waves just smashed it all like it was made of toothpicks. They'll be cleaning up for a year."

"That's just awful, I'm so sorry." Agnes was impatient now to end the conversation. She had to get back to the station. She offered more sympathies, said something about not wanting to tie up the line further, and ended the call before the woman could recount more destruction. Her mind swirled with the terrible truth that help was not coming. The immensity of the damage this storm had done—was still doing—up and down the coast was horrifying.

And what about Sunny and Herb? Had they made it out of Lake Huron? They could be on one of the many freighters stranded off the coast—and if that many had stranded, how many had foundered? And then there was Cordelia's new husband. Cordelia, at least, was safe at her new home in Cleveland. How awful if she were to become a widow so soon after marrying. And after what had happened to Lewis... Agnes shook her head; she felt so helpless in the face of all this disaster.

"Are you all right?" The postman asked, his brow furrowed. "Can I get you a cup of tea before you head back?"

"That's very kind, but I'd better push on." Agnes put on her coat and mittens, thanked the postman, and left. She stared down the quiet, snow-covered street. She'd accomplished nothing. She was supposed to have put in motion the rescue so desperately needed by that vessel out on the rocks. But the Port Austin crew was on their own, and now she had to deliver the awful news. Though her legs felt heavy and slow, she forced herself to hurry, following her own path in the snow.

Maybe she shouldn't stop to check on Maman. Keeper Duncan needed to know as soon as possible that help wasn't coming so he could come up with another plan. Then again, Agnes would be passing right by her house on the way along the coast. Agnes couldn't live with herself if something had happened and she hadn't checked on her.

She would make it quick. No getting drawn into an argument about how she'd deserted her mother during the worst storm in a century. When she reached her cottage along the shore east of town, she trudged up the snowy yard. The snowdrifts made it impossible to open the back door, so she plowed her way to the front.

The door slammed shut behind her, blown by the wind.

"Agnes, is that you?" Maman's voice came from the parlor.

"It's me." Agnes went into the parlor, but didn't immediately spot her mother. "I can't stay. I've only come to check—"

There Maman lay, sprawled on the floor by the woodstove, moaning.

"Maman!" Agnes ran to her and tried to gently help her to a sitting position. Maman cried out and said she'd rather remain on the floor. Agnes lay her back down and brought her a pillow. "Where are you hurt? What happened?"

"I tripped on the rug. My hip hurts. I think I sprained my ankle."

This was all her fault. She shouldn't have left her mother alone for so long. "How long have you been lying here?" The room was cold. Embers glowed in the woodstove.

"A couple of hours, maybe. I don't know."

"You must be chilled." Agnes pulled the afghan from the davenport and lay it over her.

"Where have you been?" Maman said in a small voice. "I've been worried sick. I thought you might not come back."

"Of course I came back." Agnes put another log on the fire and stoked the embers. Maybe she needn't feel so guilty. Maman's injury might be less physical and more a matter of bruised feelings. "I would've been here yesterday if it weren't for the storm. I was at the station. They need my help." Agnes wanted to explain herself, but without feeling like she was apologizing. What had she to apologize for? Only the outburst that preceded everything, perhaps.

"Thank goodness you're here now."

"Maman, I can't stay. I have to get back to the station."

"But you just got here."

"I have to go." Agnes faced her mother. "There's a vessel on the reef. The surfboat is buried and the lifeboat is damaged beyond use. The station telephone is out and Keeper Duncan sent me to call for help. I have to go back and tell him help isn't coming. Not from Huron City or Harbor Beach." As Agnes turned away to adjust the logs with the fire poker, which didn't really need adjusting, she explained how the boathouse had been destroyed and the signal flares blown to kingdom come. "I'll come home as soon as I can, but it might not be until this evening."

"There are a few Costons here."

Agnes whirled around. "Here in the house? Where?"

"In a trunk in the bedroom. I found them a while back. They'd been packed with your father's things."

Now this was a bit of good news. Agnes returned the fire poker to its holder and hurried upstairs to Maman's bedroom. Inside the trunk at the end of the bed was her father's uniform: a dark blue kersey coat with gilt buttons, and a matching cap with a gold-embroidered emblem above the leather bill. He'd had two such uniforms, and had been buried in the other.

Beneath the uniform were the Coston signals—two small cylindrical cartridges—and a wooden handle for holding and igniting them. Agnes put the cartridges and handle in a bag and went downstairs. She helped Maman to the davenport, the elder woman now amenable to the transfer, and covered her once more with the afghan. She brought her mother a glass of water. It was not without some guilt that she left Maman alone, again. To Maman's credit, the woman rallied in a crisis and did not protest further.

When Agnes followed her path through the snow back to the shore, a thought occurred to her. She would fire one of the Costons herself. The sooner the sailors on that stranded steamer knew help was coming, the safer they would be.

She ran along the coast until she was on a bluff and even with the stranded vessel—a straight deck freighter, it looked like. This was as good a place as any. As she retrieved the three-inch-long cartridge from her bag, a violent gust of wind knocked her off balance. She waved her arms in great circles, trying not to fall, and as she did so the cartridge fell from her hands and into the crashing waves below. She stared at the water, disbelieving. How could she have been so clumsy?

She had one chance left. Taking a step back from the bluff's edge, she took the other cartridge and placed it in the socket at the end of the wooden handle. Holding the handle in her left hand, with her right hand she shoved the spring that protruded from the end of it like a button. In doing so a sharp point pierced the cartridge. There was a sizzle and a red light shot out. She pointed the handle toward the sky so that the red light, which continued to flow, would shoot up as high as possible. Coston signals could burn for as long as two minutes and could be seen for miles.

But this flare didn't shoot up far at all and after only twenty seconds the red light fizzled to nothing. Only twenty seconds! She frowned. Costons were extremely reliable. Had the fault lain in her execution? Maybe the cartridge had deteriorated over time or had been improperly stored. And there was no telling how old they were. Agnes watched the silent ship out on the rocks. There was a chance that someone on that freighter had been watching. She put the handle and wasted cartridge in her pocket and hurried along the shore.

Although it was only eleven o'clock in the morning when she arrived at the station, the surfmen were having dinner. They all stopped eating and turned expectant faces toward her. Out of breath and both cold and warm at the same time, Agnes found it hard to speak. Mrs. Duncan offered her a glass of water. She gulped it down. From the head of the table, Keeper Duncan asked what she'd discovered. When she delivered the news that no one was coming to help, he seemed unsurprised that the damage extended well beyond their town. It was the worst storm any of them had ever seen.

Agnes almost told them about the Costons she'd found in her father's chest, but since no one mentioned having seen the one she fired, there really was no need, was there? From a signal flare standpoint, they were no worse off than they'd been when she left, and she didn't want them to think she'd fired it improperly.

Keeper Duncan had already pushed his chair from the table and was ordering his men back to work. The lifeboat was useless to them now. Even if they were to bail the water from it, they'd need a team to carry it back to the station in order to launch it from the rails. And so he ordered his men to do the only thing they could, given the circumstances: Dig out the surfboat.

Agnes was famished. Lizzie, who hadn't been in the room until now, fixed her a plate of hash and a scoop of cabbage salad and sat down beside her with a long sigh. She had been tending to Nathaniel, who'd come down with a fever after that morning's rescue attempt. Lizzie said he'd shown signs of illness the night before, after returning hours late from his treacherous beach patrol. Lizzie had wanted to tell her brother that Nathaniel was unfit to go out that morning, but Nathaniel wouldn't let her.

"And now he's feeling worse," Lizzie said. She chewed on a fingernail. "Even my brother agrees Natty's not fit to go out a second time."

A lump formed in Agnes's throat. She mumbled some consolatory words about Nathaniel and quickly changed the topic. She described her arctic trek into Port Austin, how Maman had been injured and was sure to hold a grudge for weeks after Agnes had abandoned her not once, but twice. Agnes tried to do what was expected of her, she lamented to Lizzie, but sometimes it was near impossible.

Lizzie stood, taking Agnes's empty plate. "Why must you do everything she expects of you?"

The words hit Agnes like a slap. Stunned, she carried her glass to the sink without answering. Beyond the kitchen window the crew labored at a Sisyphean task: shoveling wet sand out of the surfboat's twenty-five-foot hull only to have the next wave dump it back in.

"Truly, Agnes," Lizzie persisted. "Maybe fulfilling her every wish is not so noble or worthy an endeavor as you think it is. Who knows, maybe your mother would be better off if you didn't."

"If I didn't?" Agnes turned from the window. "You don't know my mother like I do."

"Don't you want more out of life, Agnes?"

Of course she wanted more. But who was Lizzie to judge? "My life is just fine." Agnes lifted her chin. "I'm sorry if you find it worthy of pity."

Lizzie came and stood next to Agnes. "I didn't mean it like that." She spoke softly.

"What do you mean, then? You seem cross. Have I done something to offend you?"

"You haven't offended me. I just—it's just that I…I care about, you, Agnes. I want you to be happy." She put her hand on Agnes's shoulder.

A ripple of pleasure coursed through Agnes's body. "I am happy." Her voice cracked. She covered Lizzie's hand with her own. "Our friendship makes me happy." Her cheeks warmed and she looked at the ground. Maybe she'd been wrong about Lizzie. Maybe Lizzie had feelings for her after all. Without looking up, she dared to ask, "Why, what do you think would make me happy?"

Keeper Duncan rushed into the kitchen then, a burst of cold air with him. "Lizzie, I need you on beach patrol. Now. It's snowing again and the men are busy digging out the surfboat. Put on a suit and don't forget the lantern."

Lizzie hesitated. The keeper looked at her as if to say, "What are you waiting for?" Lizzie gave Agnes a look that she couldn't quite read and then left the room.

A new hopefulness filled Agnes's chest. Lizzie had been about to say something important. If only Keeper Duncan hadn't interrupted. Well, there would be time, later. Agnes wouldn't leave the station until she knew where Lizzie's heart lay. Suddenly there were so many possibilities for her future, and they all included Lizzie.

It took Agnes a moment to collect herself. She forced her thoughts back to the rescue. "How are you going to row it?" she asked Keeper Duncan, who was getting a mug from the cupboard. It took six men to row the surfboat, plus the keeper steering at the back. With Nathaniel sick, they were down to a crew of five.

The keeper filled a mug with coffee. "We can handle it," he said. Then, more to himself than to her, "We don't have a choice."

"As I said earlier, I can—"

"It's no task for a woman," Keeper Duncan interrupted.

Agnes's head spun. It was exasperating, to be underestimated time and again. "You sound like Amos, and look what happened to him!" she said without thinking. And though Keeper Duncan looked at her strangely, she wouldn't take back her words. Instead she told him how Amos had refused to let her row the day the lifeboat capsized. "Amos wouldn't have died if I'd been at the oars. I'm strong and I know the commands. I know this reef."

Keeper Duncan finished his coffee quickly and put the mug in the sink. "I'm sorry, Agnes. I can't have you getting yourself hurt. I've sent for a volunteer from the village." He was headed for the door.

"I've done it before." Agnes spoke quickly. "Years ago when my father was the keeper, and the station wasn't in operation for the season yet. A yawl had capsized a couple miles off shore. There was a heavy sea running and it was cold and the two men clinging to the hull would've frozen if we didn't get out there fast. My sister Sunny and I rowed out with my father and a volunteer from the village."

Keeper Duncan put his gloves back on. "And you saved the sailors?"

Agnes held his gaze. "They were all saved."

"Mrs. Inby, you're a woman of many talents." Keeper Duncan said this earnestly as he moved toward the door.

What Agnes hadn't told him was that the four of them hadn't made it over the breakers, that the boat had filled with water and been driven back to shore. Agnes was sent to town to gather volunteers who then made the rescue while she watched from the station. Be that as it may, she had made a valiant effort. And her father had had enough confidence in her abilities to put her on the boat in the first place. If her father had been keeper in 1910, Amos might still be alive.

She watched Keeper Duncan expectantly. She could see herself on that surfboat, rowing out to the broken-down vessel. He must see it, too.

"All the same," Keeper Duncan said, opening the door. "It's best you stay put. You can help Lizzie and Mother prepare the coffee and have warm blankets ready. Those poor sailors will be near frozen." The wind slammed the door shut behind him.

Agnes pounded her fist on the table. Rubbing her hand, she looked around until she was certain no one had been watching.

By early afternoon the lifesavers had freed the surfboat of sand. The five surfmen and Keeper Duncan dragged the clinker-built craft away from the water, toward the building. Agnes opened the door to ask if she could be of any use before they rowed out to the vessel.

"We're not going out just yet," Keeper Duncan said as he carried the boat at the bow and led the men toward the rear of the building. "The surfboat sustained a fair amount of damage slamming into the beach. We've got to patch her up first."

Another delay and it was already past one o'clock. They were running out of time. Agnes donned her coat and followed the surfmen behind the station, where working conditions were slightly less frigid, sheltered somewhat from the wind coming off the lake. Her breath caught when she saw the destruction: five breaks in the gunwale, a large hole in the after platform, and several holes in the boat's wooden bottom. Repairs were going to take a while. Could the stranded sailors wait that long?

One of the surfmen, a moose of a man who had joined the station on a temporary basis that fall, was preparing to fill the smaller holes with oakum. Ice clung to his blond eyelashes, so that it appeared he didn't have eyelashes at all, only tiny arcs of diamonds. He looked as though he hadn't taken a break in hours. He was moving rather slowly.

"Can I help? I know how to do that," Agnes offered. "I made my own skiff and I do the repairs myself." In watching and helping her husband over the years, she'd learned plenty about boat construction and repair.

When Moose didn't respond, Agnes looked to Keeper Duncan.

"Go inside and thaw out a bit," the keeper told him. "You'll be no good to anyone with frostbitten hands."

Moose went inside and Agnes took his place. That was more like it. She could get the repairs done faster—probably better, too. Another surfman was cutting a canvas tarpaulin to make a patch for one of the holes in the hull. Canvas patches weren't ideal, but they hadn't the time for proper repairs, lest the stranded sailors die of hypothermia first. The surfboat needed to be just watertight enough to get them to the vessel and back.

Agnes pulled several strands of oakum and rolled them on her thigh. Using a mallet and caulking iron, she set about driving the oakum into the cracks in the hull. It was painstaking work, lining the oakum up with the cracks and then using the mallet and caulking iron to gently push it into the open spaces. She had the patience for it. In fact she rather liked it. Were it not for the cold, she'd be enjoying herself.

She lined up the oakum with the cracks and pushed it in with the mallet and caulking iron, an inch at a time. Amos once told her, as they repaired her skiff one spring, that she swung the mallet too hard and was liable to cause more damage. Hearing his words in her head, Agnes swung the mallet lightly.

She thought about her mother, at home alone, and reminded herself that what she was doing at the station was a matter of life and death, and could therefore be justified, even to Maman. To separate herself physically from Maman was to enjoy a certain freedom. Agnes could breathe. She could *think*.

Maybe that was the answer. Maybe she should flee Port Austin, like Sunny and Cordelia had done. Let one of her sisters come and take care of their mother. If Sunny opened a restaurant here like she'd long dreamed, then Agnes would have some relief. She could travel, maybe go and see the magnificent Niagara Falls. The mere thought of it filled her with lightness and optimism. Or what if she found other work entirely? What if she got her license and became a captain? What better way to be free! It was unusual for a woman, sure, but not unheard of. Lizzie could work on the boat with her and they would sail the Great Lakes just as Lizzie dreamed...

Hour after hour Agnes and the surfmen made repairs to the boat. Her world became the mallet and iron and oakum. Despite the bitter cold, a floating, transcendent feeling came over her like what often happened when she painted china—a sense that all was right with the world, and everything else disappeared, that she and the piece of china were all that mattered.

It was well after dark when their work was complete. Keeper Duncan inspected the repairs while the crew waited inside. Agnes sat in the warm kitchen where Lizzie and her mother were making supper. Keeper Duncan came back inside, his expression grave. The patches were rather clumsy, he said, prompting Agnes to worry he'd order them redone. Despite all their efforts, the boat could use more repairs, the keeper said. Chief among them was the self-bailing mechanism: the tubes and valves that carried water through to the bottom of the boat when pressure became too great. However, he said at last, the work was good enough to get them to the vessel and back. More thorough repairs would have to wait until the storm was over.

Chairs scraped back from the table as the crew rose to go out.

Keeper Duncan stopped them with a raised hand. "We'll go at daybreak," he said. "It would be foolhardy to attempt a rescue now, in the dark with only an oil lamp to light the way, and with the boat in the condition it's in. Breakers are still pounding the shore carrying all kinds of debris we wouldn't see in this dark."

Agnes chewed on a fingernail. That poor vessel's crew would have to wait yet another night. She feared for their lives. Hoped they'd seen her signal, such as it had been. For all she knew that was the *Titus Brown* out there on the reef. It might even be the *Marguerite*, the steamer captained by her new brother-in-law.

That evening after supper, from the warmth of the kitchen, Agnes looked out the window into the darkness. The snow had stopped again. Matted gray clouds blocked out the moon, rendering the lake black. Agnes watched the darkness, wishing she might somehow help those stranded sailors with her watching. Though she couldn't see the vessel, she felt its heavy presence, alone and broken on the rocks, waiting.

Lake Superior

In the dark Cordelia lay prone on the life raft, her fingers wedged between the wooden planks. They were arranged like sardines: Cordelia in the middle, between Mack and Richard; the watchman and Ollie on either end. She lay with her chest pressed to the wooden platform, her hips twisted slightly so that her right leg rested on her left.

The *Marguerite* had sunk less than an hour ago, and her body had gone mostly numb not long after. Her mind, too. She knew they were in grave danger and yet, strangely, she was not afraid. Her thoughts were on the practicalities now: Hold onto the raft. Stay awake. A thick cloud cover blocked any moonlight. Unable to see in the darkness, Cordelia's other senses heightened. She knew when a larger-than-usual wave was coming without seeing it. She felt it. Felt the wave pull the raft into its arc before sliding them over and down its back.

That was the best case.

Other waves crashed over their raft and when this happened the frigid water took her breath away. Those waves were an agony. Icily sharp, the crashing waves assaulted them, and she and the others would cry out. The rush of arctic air that came after felt colder still.

The raft had not flipped over, although it had come close, once.

"What do you reckon our chances are?" Mack, the third mate, now asked of no one in particular.

"Better than those who went for the lifeboat," Ollie said.

She hated Ollie for saying it. Maybe the crew had launched the lifeboat after all. Maybe Edmund was on it.

"We're not a dozen miles from land." Richard's voice came from behind Cordelia, just above her head. "We'll drift to shore sometime tomorrow. Stay awake and alert. Huddle close and we'll be all right."

Though Ollie was first mate, it was Richard—older, more experienced—who took charge, encouraging the others to talk so that they might ward off sleep. Richard asked Ollie, who'd grown up in a small town near Ann Arbor, about the Wolverines. "Squib's out with a sore shoulder," he said, trying to sound natural, like he was sitting at a bar with his buddies, and that made it worse. When Richard asked about Michigan's record against Cornell, Ollie said they were two and eight. "It'll be a fight but they've got a real chance."

There was silence for a while and then the third mate said, "I have a son. Born on the fourth of November."

"Mack?" Richard said. "I didn't know your wife was in the family way. Congratulations."

"I got a telegram in Cleveland. He's our first."

Cordelia offered a weak congratulations. She hadn't spoken in a while and found that when she did her throat hurt.

"A few years and we can bring him on as a deckhand," Richard said.

"I'd like that," said Mack.

The watchman couldn't be prodded into conversation. He only made grunting noises now and again. And so it was Cordelia's turn. She didn't feel like talking. She was exhausted and wanted only to close her eyes. No, her exhaustion was precisely why she must talk. A story from her childhood, then. At eleven years of age she'd won the Port Austin spelling bee. The townspeople versus the schoolchildren. What had been the winning word? Her memory was hazy. Felicitations? No, that wasn't it. Follicle? No. It had started with an F. The word escaped her now but she'd never forget how proud she'd been.

A gust of arctic wind made it impossible to take in breath. She was being drowned in cold air. Her body tensed with panic and then the gust was gone. She inhaled gratefully. She still wore her life belt, and her wool coat over that. Under her life belt she wore a woolen sweater and skirt, and her silk stockings and chemise. Her laced boots were still on her feet. Yet for the warmth the wet clothing provided she might as well have been wrapped in paper.

Sometime that night the storm clouds thinned and the moon shone through, illuminating the cresting waves. The five survivors lay in a row as before, too cold to move. Moving required energy they couldn't afford to expend. Cordelia drifted in and out of sleep. With Richard behind her she hadn't seen his face since he first climbed onto the raft. All she saw was the back of Mack's head. What little conversation there had been had dwindled, although Richard tried to revive it now and again. The watchman, at the raft's edge behind him, hadn't said a word.

The moonlight dimmed as clouds passed in front of it. When the clouds were gone and the light returned Cordelia could just make out, over Mack's shoulder, the crest of a wave. The wave reached higher than any that had pitched them back and forth for what seemed like hours, and maybe actually was.

The massive wave approached as if in slow motion. She tightened her grip on the wooden plank and curled into a fetal position. From somewhere outside herself she watched the wave come. "Wave," she said, her voice cracking. Then again, trying for more volume, "Wave."

And then it was upon them, drawing the raft into itself, pulling them up to a near-vertical position. Ollie, at the higher edge of the raft, fell backwards into Mack, and Cordelia lost her grip and was separated from the raft and pushed under the water.

A rush of warmth.

She kicked her legs and clawed at the water, careful not to let the life belt slip over her head. It was hard to tell which way was up and she was afraid to commit to a direction. All at once her cork life belt buoyed her to the surface.

She pushed the wet hair from her face. In the moonlight Mack was visible a short distance away. There was nothing else, no one else, only water. Where was the life raft? She spun around and cried out at the sight of its metal barrels. Just a few strokes away. With renewed strength she swam to it and grasped the rope festooned along the side. Instead of climbing up she hesitated. The air was so much colder. It wouldn't hurt to stay in the water for just a minute. Her body relaxed in the relative warmth. The lake beckoned her to linger.

No. The frigid water would kill her more quickly than the colder air. She knew this. Holding onto the rope, she tried to pull herself up but couldn't. The huge oil drum was too tall. There was a small ledge, about halfway up, and she put her right hand there for leverage. She pulled on the rope with her left hand and her torso came out of the water. She moved her right hand from the drum's ledge to the wooden platform. That was all the strength she had. She would hang there, her feet still in the water that swelled around them, until she couldn't. It wouldn't take long. She had tried.

There was movement above her and Mack appeared at the raft's edge. He grabbed her arm and pulled. He needed her to help him. It was hard to breathe and she was lightheaded, but Cordelia summoned new strength to pull her legs from the water. A moment later she was on the raft again. Every part of her hurt. Stabbing sensations pierced her legs and arms. Her head throbbed.

Someone else was climbing onto the raft. Collapsed on the platform, Cordelia had closed her eyes and didn't know who it was. Mack was yelling into the night air, calling for Ollie and the watchman. Now Richard's voice joined in the yelling. She forced herself to sit up and look, but there was no sign of either. She turned away from Richard and Mack. When the raft crested she glimpsed the back of Ollie's head in the valley between waves, his sandy hair shining in the moonlight like a little beacon. She called his name but her voice didn't sound right. It wasn't all there. Ollie didn't respond.

The raft dipped and Cordelia couldn't see beyond the next wave. When the raft crested again the little beacon was gone. A life belt floated pale and empty where he had been.

For a minute more they called for the watchman. Cordelia joined in, horrified at the thought of Ollie, who at that moment was sinking to the bottom of the lake. It hurt to yell and her voice croaked. It was no use. The watchman, who'd been silent for so long, might have been dead even before the raft flipped.

Now only three, they settled onto the raft once more. Richard was in the middle. Cordelia laid on her side, facing the oncoming waves. No one said anything for a while. No matter how long it took, she must stay alive. Edmund was out there, somewhere, on the lifeboat. He would be looking for her. She would stay alive for him. Finally Richard urged Mack and Cordelia to speak, to say anything, just to keep their wits about them.

Tell us about Christmas dinner, Richard said in a voice at once distant and near. Tell us what you and Sunny are going to make. Richard knew of Sunny Colvin and her excellent baking, once claiming that if he weren't so fond of Edmund he'd try to get a job on the *Titus Brown* for the food alone.

Christmas dinner was Cordelia's favorite, yet her dry mouth could summon no saliva, not even at her own descriptions of Sunny's plum pudding and chestnut stuffing, spiced gingerbread and sugar plums.

I could no sooner make a good mince pie than I could steer the *Marguerite*, Cordelia said.

I'm so thirsty, Mack said.

Don't eat the ice, Richard warned. Your body temperature will drop faster.

How'd you know? Mack asked.

I've seen you eat icicles off the wheelhouse.

Mack laughed once. A small, weak laugh.

Water. Mack needed water. Cordelia checked the oncoming waves and, finding none that might flip them, unclasped her necklace. With great effort she rose on one arm and dipped her necklace over the side of the raft. She pulled it up and offered the drops of water to Mack, who took them gratefully. She would get some for herself later. After she rested a while.

She tucked her chin and tried to breathe into her coat where her breath might warm her body. Pain stabbed at her fingers, which clung naked to the planks. The ice-caked raft pitched high and low in the darkest hours. If they held on until the sky lightened, they would survive. Maybe it wouldn't be long now until sunrise. She wouldn't give in to fear. She would fight the overwhelming urge to sleep. She stared at the moon as if it held the power to save her. She dared not look away. As long as she could see the moon, she was alive.

Port Austin Reef, Lake Huron

It was pointless staring out the window any longer. The life-savers would have come by now, if they were going to come today. Sunny allowed herself one last look out the pantry porthole. Several hundred feet forward, the forecastle was an icy tower turning gray in the waning daylight. It leaned to starboard like the rest of the *Titus Brown*, quiet and dark at the end of the long expanse of straight deck. A mile or two away, the snow-covered coast lay silent, as if it were uninhabited. She squinted. No sign of a lifeboat anywhere. The sky was darkening, the temperature dropping.

Why hadn't the lifesavers come? They'd fired a Coston signal, hadn't they? The bursting red light had lasted only a few seconds, yet at the time it had been unmistakable. Now, hours later, with darkness closing in and no sign of their rescuers, Sunny doubted herself. Maybe it had been her imagination, after all. That afternoon Cleve and Herb had looked at her with concern, like she was addled. So had the watchman. It was infuriating. Only Stilts seemed to believe she'd really seen the flare.

Shivering, she left the pantry for the warmth of the galley cook-stove. With the boat's terrible starboard list, water still covered nearly half the galley deck, its ebb and flow extending the icy water's reach to the cook-stove. Sunny's stockings and skirt were soaked through, and she couldn't rid herself of the chill that had settled in her bones. She rubbed her arms for warmth, and then tucked her hands under her arms. Her fingers ached. She couldn't feel her toes. Herb had gone to their cabin in search of more dry clothing, but even a change of clothes wouldn't be enough to warm her now.

Freezing or not, she had a job to do. After adding coal to the firebox, she helped Cleve take supper to the crew huddled in the mess room. The men sat in the cold dark, their blue-lipped faces lit by kerosene lamps. They passed around fried potatoes and the last of the ham. There were plenty of apples.

The first mate was talking. His breath formed small clouds. At daylight, he said, they'd go up on the boilerhouse roof and see if the port lifeboat was in usable condition. The starboard lifeboat was long gone, washed away soon after they'd fetched up bottom.

"Why not check now?" It was the new assistant engineer, the one who'd signed on at the last minute to replace Ernie. Ernie had made the right choice in going ashore, hadn't he? Sunny had never warmed up to Not Ernie.

The first mate shook his head. "Removing the ice will take time. And it'd take us an hour to row to shore in these conditions. It's too risky to attempt it at night."

"We should've done it today." Not Ernie pointed at Sunny. "If she hadn't lied about the flare, making us think help was coming, we'd be off this boat by now!"

Sunny nearly dropped the empty bowl that had held the potatoes. No one had ever attacked her in this way. She looked from the engineer to the first mate. "I didn't lie! I saw a signal. I did!"

Herb was in the doorway then, carrying an armful of blankets and dry clothes. In a flash the clothes were in a heap and his hands were on Not Ernie's lapels. Herb was a big man and he shoved the gangly engineer against the bulkhead with little more effort than it took to push open a door. Sunny felt a thrill of fear. Herb was the gentlest of men and this was something the likes of which she'd never seen.

The first mate leapt from his stool. He moved between Herb and the engineer, a hand on each man's shoulder. "That's enough!" Herb let go of the engineer and took a half step back, still glaring. The first mate put his hands out, palms down, as if to tamp down the tension in the room. "Now there's no doubt in my mind Sunny saw a signal flare." He looked pointedly at the engineer. "She grew up on a life-saving station—daughter of the keeper, for chrissakes—I think she knows a Coston when she sees one!" A deep breath, then, "Look. We wouldn't have attempted our own rescue today at any rate. The seas were far too rough. Too rough even for Captain Hanna to make his way aft. By the morrow the wind and waves will lessen and we can take matters into our own hands."

Somewhat shaken, Sunny scooped up the clothes Herb had dropped, and together they went back to the galley. "He didn't mean it," she said quietly. "He's letting worry get the better of him."

Herb grunted, still upset. "The sooner we get off this reef, the better." Sunny lay her head against his chest. Her husband was always there for her and that made her heart full. Herb took a deep breath and sighed loudly. He kissed the top of her head, a finality to the gesture, as if to signify an end to his anger and a return to his usual affable self. "You should get those on," he said.

Sunny took the clothes to the pantry. They were Herb's clothes; she'd already gone through what dry clothing she had. Changing was difficult, given her stiff knees and prickly toes, but she managed with Herb's help. His enormous pants stayed up with a pair of suspenders. After she'd changed, they huddled under a blanket in the darkness. He fell asleep in an instant. She lay there, listening to his light snoring—more audible now that the wind was only a low moan, and the waves crashed with less force—envying him his ability to sleep under these conditions. He seemed to take for granted that they would be rescued, that the *Titus Brown*, though broken, was secure on the reef, and that they would not freeze to death before help arrived.

Despite her exhaustion, Sunny couldn't sleep. She lay there, trying to quiet her thoughts, and was starting to feel drowsy when all at once the pantry began to spin. She closed her eyes to make it stop. Her insides felt as though they were full of eddying lake water. She stared at a cupboard handle until the nausea passed.

Wide awake again, she made a promise to herself: If they survived this stranding, she was going to stay ashore for good. No one would make her get on another freighter as long as she lived. She needed to make this clear to Herb before she lost her nerve. She'd tried to tell him during the storm but he hadn't heard her. He would hear her this time.

"Herb." She turned her face toward him. Then, a little louder, "Herb."

"Hmm?" He grunted without opening his eyes. "What is it? What's the matter?"

"I want to open a restaurant in Port Austin." It was a moot point, now, but Herb didn't know she'd lost all her money and, besides, it was important that he understood her aspirations.

He opened his eyes. "A restaurant?" A long pause. "I don't know, Sunny. Let's get ashore first."

"There's a place in the village, near the shore. We could live above it."

Herb sighed. "Restaurants are a lot of work. More than cooking and baking."

Sunny shivered. She scooted backward, further into Herb, and pressed herself against the warmth of his chest. "We could figure it out together." Her icy toes throbbed. She'd toiled barefoot all day, as her shoes were worn slippery smooth, and though she'd put them back on to sleep, her feet were as cold as if she hadn't.

"I don't know, Sunny. Sailing is steady work and a good income. Starting a business is risky."

She let out a sharp laugh. "Here we are stranded on a reef, freezing to death, and you're saying *my* idea is risky?"

"Not a-one of us ever saw anything like this storm. And if I sail another thirty years I won't see another like it."

Isn't that just what he'd say? A gust of wind hit the boilerhouse. She pulled the blanket up over her nose. "Boats are lost every season. There are accidents."

"There're accidents everywhere," Herb said. "There are plenty of dangers on land, my love. Illnesses, fevers."

He was alluding to her father, who'd died of pneumonia years earlier, his illness having developed following an outbreak of grippe. It had happened in November, when Sunny and Herb were on the lakes, unscathed by the epidemic. It wasn't fair to use her father's death against her. Herb was being difficult to a maddening degree. Sunny needed to explain why this was so important to her. But she couldn't find the words to describe the ways in which she felt herself changing. How she needed this for herself.

Instead what she said was, "If you don't want to join me, then maybe I could do it myself."

Herb shifted onto his back, pulling his arm from around her waist. "I didn't say that. It's just—you don't know what you'd be getting into. Where would you open this café?"

"Like I said, I have it all picked out." Sunny turned to face him. "The restaurant in the village, next to the hotel. The owner is selling it." Never mind that she no longer had the money.

"And what about our income? There are expenses, Sunny."

"How much do we really need?" she said, her voice strained.

All this arguing had drained her energy. Her eyelids closed of their own accord. Herb was saying something about money, about how he couldn't make the same money on shore. It was different for her, of course, didn't he see that? She made less than a third of what he did. She said nothing; he'd only say it wasn't his fault he earned more. And then she'd have to assure him it wasn't his fault, and that she was glad he made a good living. She was too tired to tell him yet again that she never intended to do this for ten years. When he'd first gotten a job as a deckhand she had stayed at the station in Port Austin with her parents. She'd assumed she'd fall pregnant and Herb would find work on land and they'd get their own place to raise their family. When after a couple of years no babies came and Herb had been promoted to steward she agreed to join him as second cook. If and when she got in the family way, she'd always reasoned, then she could convince him to find a job ashore.

Sunny was thirty-three now, and after thirteen years of marriage, no longer waited for a baby. The truth was, she felt selfish for wanting this. She took a deep breath and started to say the words, then stopped. She'd always made a point of never making promises she couldn't keep. Then, without reminding herself yet again why she shouldn't, she said the words. "I swear I'm not setting foot on another freighter, ever again."

A long pause, then, "All right, my love. If it's that important to you, we'll go ashore."

Sunny's mouth fell open. Had she convinced him at last? "You mean that?"

"You've been on this boat long enough. Maybe this storm is a sign that it's time to give up sailing. Running a restaurant won't be easy." He rubbed his forehead as if to erase a headache. "But maybe I owe it to you to give it a try."

"Thank you, thank you, *thank you!*" Sunny put her arm around him. Herb didn't believe in signs, but never mind that now. A new lightness filled her chest, tempered by one unavoidable truth. As much as she hated to, she had to tell him. "There's one problem," she said. "I lost all the money I'd been saving. It was in my pocket and I think it happened when I was washed down to the boiler room." She bit her lower lip. Please don't let this change Herb's mind. "I'll find work somewhere and save up," she added quickly. "One day I will open a restaurant."

After a long pause, heavy with the weight of her future, Herb said, "I'm not saying no. I swear I'm not. But until we have the money to make a restaurant happen, I need a job. And I wouldn't make as much money ashore as I would with Captain Hanna. One more season, at least. If we save every penny."

"I understand," she said quietly, almost to herself. If Herb returned to sailing, she feared it would only be a matter of time before he convinced her to join him, and one sailing season would turn into two, and two into three, and in ten years she'd be no closer to her dream than she was now. She had to stay strong, yet she'd never felt weaker. She pressed herself closer to Herb's body. "I can't stop shivering."

"You've been barefoot and in wet clothes all day." He kissed the top of her head. "I'll take care of breakfast in the morning. You rest. Stay under the blankets."

Sunny tried again to sleep. The uncertainty of her future added to her insomnia. And when she finally closed her eyes, all was a violent confusion: tarpaulins flapping in gusty winds, men slipping on icy decks, whistles blaring and combers slamming. And then coal. Coal burning in the firebox, glowing orange and bright and then fading to white-gray ash.

TUESDAY
November 11, 1913

Port Austin Reef, Lake Huron

Sunny opened her eyes. Had she slept? Sleep had seemed impossible the night before, what with her constant shivering and bones aching with cold. It must be morning—four, five o'clock?—though it was still dark. Herb wasn't here with her in the pantry. A clanging of pots and kettles came from the galley. He was making coffee.

He'd told her to rest today. And it was all she wanted to do. Her entire body hurt, and to stand up was a daunting proposition. But she had a job to do, no matter what Herb said. A job she would finish today, and then go ashore for good. The thought of it filled her with lightness. The money she'd lost, well, she would think about that later. Herb had given her his blessing, even if he himself was unsure what he would do come spring. His blessing for her to go ashore would have to be enough for now. She removed the blankets from her body. The cold air sent her shivering again.

With some effort she coaxed her muscles to a standing position. She peered out from the pantry to the galley. Herb was putting a pot on the cook-stove. A faint light shone through the cracks and larger breaches, casting the galley in a pinkish hue. There was no water where he stood. The lake level appeared to have lowered. And while water flowed in and out of the galley with the waves, it didn't reach as high as it had a day ago, and that was a relief: She wouldn't get splashed with icy-cold water as she made breakfast.

"I'll get the coffee." Sunny spoke softly, the cold making it hard to talk.

There was a commotion in the mess room. Heavy footfalls and men's voices. Voices Sunny hadn't heard in two days.

Then the men appeared in the galley doorway: Captain Hanna and the officers.

"Good morning, Mrs. Colvin," Captain Hanna said. "The bosun was just telling me you're the only cool-headed one aft." He spoke so calmly Sunny could almost imagine they weren't stranded on a reef.

"Just doing my job as best I can, sir." She cleared her throat, trying to speak normally and to reflect Captain Hanna's cheerful calm. "It's good to see you aft."

"I tell you this vessel is iced up thicker than your famous cookies." He surveyed the damaged galley but said nothing.

She forced a smile. "No iced cookies today, sir," Sunny said. "But we'll have your coffee presently."

"Sounds heavenly. Do you mind if we wait in here? Melt the ice from our mustaches and all that?" Without waiting for a reply, Captain Hanna stepped further into the galley. He glanced at her feet. "Mrs. Colvin, what happened to your shoes? You'll suffer hypothermia before the lifesavers even get here!"

"It's so I don't slip. The soles of my old shoes don't do well on wet decks that are sloping to starboard." She'd slept with shoes on but now that she had work to do she'd taken them off again and wore only a pair of Herb's socks. Her feet, which yesterday had been all pins and needles, had gone mostly numb and were tinged bluish-white.

"This won't do." Captain Hanna ordered the first mate to the forecastle, where in his quarters he kept a pair of shoes for ballroom dancing.

Sunny didn't want the fuss. "It's not necessary—"

"I insist," Captain Hanna said, and not long after that she was putting on his dancing shoes. They were sturdy, and although Sunny's feet were large for her frame, they weren't nearly as big as the captain's. Her narrow feet slid around inside them. She wasn't sure she'd like clomping around in over-large shoes, but she went about making coffee anyway, ignoring Herb's protestations that he could do it himself.

Sunny listened with one ear as Captain Hanna told the first mate what they'd discovered on their way aft. The life raft forward had been washed away, he said, as was the starboard lifeboat. The *Titus Brown's* bow was about ten feet lower than the stern. The massive waves stove in the forecastle, knocking out doors and windows. The top of the wheelhouse was gone, and the bulwarks forward bent in.

Then the captain lowered his voice. Sunny, pouring boiling water through the filter, paused her task so that she might hear what came next. Bits and pieces of his description were audible, most notably the words "crack" and "three inches" and "down the side."

Sunny gasped, quite without meaning to. The captain's voice went silent and she felt the men watching her. Without looking up she finished pouring the boiling water. She picked up a mug and filled it with coffee. She handed it to Captain Hanna without saying a word.

As she made breakfast her mind repeated the same thought over and over, like a skipping phonograph record: The *Titus Brown* was splitting in two. The *Titus Brown* was splitting in two. The captain hadn't said it—at least, she hadn't heard him say it—but it didn't need explaining that the crack would widen. With every comber that broke over the boat, the crack would grow, bit by bit, until the steel freighter split completely. The stern half would slip off the reef and under the water.

Her chest felt heavy. She forced a deep breath. It felt as though she would never get enough air.

Now the mate was saying he planned to take a few men atop the boilerhouse to clear the ice from the port lifeboat.

Calm yourself, Sunny. The lifesavers will be here, even if the crew has to fetch them themselves. Get back to work. She returned to the cook-stove, leaning in close for warmth, and fried up the last of the potatoes. She stepped gingerly in the captain's dancing shoes, like if she weren't careful it would be her one hundred pounds that hastened the boat's cleaving.

She flipped the potato slices. How sick the crew must be of potatoes. Yet not one of them uttered a complaint. Fact was, several of them had said little at all these past thirty-six hours, having gone quiet with cold and fear. Stilts had kept mostly to himself since Sunday night, curled into a ball in a corner of the mess room. Sunny had been unable to draw him out.

She took another deep breath. They were going to be fine. Today she was going to make it ashore. For the first time in years she would enjoy the holidays without the dread of returning to sea in the spring. She would meet Cordelia's new husband. She knew little of the *Marguerite's* captain and was curious about the man Cordelia had married so suddenly. Sunny would make French macaroons for Maman. They'd sit by the fire in the evening. And the Christmas dinner she had planned! The old traditions were the best: goose, plum pudding, chestnut stuffing, sugar plums. Ideally she would have already made the pudding, and put it away to ripen. It was richer that way. Next year. The candies and cranberry jelly she always made the day before.

The *Titus Brown* was splitting in two. Her chest tightened again, and she took another deep breath, exhaling forcefully.

Think pleasant things. Think of Christmas. Agnes's daughter, Aimee, a wonderful girl, would come up from Detroit and help decorate the house with holly and cedar and mistletoe.

Sunny would make Aimee's favorite candy fairies. They'd gather around the fire and hang stockings and—

The spatula slipped right out of her hand and onto the deck. Oh! How had she lost her grip on it?

Hands pressed lightly on her shoulders. "Come, Love." It was Herb. "You've been working so hard. You're shivering. You can barely walk." He placed the spatula on the counter.

"Who isn't shivering? And I can walk fine. These shoes are clunky, is all." She picked up the spatula and waved it at him. "It's my job to make breakfast and that's what I intend to do." She emphasized her point by lifting the cast-iron pan—when had it gotten so heavy?—and flipping the potatoes in the air. Never mind her left index finger wrapped in a strip of linen, where she'd nicked herself with a knife yesterday. It had hurt, but only a little, and the scrape on her half-numb-with-cold finger wouldn't have registered at all were it not for the blood, bright and urgent.

She looked at the potatoes. "These are almost done. Find the bowl, could you?"

Herb nodded and left for the mess room. Between waves that pounded the *Titus Brown* she heard footsteps overhead. The first mate and some others had gone up on the boiler-house roof to axe away the ice from the only lifeboat they had left. No one wanted to wait any longer for the life-saving service. With half an ear Sunny listened to them work above. It must be terribly slippery up there. One wrong step and you're in the icy water, where none of them would last long.

This cold was intolerable. Standing near the cook-stove eased her shivering some, but preparing food for the crew required moving about, not just hovering over the stove. Her woolen pea coat was buttoned tight, but it hardly mattered. The chill was trapped inside her bones now.

Not long after daybreak the sailors had de-iced the lifeboat and were preparing to lower it into the choppy water. Eight men would go ashore to get help. Sunny feared for them. They were going to brave these seas in a lifeboat, with waves four to six feet—and rogue ten footers that brought water splashing into the galley. Rowing a lifeboat would be both strenuous and dangerous, especially for men unaccustomed to it. Though she didn't disapprove of the effort, nor could she bear to watch the launch. She was grateful to have something else to do, a soup to prepare. Herb had tried to dissuade her. The men had had potatoes and coffee and that was enough, he'd said. No one could expect more. Sunny disagreed. It was anyone's guess when their next meal would be if she didn't prepare something. And it would be a rough ride to shore. A simple soup, warm and reassuring, would give everyone the extra strength they'd need.

She got the ham bone from the refrigerator and carried it to the cook-stove. With quaking hands she lifted it above the stockpot. She let go too early and the ham bone landed on the cook-stove with a clanking sound. Embarrassed at her clumsiness, she waved away Cleve's attempt to help. Her second attempt was successful. She asked Cleve to fill the large stockpot with enough water to cover the ham bone halfway. It would need to boil and then simmer for a good hour before she added the other ingredients. The carrots had been lost to the storm, and the last of the potatoes had been fried up for breakfast that morning, so it wouldn't be her most flavorful ham bone soup. But they'd salvaged enough canned white kidney beans and peas to make do.

How ridiculous she was to be worrying about flavor. Old habits.

She looked at her feet. The waves didn't reach the cook-stove, where she stood in the captain's shoes. The water level was going down. There must have been a seiche these past two days, like the one that'd stalled them in Lake Erie, only larger, and now the seiche was resolving. When she mentioned this to Cleve, his furrowed brow worried her. "What is it?" she asked.

Cleve said nothing as he poured water into the stockpot.

"Tell me. Please." She clasped the rolling bar to steady herself. The boat wasn't moving, was it?

Cleve placed the lid on the pot. "The water level's going back down and I'm wondering if that won't put greater strain on the boat. The stern's already higher than the bow, and as the water retreats, more of the stern will be out of the water, which will make it heavier in a way, and—"

"And that will make the boat split apart faster."

Cleve nodded. "I'm sure the lifesavers will be here before that happens."

He was only saying that because he thought she'd panic. Not her! Even Captain Hanna said she was the calmest one aft. Still, this wasn't good. Where had she put her life belt?

Moments later she was grabbing cans of peas from the pantry when someone shouted "Man overboard!" There were hurried footfalls on the fantail. Sunny rushed out of the pantry—as much as her aching joints and too-big shoes would allow her to rush—and looked for Herb in the galley. Where was he? That's right; he'd gone to watch the launch. A tingling at the base of her spine. It wasn't him. No, it couldn't have been him. She set the cans on the counter and hurried through the companionway. Out on the fantail the freezing wind hit her with new force.

Men were leaning over the bulwark, in the places where it wasn't stove in, searching the water. Tears pricked at the corners of her eyes. Where was Herb? Where *was* he? Then: a flash of red hair, on the port side. She covered her mouth and cried out in relief.

Stepping gingerly on the icy deck, she moved next to her husband. "Who was it?"

"Stilts," Herb said quietly, not taking his eyes off the water.

"No!" Not Stilts. Not dear, sweet Stilts. Walter. "How—how did it happen?"

"A wave hit the lifeboat as the assistant engineer was climbing in. The engineer wobbled and Stilts reached over to steady him but then he lost his balance. Stilts went over the side, just slipped off into the waves. Never came up, not even once. It happened so fast." Herb put his arm around her. "You should get back inside and rest. You don't look well."

Sunny searched the churning waves for Stilts's gangly limbs. She watched the water a long time, even though she knew he was gone. The waves crested and dipped and still he didn't surface. He'd had his whole life ahead of him and now it was done, just like that. It wasn't right. She felt sick to her stomach. The lifeboat rushed away from the *Titus Brown* without its newest deckhand. Someone returned the life preserver to its hook. "I never made the butter tarts you wanted," she said quietly to Stilts. A cold tear ran down her cheek. "I'm so sorry." She wondered if his grandmother were still alive and, if she were, how she would bear the loss.

Herb squeezed her shoulders. "Let's go in. You should lie down."

She twisted herself from his grip. "Not yet." She couldn't leave Stilts out here, alone and cold. Sunny watched the water. It peaked and flattened and Stilts did not come to the surface.

Minutes passed and Herb's hands were on her shoulders again. "You really need to get inside where it's warmer." Then, when she still didn't move, "Your soup."

"All right, all right." She closed her eyes and whispered a goodbye to Walter, then let Herb lead her back inside.

In the galley she struggled to open a can of beans.

"I can do this, Mrs. Colvin," Cleve said. "Why don't you rest?"

"Why is everyone telling me to rest?" Sunny sighed. Truth was, her limbs ached more than ever and had taken on a new weight. And somehow the cook-stove's warmth no longer reached her. Stilts's death weighed heavily on her heart, making her very tired all of a sudden. It wasn't fair. It was the new assistant engineer's fault for wobbling. It should've been Not Ernie.

More than ever she wanted off this boat. To start anew. Even if she didn't have a restaurant. She had Herb's blessing, and that was a start. She asked Cleve to tell her when the soup was boiling, and went to her nest of blankets in the pantry. Curling up, with the captain's shoes still on her feet, she closed her eyes.

Sunny awoke with an aching head. When she first tried to sit up, a dizziness overtook her and she lay back down. A different approach, then. She rolled onto her side, waited a moment for her mind to settle, and then gingerly pushed herself up to a seated position. "The soup," she said. The soup might be boiling. With one hand on a rolling bar, she pressed the other against her thigh to help her rise. Her weakened legs were ill-equipped to navigate the slanting deck. She clung to the rolling bars for support as she shuffled into the galley. She felt a hundred years old.

Cleve was at the cook-stove. "It's simmering now. I didn't want to wake you." He stopped stirring and looked straight at her. "You really should rest more."

"I wanted to open a restaurant," she told Cleve. Her body was shutting down; she could feel it. The lifesavers would be too late. "I lost all my money in the storm. It must've happened when I fell down to the engine room." She was nearing the cook-stove when the ship swayed. Metal creaked.

The *Titus Brown* was moving. This was it. They were sliding off the reef. Oddly enough, she wasn't scared. Emotions had become a distant thing. Her legs buckled and she reached for Cleve's arm to steady herself. From somewhere above her own body she heard herself talking to Cleve but her words made no sense.

Cleve was saying her name. What did he want from her?

She squatted next to the cook-stove's firebox. Her hand gripped the rolling bar above her head. The *Titus Brown* was slipping away, off the reef. She was suspended in the moment just before it dropped beneath her feet. Her stomach rose up in her throat. She closed her eyes and waited for the water to come.

When it didn't, she opened her eyes. Cleve's face was inches from hers. "Are you all right?"

Seconds passed and still the water didn't come.

The cook-stove and the refrigerator and the coffee urn slowly came into focus. "Are we still on the reef?"

"We're still on the reef." He was looking at her strangely. "Help's coming. You should rest until they get here. It's gonna be a bumpy ride to shore."

Her body became heavy, as if her pockets were weighted with rocks. Cleve extended a hand and she let him help her to the pantry. Each step hurt, every muscle ached, and she slumped gratefully onto her pile of blankets. She pulled a blanket around herself and huddled against a sack of flour, its contents turned to paste. Her eyes closed.

Sunny was trapped in the engine room. The mechanical parts disappeared and now it was an empty metal cavern, now a cave. The cave was familiar. The rush of cool air at its mouth, the trails leading through grand chambers and narrow, serpentine passageways, the subterranean waters with eyeless fish. Mammoth Cave. But she was lost. She kept walking, searching for the entrance but each turn led to another passageway where crystalline flowers lined the walls. The cave grew cold. Footsteps, now. Louder. Closer. Help was coming.

Herb's face was ashen, kind. She was awake now—yes, she had been asleep, dreaming—and he stared down at her from the doorway. The doorway to the *Titus Brown's* pantry. She lifted her head from the sack of flour, and at this small movement the room spun and she strained to focus. She waited for everything to make sense. With her fingers pressed to her temples to ease the spinning, she asked Herb what was the matter. She leaned forward, ready to be sick. After a minute the nausea passed.

"I'm worried about you," he said. "You were making strange noises."

"I'm not well," she was able to say before the pantry spun again.

She closed her eyes, becoming suspended in that realm between sleep and wakefulness where the passing of time was hard to measure, until her heart pounded in her chest and frightened her awake. It was no use trying to rest. She went to the galley.

"What are you doing? You should be resting." Herb was standing at the cook-stove, a large spoon raised halfway to his lips. He tasted something, put down the spoon. She told him about her pounding heart and her dizziness. He said she was suffering from exposure, and that he would fetch her blankets so she could sit next to the cook-stove. In the pantry, as he bent over to pick up the woolen blanket he cried out, pressing his hand to his lower back. Before Sunny could react, Cleve appeared from nowhere, rushed to Herb's side, and helped ease him to a lying position. Herb winced and Sunny watched, helpless. It'd been ages since Herb last threw out his back but she remembered how much pain it had caused him, and how frustrated he'd been, unable to do much of anything for days. They were all falling apart on the reef. The crew and the boat.

Sunny glanced at her hand. It took a moment to realize that her wedding band was gone for good, and that she'd already known this. The storm had taken her money, her jewelry, her dream. She ought to get up and help Cleve with Herb but she was too tired to move. Captain Hanna came into the galley and Sunny watched, as if from a great distance, as he got himself another cup of coffee. Cleve asked about the split amidships. One of the crew had gone to check on it, was the reply. Sunny wrapped her arms around herself and closed her eyes.

Moments later someone else came into the galley—one of the deckhands? An oiler? Her eyelids were too heavy to open. The man spoke in a low tone to Captain Hanna. She heard the important part. The crack, which earlier in the day had been three inches wide, had expanded to more than six.

Lake Superior

A muted light illuminated Richard's ice-flaked sweater, inches from Cordelia's nose. Daylight. What time was it? She'd lost track of the moon at some point—she must have closed her eyes for a time—but it was morning now, and she was alive. Hope welled in her chest. Today they would be found.

She turned her head a little, trying to look behind her, to the south. Clumps of ice that had formed on her eyelashes partially obscured her vision. For as far as she could see, there was only water. Yesterday Richard had said they were drifting south toward land but they must not have been as close as he'd thought.

Richard lay before her, his eyes closed. His black hair was covered in ice flakes, as were his eyebrows and lashes. Cordelia turned her face to the sky. The sun hid somewhere beyond the thick gray that pressed down on them. The life raft rose and fell. She couldn't feel her feet.

A wave reached over the raft. She braced herself. The wave rose up behind Richard and folded over on itself, onto them, the icy water stinging her face and hands. Worse was the wind that came after.

She tried to stretch out her legs, which she'd kept bent into her chest, and this attempt at movement produced stabbing sensations in her thighs and calves and so she remained in a fetal position, curled into Richard's chest. There was a weight on her legs. She craned her neck, slowly, each movement difficult and painful, to see what it was. Richard's pea coat covered her lower half. She looked up at the wheelsman's face.

When had he last spoken?

Rich— Her voice didn't work as it should. She tried again. Richard.

He didn't stir.

She swallowed hard. She didn't want to be alone. Richard, she repeated, an attempt at urgency in her voice that didn't sound like her. Richard, wake up! But her speech came out all wrong.

The wheelsman moaned but didn't open his eyes.

She pushed at his chest to rouse him. His ice-flaked lids opened. But he wasn't right. It was like he didn't see her. Like he wasn't really there. She jerked back her hand and looked away.

A dull pain in her abdomen. She needed to urinate. What could she do but empty her bladder where she lay? The warm urine, not enough of it, ran down her thigh. It soothed her for an instant before turning cold.

Richard was too quiet. She must rouse him. Richard. He didn't respond. He could not leave her alone on this raft. No. There was a third person. On the other side of Richard. Someone had climbed onto the raft after the *Titus Brown* broke in two. Ollie? The watchman? The events of recent hours hovered on the horizon and refused to come into focus.

Her mouth was too dry. Her world was freshwater all around and yet too far away. A wave passed beneath them and then, with great effort, Cordelia turned her body to face the raft's outer edge. That was as far as she got. She hadn't the energy to unclasp her necklace, let alone to lean over the side of the raft and dip it in the water. Her fingers couldn't have worked the clasp anyway.

She closed her eyes. Just a little rest. It was dangerous to sleep but she couldn't fight it anymore...There was a faint crying in the distance. Seagulls. Hope tingled in her limbs. How far from shore could a seagull fly? She opened her eyes and searched the gray skies but saw nothing. A moment later the seagulls' cries were gone.

Now there was something in the distance. Could it be? A small boat—the life-saving service! There it was, a lifeboat coming toward the raft. Something was off. The lifeboat was rowed by just one person. And there was no one to steer. But look who it was! She would admit it now: She had given up hope. But here he was! Where had he been all this time? And why was he alone? Funny, he still wore his captain's hat. He rowed up alongside her.

Edmund, she said weakly. I thought you didn't make it.

I had some trouble.

You're here. You found me.

I'm sorry, Cordelia. I should have known better. November is always dangerous.

It's not your fault... but I don't know where I should be going.

You need to be strong.

I need your help. I'm drifting.

You're almost home.

But where? Where is home? Come closer. Help me into your lifeboat.

Edmund shook his head. The lifeboat moved further from her.

A wave splashed Cordelia's face and she squinted against it. When she wiped her eyes and opened them again, Edmund was gone. The empty lifeboat rocked in the waves.

Edmund!

Hands gripped the raft's edge. But not Edmund's hands— too pale. Arms reached up and over, crooked for support against the edge of the raft. Then a head and torso. A terrible gash at his temple.

Where to? The young man asked with a smile.

Where...? Take me to Edmund. He was just here.

Sorry, can't.

With you, then. But where are you now? You don't look well. You're bleeding.

Come on, where's your sense of adventure?

I came on this trip, Lewis. That's an adventure.

Not the kind I'm talking about. Not sailing or hiking or flying. No, no, no.

I don't know what you're saying.

I'm talking about the adventure of not knowing...

Not knowing what? Lewis, you're—

Still smiling, Lewis climbed the oil drum, dove backwards into the air, and disappeared into an oncoming wave.

Cordelia stared at the wave as it crested. It rolled beneath her raft, and on the other side of it Edmund's lifeboat reappeared. There was a figure at its far end. But not Edmund. This man held a steering oar and wore a keeper's uniform.

Father!

She could almost smell the sweet, grassy scent of his kersey coat. She was home again—the warmth of a wool blanket and the sound of crackling fire. Her father would take care of her now.

The boat came closer. Squinting wrinkles etched at the corners of his eyes. But he wasn't smiling. Her father looked forlorn. No words passed his lips, only the silent shaking of his head. She'd disappointed him, somehow. She called out to him again; he didn't answer. He pointed south. Cordelia followed the direction of his pointing finger, and she was just able to make out a pine tree.

The shore! She turned back to her father but he was no longer there. The lifeboat, too, was gone.

Father! Edmund...? She wanted to cry, but no tears came. A great weariness blanketed her, and her eyelids closed. It would be the easiest thing in the world to fall asleep... No. She must try to stay awake. It wouldn't be long now. The lone pine tree spread, becoming many. She nudged Richard. He didn't stir. She told him about the trees, told him that if he'd just open his eyes he would see them, too.

There were sounds of movement behind the wheelsman. With great effort she lifted her head to see who it was. Rising up on the other side of Richard was Mack. Mack was the other person on the raft.

Mack, she said. There are trees.

His face was a blank. Foam bubbles lined the corners of his mouth.

Richard opened his eyes—at last—and said the third mate's name.

Mack gave no indication of his having heard them. He crawled away from them then, past their feet toward the end of the raft. He flopped onto his stomach and made swimming motions with his arms, like he was trying to swim off the raft and into the water.

No! Cordelia cried.

Richard roused. He sat up and extended a long arm and grabbed Mack by the ankle. Mack kicked his leg, trying to free it from Richard's grasp, but Richard hung on and pulled himself closer. Then Mack kicked like an angry mule, with such force that Richard lost his hold. He rolled past Cordelia's head and over the edge. She reached for him but he was too far away.

Down past her feet, a splash. The raft was empty where Mack had been. He was in the water now, swimming away from them. Swim toward the trees, Cordelia said. She checked again but now the trees were gone. The shore was gone. And Mack was swimming the wrong way. He swam into the oncoming waves and didn't stop.

There were grunting noises. Richard struggled at the raft's edge. His arms rested on the wood planks but his lower half hung down the side. He needed her help. Wincing with each painful movement of her muscles, she inched closer and reached for him. He wouldn't grab her hand. He remained hovering at the edge.

Try, she said, or tried to say. The wheelsman slipped out of sight.

Richard! She yelled but nothing came out. She dragged herself to the raft's edge. His foot had caught in the rope along the side and his upper body was beneath the surface. She leaned over to grab his boot. With all her strength she couldn't lift him. She lay on the raft, her cheek pressed against the cold wood, her fingers wrapped around the edge. She looked away from where the raft trailed Richard behind it.

Everyone had left her. Edmund was gone. And Richard and Mack. Even the jacket from her legs. Soon she would be gone, too. A wave rolled toward her, gathering height. Let it happen then. Death will be a relief. Why had she ever feared it?

She loosened her grip and watched the wave come. She wouldn't fight this time. She would lose her balance and slide off the raft with the help of this approaching wave.

Seagulls cried out in the distance. It was too late for them now. Edmund was gone and she was drifting again. The wave pulled her raft into its wet embrace and she closed her eyes.

Port Austin, Michigan

At long last the storm had passed and it was merely a blustery November morning. Agnes hurried from Lizzie and Mrs. Duncan's cottage, where she'd slept in a spare room and Lizzie had slept in her own. Lizzie had been avoiding her since yesterday afternoon. It seemed that way, at least. Agnes perseverated on the conversation they'd had yesterday in the kitchen. Lizzie had been about to say something important. Could it be she had intended to declare romantic feelings for Agnes? If only Keeper Duncan hadn't interrupted them. The moment had been lost and Lizzie had become distant.

Agnes ran to the station. She would have to figure all that out later, after the rescue. Right now she had a job to do. Pray the lifesavers had not left. She would convince Keeper Duncan she belonged on that surfboat if it was the last thing she did.

The surfboat was still on the launching rails. Good. And the shipwreck? She ran past the station and up the beach. The vessel was still there. It was curious that the sailors hadn't tried to come ashore themselves. Were they all right? They'd been on that reef for at least a day and a half. They would be rescued today, at last, for while the surf was rough, these were the seas the lifesavers' surfboat was built for. With its flat bottom, little keel, and seven-inch draw it could ride heavy seas like a duck.

She hurried to the main building, arriving just in time to help serve breakfast. Lizzie greeted her warmly, if neutrally, and Agnes wondered anew if she'd done something to offend her. Nathaniel wasn't coming down to eat, Lizzie was saying. Although his fever had broken, he was far too weak to take part in the rescue. With Irvin's broken leg, and another surfman dismissed the week before, there were only five men left. It was just as Agnes had suspected.

Lizzie had saved a place for Agnes next to Keeper Duncan, which surprised Agnes a little. Normally the two women sat together. Lizzie said she wasn't eating, that she had no appetite. Agnes furrowed her brow, but Lizzie offered no explanation.

Agnes must waste no time making her case to the keeper. As they sat down to eat, she once again volunteered to row. "I'm strong enough—I once helped my father rescue sailors from a laker that had grounded two hundred yards offshore," she said after the keeper had taken a forkful of eggs. As long as he was chewing he couldn't tell her no. "My father launched a hauling line to the vessel. But instead of using the breeches buoy, he ordered the men to pull the surfboat out to the vessel because it would be faster that way. I helped with the hauling. All afternoon I stood in two feet of snow and slush and I hauled that line. It took us hours and it was cold and windy, but we rescued all of them." Finished with her faithful account (perhaps she'd embellished a little as to the amount of snow), she waited for Keeper Duncan's judgment. Lizzie looked at her brother, as if daring him to say no.

Keeper Duncan wiped his mouth. "The fact is we'll be much faster with a full crew, and the man I sent for from the village had taken ill." He breathed in deeply, as if considering the matter one last time, then exhaled with a loud sigh. "You'd best get suited up then. We'll find you a pair of boots."

Agnes sat there, momentarily stunned. She almost thought she'd heard wrong. Keeper Duncan was giving her a chance to make up for that day years ago. Something opened up in her chest, a long-held regret released. It was too late for Amos, but she would save someone else.

Agnes was putting on her oilskin when Lizzie approached.

"You talked him into it, then. Well done." Lizzie sounded like she was trying to convince herself this was a good thing. She put a hand on Agnes's shoulder. "Be safe out there, Aggie."

Aggie? A flicker of anticipation. Agnes had not offended her, after all. It'd been something else troubling Lizzie.

"You're the bravest person I know. But please, don't be too brave. I—I don't know what I'd do if something happened to you." Lizzie turned to leave, hesitated, then spun back around and kissed Agnes on the cheek. On the cheek but so close to her mouth that Agnes wasn't sure which had been Lizzie's intended target.

Agnes floated above herself. Her cheek burned where Lizzie's kiss had landed.

Lizzie embraced her. Then, whispering in her ear, "I'm so proud of you. Come back to me." She squeezed Agnes tight, and then in one motion released her grip and turned to leave.

Agnes stood there, dumbly touching her cheek as Lizzie left the room. Her knees buckled and she leaned against the table for support. A smile spread across her face. With Lizzie's kiss she had become all-powerful. She had more than enough strength to row to the broken-down vessel and back. She could row there and back a dozen times if she had to!

"Are you all right?" It was Keeper Duncan's voice. Suddenly he was in the room, although she hadn't noticed him enter.

Agnes straightened. "Yes. Perfectly." She put on the canvas hat she'd been given. "I'm ready." The keeper opened the door and she followed him outside, a secret smile on her lips.

It wasn't snowing anymore and the winds had died down to near twenty miles per hour. The waves churned aggressively, if not as violently as the day before. Agnes and the crew dragged the 700-pound vessel up onto the launching rails.

They'd packed it with all the supplies they'd been able to salvage, as well as blankets for the survivors. Although the hastily patched surfboat wasn't motorized, it did have a sail.

Keeper Duncan ordered everyone to their places. Agnes, hyper-alert and energized both by Lizzie's kiss and the danger of what lay ahead, stood between two surfmen on the port side of the cedar and oak surfboat. A lifeline hung in shallow 'U's along the sides. The boat's name was painted in black near the stern: *Mettle*. Three surfmen stood on the opposite side. The man across from her, Moose, the one whose work repairing the surfboat she'd taken over the day before, looked away. Clearly he didn't want her there.

The man to her left gave her a nod. "Match your strokes to mine," he said.

Keeper Duncan climbed into the surfboat and at his signal the six of them pushed the boat down the railway. Once it got going the two men at the bow climbed in, followed by Agnes and the surfman opposite her, and just before the surfboat splashed into the water the two men at the stern climbed in.

They raised their long oars straight into the air and once they hit water the oars came down and they were off, and immediately in the thick of it.

Agnes watched the surfman in front of her and synchronized her movements with his. Keeper Duncan moved to the stern to steer. He called out orders, shouting at them to row harder or to ease up. It was control in the midst of chaos and the observing part of Agnes was amazed at how she and the men all worked as one. She was almost giddy at how they teetered on the edge of destruction. She couldn't feel the cold, couldn't feel anything but the imperative to keep the boat going, keep it upright and get it over the surf. To not get thrown back to shore.

Keeper Duncan steered with a long oar. As his crew rowed, he maneuvered the boat to avoid the heaviest breakers. When a breaker couldn't be avoided, he made sure they met it head on. Facing the stern, Agnes couldn't see what was coming; her only clues were the rise and fall of the bow and what she saw in her peripheral vision. That and the commands from Keeper Duncan.

"Ease up, ease up!" Keeper Duncan shouted above the waves and wind.

Agnes slowed her movements, mimicking the surfmen in front of and beside her. The *Mettle* was about to crest a wave, and the keeper was checking their motion so they wouldn't fall too heavily on the backside of it. His skill quickly became apparent and he had her full trust. As with Agnes's father, Keeper Duncan knew just how much speed was needed in a given circumstance. He knew how to dodge the sea, how to avoid meeting a wave right as it was breaking.

They crested the wave and rowed on. Moments later the keeper steered the pole hard to turn them to port. He was avoiding something. Shipwreck debris, probably—a broken crate or a door or a barrel. Seconds later a massive log swept past on the starboard side. Agnes felt a thrill of terror. A wooden door narrowly missed them. Any large debris hitting them at the wrong place could spell disaster. But Keeper Duncan had avoided everything so far.

At last they'd made it through the gauntlet of breakers. This victory boosted Agnes's confidence, but they were only just beginning their journey to the shipwreck. There was debris to mind and six-foot swells to tackle and icy water to avoid at all costs. No one could last very long in it, with or without a life belt.

The lifesavers rowed out of Alaska Bay, the keeper steering them northwest past Turnip Rock and Thumbnail Point. The trees on Turnip Rock were covered in snow. A fleeting memory: Sunny and Agnes, in their youth and to their mother's consternation, climbing the rock outcropping and picnicking atop it. Their own island for the afternoon.

From Turnip Rock it would be more than a mile to the vessel, which had grounded not far from the reef lighthouse. The reef extended from the shore all the way to the lighthouse, of course, so although they'd survived the breakers, the shallow water meant unpredictable waves.

Agnes glanced down. An inch of water had collected at the bottom of the boat. The water probably came from sea spray. Or. Or it was seeping up from underneath, through cracks they'd missed or cracks they'd inadequately patched. It could be that the canvas patches were giving way. Her chest tightened.

There was nothing to do but row. Forcing from her mind the water at her feet, Agnes rowed in pursuit of a perfect synchronicity with the men. She was all arms and upper body, a working part of the machine. Her skin was damp with sweat beneath her storm suit.

Keeper Duncan called out: "How many are on board?"

They couldn't be at the vessel so soon, could they? Agnes glanced over her shoulder, in the direction the keeper was looking. She caught a glimpse of a lifeboat that quickly disappeared behind a cresting six-foot—maybe eight-foot—wave. The shipwrecked crew! They were alive, and attempting their own rescue. As she rowed she watched the water for the lifeboat to reappear. It was making a direct line for the shore. The two boats were briefly within shouting distance, and Keeper Duncan called out again.

"Sixteen!" shouted a man from the other boat.

So they would have to make two trips. The surfboat could hold ten to twelve shipwreck victims. Sixteen was out of the question. Especially so today, when they had to be extra careful not to overload it, given the slapdash repairs.

Agnes glanced again at the water collecting in the bottom of the boat. She frowned. Was there more than before or was it just her imagination? Never mind. Keeper Duncan would order them to bail if he thought it necessary.

Keeper Duncan shouted back to the lifeboat. "Mind the breakers!"

From the corner of her eye Agnes tracked the sailors' progress until she could no longer see their lifeboat. With luck they would make it to shore safely. There would be no surfmen to help them if their lifeboat capsized in the breakers.

At last the *Mettle* arrived at the stranded vessel. A straight deck freighter, as she'd suspected. What a nightmare they had survived. The steel ship was coated in ice and tilting to starboard. The smokestack had collapsed and there was extensive damage to the boilerhouse and bulwarks. These sailors were lucky to be alive.

Keeper Duncan steered them to the lee of the freighter's stern. He did this with apparent ease even though there wasn't much of a lee at all. Waves broke high on the freighter's iced-over steel sides. It was a wonder the crew was able to get its own lifeboat away.

Up on the fantail several sailors waved and one lowered a rope ladder. They all wore life belts, and when one of them turned around Agnes inhaled sharply. Hair at the nape of her neck stood on end. Of the stenciled letters on the back of the sailor's life belt she could make out only "R-O-W-N" but that was enough.

A man Agnes took to be the skipper on account of his cap waved his hand and shouted, "I'm Captain Hanna, and this is the *Titus Brown*."

Port Austin Reef, Lake Huron

Sunny, huddled near the cook-stove, needed to get back to work. She rose, perhaps too quickly, and her vision blurred. She grabbed the rolling bar next to the stove and stared at the firebox until the falling-over feeling passed. That she should be seasick now—when the boat no longer moved!—made little sense. She'd been so rarely afflicted all these years.

The dizzy spell passed and she went to continue her work, uncertain what, specifically, that was. What time was it, and what meal was she supposed to be making? She scanned her surroundings with a flutter of panic at how foreign everything appeared. It was as if she'd been placed in the galley of a different boat.

Soup. The word came to her just as she recognized the refrigerator—the piece of equipment that had excited her most about the *Titus Brown* when she'd first come aboard. She'd been dazzled by the white enamel and the promise of dry storage.

Yes, she'd been making hambone soup for the crew. But not all the crew. Some had left on the lifeboat to get help. And Stilts. Something had happened... She remembered now—oh, poor, dear Stilts! Tears welled in her eyes. He'd wanted butter tarts and now he'd never get them. She should have made them sooner... The men on the lifeboat, what had become of them? She shook her head. She wasn't usually prone to worry. They would be all right. The first mate was strong. All the men who'd left were strong, the strongest of the crew. They'd taken the coal passers and firemen. Those men would make it to shore, and they would find help for the rest of them.

She lifted the lid and smelled the hambone soup. It was ready. She would ladle the soup into coffee mugs. Where was her ladle? There was Cleve, standing in the doorway. She asked him to please find her the ladle, for she'd forgotten where she put it.

"Come again, Mrs. Colvin?"

She repeated her request. Cleve was looking at her as if she'd asked him to swim to shore.

"Mrs. Colvin, you're talking strangely."

She asked him what he meant by that.

"Pardon me for saying it, but it almost sounds like...like you've been drinking."

Drinking!

"Please don't take offense. I know you haven't been. It's just that you're slurring your words."

Something was wrong with Cleve's ears. She found a mug for the soup. There was the ladle—right there on the counter. Had it been there all along? She dipped the ladle into the stockpot and filled Herb's mug.

Cleve took over the ladling and Sunny went to the mess room to give her husband his soup. A sea of pale faces returned her gaze. Some of the men had towels wrapped around their heads. Some wore socks for mittens. But Herb wasn't one of them. Where had he gone?

There was a hand on Sunny's shoulder. She looked at it. Cleve's hand.

"Are you looking for Herb?" Cleve asked.

Sunny nodded, afraid to speak. She didn't want the men to think she was drunk. As it was they were looking at her oddly.

Cleve said Herb was in the pantry, and he guided Sunny as if she were an old woman. She ought to brush his hand away, the whippersnapper, but the truth was she could use some help steadying herself. Walking had become difficult given the ache in her knees.

Herb was in the pantry, as Cleve had said. That's right, Herb had thrown out his back. He couldn't sit up. He leaned his head forward and she kneeled beside him and lifted the mug to his lips.

Herb swallowed and smiled at her. "You're an angel."

"I'm a cook." She hoped the words came out right. She waited for Herb to tell her she sounded funny, but he didn't.

He finished taking the broth and Sunny stood, slowly. She carried the empty mug to the galley sink. A commotion rose up somewhere beyond the galley. The mess room. She made her way to the voices, using the rolling bars and bulkheads for balance. Their mumblings made little sense, as if they were spoken far away or in another language. She understood their gestures toward the stern, however, and Sunny slipped past them and out onto the fantail.

Stepping as gingerly as she could in the captain's shoes, Sunny went onto the after deck. Though she wore every dry article of clothing Herb had left, it wasn't enough to block out the cold or stop her from shivering.

There were others on the fantail, including Captain Hanna, and she looked in the direction they were pointing. In the near distance a spectral shape appeared on the crest of a wave, hung there a moment, and then disappeared. Sunny squinted, not sure she could trust her own eyes. None of this felt real; she moved as if in a dream. Cleve had said she was talking funny. Maybe her eyesight was going now, too. And what about her mind? Maman would tell her she had kinks in her thinking machine and put her on a train to the Eloise asylum.

She watched and waited. The ghostly shape crested another wave. She looked to the Old Man, to see if he had seen it, too, or if it was only her imagination. Like the signal flare. Yes, he was looking right at it. He was pointing. The shape disappeared again when the wave slipped from beneath it. For a moment it seemed the form would not reappear.

But it did. It grew larger, closer. "Is it...?" Sunny began. It was hard to hope, after so long.

"The life-saving service," said the watchman, whom Sunny hadn't noticed was standing nearby. "Here at last."

Now the ice-covered boat resembled what the watchman said it was. The boat neared, its white bow bearing the familiar U.S. Life-Saving Service emblem. The men rowed vigorously. Relief gathered behind Sunny's eyes and she wiped them with her sleeve.

Captain Hanna touched her shoulder. "Get Herb," he said. "You two will go with the first group."

She went to the pantry. Together with Cleve she helped Herb to stand. He moved very slowly out of the pantry, but at least he was moving. When they reached the galley, however, Herb stopped. He could walk no further, he said. The pain in his back was too much. Sunny left him with Cleve. She would find help.

By the time she reached the fantail, two lifesavers had boarded the *Titus Brown*. She wanted to run up and kiss them. She'd never been so relieved to see anyone.

"Are we glad you're here," the captain was saying. "We sent eight of our crew in the lifeboat this morning."

"We passed them on the way," one of the lifesavers said, his oilskin covered in ice.

"Ladies first." Captain Hanna gestured toward the lifesaver who had his arms outstretched, ready to help Sunny to the rope ladder.

"I'm not a passenger," Sunny said, forming her words carefully. "I'm a member of the crew. I'll go in order of rank."

Captain Hanna looked at her for a moment, like he was going to object. He nodded instead. "Of course."

"Herb needs help," Sunny said. "It's his back."

Captain Hanna spoke to the two lifesavers, who passed her and went into the *Titus Brown's* after deckhouse. She waited on the fantail for them to carry her husband out. Poor Herb. He was in tremendous pain. And he hated to have to admit it, let alone accept the help of others.

The lifesavers brought Herb to the bulwark where the rope ladder hung and, one holding his hands and the other his feet, lowered him over the side. Sunny held her breath. The men timed the transfer with a cresting wave, and as it lifted the surfboat to within a few feet of the gunwales, Herb was lowered into a lifesaver's outstretched arms. He'd made it.

Some of her crewmates used the rope ladder to climb down the ten feet from stern to surfboat. Others timed the rise and fall of the rescue boat, and when a cresting wave shrank the drop to three or four feet, made the jump. All the while, waves pounded the *Titus Brown's* weather side and freshwater spray soaked them.

When it was Sunny's turn, she summoned all her strength. This was it. The lifesaver bracing himself against the stern bulwark attempted to lower her to the surfboat, as they'd done with Herb. She shook her head. She would use the rope ladder instead. What came next happened in a blur: One leg, then the other, over the railing. Down the rope ladder and onto the surfboat. A lifesaver's arms around her, guiding her to a seat near the stern. A thwart for her to sit on. The boat bobbing in the waves as someone wrapped her in a blanket. She hung her head in relief. It was over. Almost.

"Sissy! Thank heaven you're all right!"

What was that voice? It came over the wind and waves. It was high-pitched, for a man. And no one called her "Sissy" except Agnes. Slowly she turned toward the voice. Yes, she had surely lost her mind, for she imagined she saw Agnes, dressed like a lifesaver and sitting behind an oar. These were hallucinations—her sister's pale cheeks and dark lashes, the spray dripping from the rolling brim of her canvas hat.

"Is that really you, Agnes? What are you...?"

"Hush now." Agnes tucked the blanket around her.

The surfboat rose and fell. Someone had lain Herb flat near the stern and covered him with a blanket. Sunny judged the distance to the gunwales in case she got sick, then focused on the horizon to keep her nausea at bay.

The surfboat, loaded with survivors, pulled away from the *Titus Brown*. The space between the small surfboat and enormous freighter opened up quickly. Captain Hanna lingered on the fantail, watching them a moment before disappearing into the boilerhouse.

They were away.

Now at a distance from the *Titus Brown*, its smokestack was visible. The thick black cylinder lay flat against the boilerhouse roof as if it were taking a nap. The freighter appeared so pitiful there on the reef, broken.

Water collected at Sunny's feet, not that it mattered much—her feet were already numb. She huddled inside the blanket, feeling weak and tired as Agnes rowed with such strength. What was she doing here? It made no sense, and yet she was terribly glad of it. With Agnes here, it was like Sunny had already made it home.

Her sister rowed rhythmically. Like a moving part of the *Titus Brown's* engine, each move efficient, precise, identical.

Sunny hummed herself a lullaby. The one their father used to sing. Waves broke over the stern and her eyelids became heavy. Climbing down the ladder and worrying over Herb and bracing herself in the biting wind had taken what strength she'd had left, and they were still a good distance from shore. Her eyelids lowered, and, despite the surfboat's rising and falling and the stinging spray and the keeper's shouting, she drifted off to sleep.

Lake Superior's Shipwreck Coast

What was that sound? Like a child rapping softly on a door.

Nothing. Only the waves.

There it was again. She hadn't imagined it.

And the scent of pine and wood smoke—that was real, too.

Cordelia squinted in the daylight. A frothy curl rolled toward her and she shut her eyes against it. When the comber didn't hit she opened her eyes again. The waves were breaking at a distance, not here.

Again came the rapping.

This time she felt it as much as heard it. The water was pushing the life raft into something. With great effort she tried to lift her head—a shooting pain in her neck—and gave up. She couldn't move.

After a time the water spun her raft just enough that she could see the wide, flat rock it had come to rest against. She closed and opened her eyes. The rock was still here. Beyond it was sand. More rocks. Pine trees. All blanketed in snow.

We made it to shore, she told the others. There was no reply. Edmund?

He wasn't on the raft. He had gone ashore without her. On the lifeboat.

No, that wasn't it. He was gone and she was alone.

The raft moved and there was a better view of the land. Not far off was a forest. No houses, no smoke rising up from chimneys. The sun was overhead. She would wait here on the raft. Someone would find her.

A long time passed and no one came. There was something, a structure, a distance away. It hadn't been there before. Had it? She squinted. A very small house, set back from the shore. At a break in the tree line.

She would go to that tiny house. Crawl, if she had to. Someone would be there.

She urged her muscles to move her off the raft but they would not comply. Gravity had become too strong. Her head was too heavy and her neck would not lift it. The slightest attempt brought a searing pain.

Maybe someone was in the dwelling even now. In that small house nestled among the evergreens. She would watch and wait.

Who lived in such a tiny house?

Port Austin, Michigan

If the situation weren't so dire it would be comical: Sunny dressed as a fireman and Agnes as a lifesaver. The things Maman would have to say about their unladylike appearance! As Agnes rowed, she stole worried glances at her sister, who'd quickly fallen asleep, sandwiched between two crewmates. Was it a restful sleep or a lapse into unconsciousness? Agnes wished she could wrap Sunny in her arms and warm her, as she was clearly suffering from exposure, but the most important thing she could do for her sister was to keep rowing.

Agnes glanced down and immediately wished she hadn't. The water now covered her feet. She gripped the oars tighter, her thoughts racing. The surfboat would start leaking faster with the added weight of the eight shipwrecked sailors. And they still had to go back for the eight who awaited them on the freighter.

"Faster, now, faster!" Keeper Duncan shouted over the waves.

Keeper Duncan wasn't steering them back to Alaska Bay and the station. Though the rowers faced astern, and so couldn't see exactly where they were going, it was clear from the orientation of the lighthouse that they were headed straight for the beach. The keeper must have decided the surfboat was filling up too fast, that they'd never make it all the way back to the station. The race was on to see which happened first: they reached shore or the water reached the gunwales. Matching her motions to those of the surfman in front of her, Agnes rowed with a new vigor. The *Titus Brown* grew smaller in the distance.

Keeper Duncan ordered Agnes and the lifesaver next to her to bail water. She worked quickly. They'd made some headway when the keeper ordered them back to their oars. They were nearing the breakers.

Agnes took a deep breath. This would be the most treacherous part. If they capsized, the shipwreck victims—her dear sister and Herb—would be in grave danger, for they all were in a weakened state, having used up their energy fighting the storm and then staying alive on the reef.

A wave overtook their surfboat, forcing the stern up and pushing the bow down. Agnes leaned forward to compensate for the tilting. The wave passed beneath them, the boat shifting and then the stern dipping as the bow lifted up. She pressed her feet to the footboard to steady herself. The bow came down on level with the stern. They'd made it past the first breaker.

Another was soon upon them. It lifted the stern high, but the wave, instead of passing underneath, carried the surfboat before it. Now they were in danger of flipping stern over bow.

"Faster!" Keeper Duncan commanded.

Everything came into sharp focus: the boat's tilting, the cresting wave, the oars moving all together. Agnes rowed as hard as she could. The wave mustn't overtake them. Six rowed as one and the keeper steered and soon they were running a distance before the wave—they were surfing!

When they came out of it upright, relief coursed through Agnes's body. Sunny, slumped on the thwart beside her and wedged between two other survivors, had no idea how close they'd just come to capsizing.

Keeper Duncan changed tack, likely because of the close call. He shouted his decision to back the boat over the breakers. Agnes had seen this done many times. It was one way to deal with roiling surf like this. The two lifesavers at the stern turned around to face the shore. As the next breaker approached, Agnes and the lifesavers facing the waves stopped rowing, and the two stern rowers now facing forward backed the boat into the breaker. This gave the surfboat enough backward motion to carry it safely over the cresting wave. That accomplished, Agnes and the other lifesavers facing the waves resumed rowing them toward the beach, only for a moment until the stern rowers took over and backed the surfboat over another cresting wave.

This push and pull of the oppositely facing rowers continued until at last came the glorious friction of sand pushing up against the hull. Following the lifesavers' lead, Agnes climbed out and helped pull the boat a safe distance onto the beach. Lizzie and Mrs. Duncan were there, standing next to a horse and sleigh. They must have been watching from Thumbnail Point to see where Keeper Duncan would bring the survivors ashore. It wasn't a given that the hastily patched boat would make it all the way to the station, and indeed it would not have.

Agnes tried to rouse Sunny. Her sister hadn't spoken or even stirred since falling asleep. Please let them not be too late. "I've got to get the rest of your crew," Agnes said, not knowing if Sunny was listening. There was only a slight flutter of her eyelids. "The keeper's sister and mother are here. They will take good care of you." There was no response. Agnes's stomach twisted with worry. With Keeper Duncan's help, she lifted her sister out of the boat. He carried Sunny to the sleigh, even though Agnes said she could do it.

"Save your back for rowing," he said. "You did very well, but you've got more to do."

Agnes grabbed the blanket and covered her sister. "I'll see you soon," she said, and kissed Sunny's cheek. It was like kissing marble. She wanted to stay with Sunny, to make sure she would be all right. How could she leave her sister in this condition?

"I'll look after her for you."

Agnes had been so absorbed in her concern for Sunny that she hadn't seen Lizzie approach. Lizzie wore a serious expression, her brown eyes peeking out from under a fringe of bangs tucked in her wool hat.

"She's very ill," Agnes said. Any awkwardness she might have felt in the presence of this beautiful woman who had kissed her that morning was overshadowed by the seriousness of Sunny's condition. "I'm terribly worried about her."

Lizzie, frowning, looked at Sunny. "I'll ride with her to your cottage, and make sure she's looked after."

"Would you? That would put my mind at ease." There was so much more Agnes wanted to say. The words, whatever they were, would have to wait. On impulse Agnes wrapped her arms around Lizzie and held her tightly. Then, pulling back, "I should help with the bailing."

Lizzie nodded. "I'll see you when you get back."

As soon as the water was bailed from the *Mettle*, Agnes and the crew dragged the surfboat to the lake's edge. No launching rails this time. Agnes took her place on the port side. Keeper Duncan, standing in the center, gave the command and they moved the boat into the water. The two men furthest forward pulled lines attached to the bow. As they entered the churning surf, the surfmen at the bow tossed their lines into the boat, climbed in, and grabbed their oars. Agnes and the surfman opposite her, as well as the two men closest to the stern, continued pushing the boat into the surf. Water splashed up to her thighs and icy spray stung her face. She blinked quickly to clear her vision.

The boat neared a breaker as she and the surfman opposite her climbed in. In one swift movement she took her seat on the middle thwart, grabbed her oar, and placed it in the oar lock. Holding the end with both hands, she leaned back and pulled the oar through the surf. The bow dipped down behind her and as it rode down the back side of the breaker the last two men climbed in at the stern. Keeper Duncan moved to the stern, maneuvering the boat with the long steering oar.

It was harder going, this time around. It took an eternity to get out of the boiling surf. When they finally passed the last of the breakers, Agnes looked to the shore. There was no sign of the horse and sleigh carrying Sunny. They must have gone inland, cutting across the forest to the road, to avoid the rocky coast surrounding Thumbnail Point.

As she feared, the *Mettle* was leaking faster now than it had on the first trip. By the time they arrived at the *Titus Brown*, the water was past her ankles. The shore was nearly two miles away, an impossible distance with these leaks. She bit her lip. The boat would surely fill with water before they reached land. May the sail save them all.

Quickly, the remaining survivors boarded, Captain Hanna last. Keeper Duncan pivoted the boat and they made for shore. They weren't halfway to land when he ordered them to put up the sail. Agnes kept rowing as several surfmen hoisted the sail. With the combination of human and wind power, the boat moved much more swiftly. Despite this, the water was at her calves by the time they reached the breakers. And by the time the hull brushed against the sandy beach, the water inside it was mere inches from the gunwales. Agnes slumped on the thwart, exhaling loudly. They'd made it, but barely.

Word of the rescue had spread, and this time they were welcomed by townspeople carrying pails of hot coffee. A small crowd of at least two dozen waited on the shore, the surfmen's wives among them. Lizzie wasn't there; maybe she was still at the cottage with Sunny.

"Agnes! I heard you were part of the rescue and I had to come see for myself." It was the church organist, a member of her china-painting group. She offered Agnes a mug of coffee. Then someone wrapped a blanket around Agnes's shoulders as the organist peppered her with questions. How had she come to be on the rescue? Was she scared? Had she done this before? Did her mother know?

Exhausted, Agnes answered quickly and, after confirming Sunny and Herb had been taken to the cottage, made an excuse to leave. She sat on an outcropping of rock a short distance from the group of shipwrecked sailors and their rescuers and the coffee-and-blanket-bringers.

Agnes had helped rescue sixteen sailors from a broken-down steamer nearly two miles off shore. She'd rescued her own sister! Let them not have been too late. A few yards away, the *Titus Brown* sailors huddled under blankets, sipping their coffee. Each of them was someone's husband or brother, father or son. She thought of Amos, and how she might have helped him. She would take solace in the fact that she had saved lives today, in a rescue she might not have dared attempt were it not for her regret over losing Amos. She'd been right to trust in her abilities. From now on, she would trust in herself more.

It came to her then, the change she would make in her life. She loved being out on the water, the fresh air and the freedom of it. And she was more than competent at sea. Today had proved that. Why couldn't she captain her own boat, not for pleasure, but for business? There were details that needed working out, details like which boat and what business and how to get licensed. But she would figure it all out. Not far from where she sat, the *Titus Brown's* captain talked with his crew, all of them huddled under wool blankets. Yes, she would be a captain one day. Not of a freighter, no. Something smaller, more local. Smiling at the thought, she brought the white china mug to her lips. The coffee had already gone cold. No matter. Coffee had never tasted better.

But where was that sleigh? Agnes glanced over her shoulder for any sign of it, anxious as she was to get to Sunny. What a haunting sight she had been, with her bluish face and her closed eyes. Never had she looked so frail. When the sleigh at last returned to the beach, Agnes told Keeper Duncan she'd like to ride with the shipwrecked sailors to town so that she could go straight to Sunny. He agreed, and said he and the crew would take care of returning the surfboat to the station. Someone was bringing the carriage.

"Mrs. Inby, what you did today was astounding," Keeper Duncan said then. "We needed every last rower to get to the vessel and back twice. Thank you."

"Thank you for allowing me to help. It means a lot to me."

"You're a remarkable woman, Mrs. Inby, and—"

"Please, call me Agnes." She could give him that, at least.

"Agnes," he said, smiling. "I want to apologize for underestimating you. It was only out of a desire to protect you, you see, and... At any rate, you're a superb oarswoman. And please do call me Elzie."

"I'm happy to be of service, *Elzie*." Agnes handed her mug to a volunteer and climbed into the sleigh. "My father would have been very impressed by your steering today. Maybe even a little envious." Agnes smiled.

Elzie looked at the ground and if his cheeks weren't already pink with cold she might have seen them redden. The sleigh jerked to a start and Agnes waved goodbye.

The proprietors of the hotel in the village, the son of whom had brought the coffee to the shore, had offered to take in the survivors. The hotel would provide hot meals and warm beds until the sailors could travel home. No one was going anywhere for the time being. It had snowed so much over the last three days throughout the Thumb that train service had halted. Word was it might start back up tomorrow. If not tomorrow, then Thursday.

On the sleigh ride into town, Captain Hanna tried to assuage Agnes's fears for her sister. He described the strength and bravery Sunny had shown, and suggested it was exhaustion that had knocked Sunny out during the rescue. With rest, he surmised, she would be fine. Agnes wanted to believe him. Still, she alighted from the sleigh before it crossed Bird Creek, and with what strength her hours of rowing hadn't sapped from her, she ran the rest of the way home, terrified Sunny might have already succumbed to exposure.

WEDNESDAY
November 12, 1913

Port Austin, Michigan

Immediately after rising, Agnes crossed the hallway to check on her sister. She opened the door slowly so that it wouldn't creak. Sunny was still asleep. Her feet were wrapped in towels and elevated on pillows, and she lay so still under the pink and green quilt that it wasn't clear if she was breathing. Agnes tiptoed closer.

The events of yesterday had already taken on a dreamlike quality. Following the rescue, Sunny, puffy-faced and blue-lipped, had slept the entire afternoon. She'd woken only briefly when the doctor came to check on her. Sunny suffered from hypothermia, the doctor had said, which came as no surprise, and her feet were frostbitten. He'd told Agnes to give Sunny's feet a warm-water bath and then loosely wrap them in clean towels. He warned her to keep an eye on the frostbite, lest it turn gangrenous. "Watch for her skin to become pale, hard, cold, or numb. Those are danger signs," he said. "And under no circumstances should she walk on her frostbitten feet until they've healed."

Now Agnes came to Sunny's side. She held her breath, waited: There it was—the rise and fall of her sister's chest. Agnes placed a hand on her sister's forehead. No fever, thank goodness. Sunny stirred. Agnes stilled, not wanting to wake her. Once Sunny had quieted again she left the room, closing the door with the faintest *click*. She would check her feet later.

Agnes put on a shirtwaist and skirt and went downstairs to the parlor, where Herb slept on the davenport. Maman prized that davenport and Agnes couldn't imagine her mother allowing any of her daughters to use it as a bed. Only Herb, whom

Maman adored. He had injured his back during the storm but last evening said he was doing better.

Avoiding the loose floorboards so as not to wake anyone, Agnes went to the kitchen. She stopped short at the doorway, at the sight of the familiar forest green wrapper over flannel pajamas. Maman, her back to Agnes, sat at the table with her morning tea.

Agnes took a deep breath and put on a cheerful expression.

"Good morning," Maman said without turning around. The woman's hearing was impeccable.

"Sunny is resting peacefully, no fever," Agnes said, going to the cupboard for the new cereal she liked. "I'll check her feet when she wakes." She heated the shredded wheat biscuits in the oven for a few minutes.

"I've looked in on her twice this morning. I was up early," Maman said, adding plaintively, "I couldn't sleep, on account of my ankle and hip."

Agnes sighed inwardly. Maman would not let her forget her injuries anytime soon. "Can I get you some liniment?"

"I used up what we have."

"Then I'll get some at work today." Agnes, determined not to be troubled by her mother's complaints, waited by the cookstove until her cereal was ready, then poured hot milk over the crisped shredded wheat and carried it to the table. Her chair was heavy and uncooperative as she pulled it back. Liniment would do her own sore muscles some good.

Maman raised her mug to parched lips and sipped without making a sound. "Did you know I visited your father's parents in this house three times a week until they passed? And that was on top of my duties at the station." Maman stirred her tea slowly and set her spoon on the saucer. "I don't want to be a burden, you know."

Agnes forced a chipper tone. "You're not a burden, Maman. And you're in better health than you think. You just need to get out of this house more often, see your friends more."

"Well if my own daughter doesn't want to spend time with me, I suppose I'll have to."

"Maman—" Agnes stopped herself. She wouldn't do this anymore. To say anything further would be to repeat conversations they'd had a thousand times. "I helped save Sunny's life. And Herb's. I rowed for miles to save that crew."

Maman didn't respond, only sipped her tea.

"The doctor said your hip is bruised, not broken." Agnes spoke more harshly now. So much for not being bothered by her mother's complaints. "If it were broken you'd have trouble sitting up, let alone walking. And he said your ankle will be fine." Then, backtracking just a little: "Should I go now to get the liniment, and bring it back before I start work?"

"If it's not too much trouble."

Agnes finished her cereal and said she was going to the store presently, where she'd purchase liniment for Maman and aloe for Sunny's feet, as well as a few ingredients for dinner. If Herb's back allowed it he would likely offer to help cook, and Agnes would be more than happy to accept.

On her way to Bisbee's, she paused to watch the lake. The waves had diminished considerably since the day before when she'd rowed with the lifesavers. In another day the lake might be completely calm, with only the ghostly presence of the broken vessel on the reef to remind them of the monstrous forms the water could take. This lake could become so furious, with waves rising thirty feet in the air, sinking ships and drowning sailors. And then, no matter how tremendous the seas had been, no matter how angry, the lake would return to its unassuming presence, as if nothing had happened.

And that same song would play, on and on into forever.

Mr. Bisbee told her she wasn't needed at the store, as the town was still half-buried in snow, but that he expected things to pick up Thursday. And so after getting groceries—the selection for which was scant, as there'd been no deliveries in five days—she stopped by the hotel to inquire about the *Titus Brown's* crew. The proprietor confirmed that all were doing fine, including the ones who had rowed themselves to shore—except for the one sailor who'd drowned trying to get onto the *Titus Brown's* lifeboat. The poor soul. A storm like this and there were bound to be more deaths. Those vessels stranded further down the coast, what had become of them? She'd buy a paper as soon as the trains could get through, which the hotel keeper expected would be later that day.

Outside the hotel she ran into Lizzie. Agnes stood up straight, her mouth forming itself into a smile all on its own.

"I was just coming to see you," Lizzie said. "I thought you might be at Bisbee's."

"You were—Oh! Well, it's a slow day, and I wasn't needed..." Agnes's face warmed. She hadn't seen Lizzie since yesterday at the rescue, and that was only briefly. They hadn't had a chance to talk about Lizzie's kiss and what it meant. What did Lizzie want to say? Agnes searched Lizzie's features for clues as to what she might be feeling. Did she regret kissing Agnes? Maybe Lizzie meant to explain that it was just a friendly kiss and nothing more.

Lizzie stepped into the alcove, out of the wind rushing down the street. "How is your sister?"

Agnes moved into the alcove with her. "Much improved, thank you."

"That's good to hear." Lizzie looked at the ground, then at the street, and then at Agnes. "I...I wanted to tell you something."

Agnes got very quiet. There was something in Lizzie's tone that worried her. Across the street a man shoveled snow from the sidewalk in front of a café. The café that Sunny had hoped to buy. A thick scarf covered his face and neck but his gray hair blew loose in the wind. Finally, Agnes said, "What is it?"

Lizzie bit her bottom lip. "Nathaniel's asked me to marry him." The words came out in a rush.

Agnes felt like she'd been punched in the gut. She leaned against the brick building lest she fall over. "Oh. I see." Disoriented, she looked across the street, where the gray-haired man leaned against his shovel, catching his breath. She forced a smile. Good manners required she say something. "Congratulations, then." That should suffice, yes? She had to get out of there. This was not at all what she'd expected. Not after yesterday. She held up the paper bag she was holding. "I don't mean to rush off, but I'd better get this home to my mother. Liniment. She fell during the storm."

"Wait." Lizzie put a hand on Agnes's arm. "I haven't given him an answer yet."

Agnes stopped mid-stride, nearly falling off the step. "Why—why is that?"

"Because I'm in love with someone else." Her hand was still on Agnes's arm. "But I don't know if she feels the same."

Agnes stared, incredulous. Lizzie's meaning slowly sank in, and a smile spread across Agnes's face. "She does." Her voice quivered. "She most certainly does feel the same."

Lizzie beamed, then quickly grew serious. "But there are complications, aren't there?"

Agnes shrugged. She would not be daunted by *complications*, not now. "There are always complications, aren't there? Ours" —ours!—"are just of a different sort."

"Yes." Lizzie nodded. "Yes, you're absolutely right. I knew you were brave. I knew it!"

"I have an idea." Agnes leaned closer to Lizzie, nodded at the building across the street. "Meet me at that restaurant in an hour and I'll tell you all about it."

Lizzie squinted at her. "What are you up to, Aggie?"

"You'll see." She kissed Lizzie on the cheek and hurried down the street, turning around once to wave at the young woman who'd just changed the course of her life. The beautiful woman who stood in the alcove, waving back.

At the cottage she found Maman in the parlor with Herb, the latter sitting in a wingback chair next to the hearth, an afghan covering his legs and a cup of tea on his lap. Agnes put away the groceries, handed Maman the liniment, and put her coat back on.

"Are you headed to Bisbee's, then?" Maman asked from her perch on the davenport.

"Not until tomorrow. I'm meeting a friend."

"A friend?"

"Lizzie Duncan, the keeper's sister."

"Oh," Maman said, "I thought maybe you were meeting the keeper himself. I thought you'd help me with some mending, but I suppose I can do it on my own."

Agnes felt a familiar pang of guilt. Even though she would never keep Lizzie waiting, she imagined what it would be like if she yielded to Maman's wishes, as she always had. The scene flashed in her mind: sitting on the davenport mending shirtwaists, quiet and dutiful with Maman, as if she'd never lost her temper so magnificently; the resumption of her quiet, steady acquiescence to Maman's demands; the rendering of her declarations of independence as transitory as a November gale, all rage and wind and fury that settled down into nothing.

You can't spare her every disappointment. Lizzie's words echoed in her ear. *And why would you want to?*

That was the old Agnes. If she was going to live the life she was planning, she had to be willing to disappoint Maman. There was no getting around it. She might as well start now.

"Perhaps I can do some mending this evening."

Without looking up Maman said, "Suit yourself."

The guilt didn't go away. But this time, Agnes decided, she would let the guilt wash through her and keep going. Remembering something, she went upstairs to her room. On her dresser lay the brooch she'd painted with delicate blue and yellow flowers. She put it in her pocket. With a cheerful goodbye to Maman she left the cottage to meet Lizzie. Following the path she'd trod in the snow, she walked at a normal pace at first, and then, her thoughts on the narrowing distance between herself and Lizzie, her footsteps quickened, and by the time she crossed the bridge over Bird Creek she was running.

Port Austin, Michigan

Framed by a pale lace curtain, a nine-pane window trapped triangles of snow in its nine corners. A spindly, leafless branch blew against one of the panes, its icy finger tapping on the window. Sunny had known these lace curtains for most of her life. Maman had made them to hang in her childhood bedroom at the station. The bed was familiar, too, with its dark wood posts and headboard. This was the bed where she and Herb spent their winter nights.

On a small round table next to the bed, someone had placed a pitcher of water and a glass. She reached behind her to feel for Herb but there was only the green and pink quilt. How long had she been asleep? The events that led to her being here were trapped in a fog of jumbled scenes: Climbing down from the *Titus Brown* to the lifesavers' boat. Riding in a sleigh. And Agnes—she had seen Agnes. It seemed as though she'd seen her on the surfboat, but that made no sense. Agnes must have been waiting for her on the shore.

Was it a new day, now? The overcast sky revealed little as to the time, only that it wasn't night. And where was Herb? The rest of the crew? Agnes? Panic rose in her chest. She couldn't remember if everyone had made it off the boat. She wanted to call out, but her throat burned.

With some difficulty, she rolled toward the bedside table. Every muscle was weak and aching. Her feet were wrapped in bandages. Reaching for the glass, she misjudged the distance. The glass hit the floor and shattered. Seconds later Agnes was at the door.

"You're awake!" Agnes beamed.

"I was..." Sunny's voice was raspy and it hurt to talk. "Water. I'm sorry—"

Agnes waved away the concern. "I'll take care of it, Sissy. Don't you worry yourself one bit. I'm just so happy you're finally awake." She left the bedroom but not without pausing at the threshold, her hands on the door frame, to gaze at Sunny. What else was that in her smiling expression? Relief? Sadness? Worry.

Agnes returned a minute later with a broom and dustpan. She swept up the broken glass, carried it away, and brought Sunny a new drinking glass.

It was a relief to see her after so long. Now her older sister sat on the edge of the bed, and Sunny rolled toward her as that side of the bed dipped slightly. Agnes poured a glass of water and held it out. Slowly and with great effort, Sunny sat up and accepted the glass carefully, with two hands.

"I thought I might lose you," Agnes said. "How are your feet feeling? *Can* you feel them?"

"Hurt. Like needles," she said, economizing her words to minimize the pain.

"Good, that's good! The doctor said it would be a bad sign if they were numb."

Sunny sipped her water. The coolness soothed her throat. "Herb?"

"He's fine. He's downstairs by the fire. His back is much better. He's been so worried over you. Maman is fussing over him, of course."

Maman always fussed over Herb. "What—" Her voice faltered. She tried again. "What day?"

"What day is it? Wednesday. It's Wednesday afternoon. You've been in bed for a full day and then some. You were unconscious when we brought you ashore."

"We?"

"Oh, you mustn't remember. I helped row the surfboat! I had no idea it was you out there. In fact I had a feeling it was Captain Blythe." Agnes didn't say anything for a moment, like she was trying to figure something out, and then she brightened. "Everyone made it, including the sailors who came ashore by themselves." Then, in a lower voice, "Although I understand one of the crew drowned before we got there. I'm so sorry."

Stilts, she remembered now with a sinking heart. Stilts had not made it. She drank more water and waited for her voice to come back. "You were rowing?"

Agnes explained how the station had been short three surfmen, and that she'd convinced Keeper Duncan she could row well enough to stand in.

"You've always been strong."

"As are you! When I checked on your crewmates recuperating at the hotel, they told me how you barely slept a wink the entire two days, that you were making sure they were fed and in good spirits. They credit you with keeping them alive."

"I saw a flare. I think. Did I?"

"You saw it? Yes—that was me! I wasn't sure anyone had." Agnes placed her hand on Sunny's. "I sure am glad you're home, Sissy. I didn't think I'd lay eyes on you 'til the end of the month. And then with this storm... I was so worried."

It took a while for Sunny to collect her thoughts. She spoke slowly. "I whistled up the storm. To come home early."

"Ha! And in such dramatic fashion, too." Agnes kissed her cheek. "I should stop talking and let you rest your voice."

"I'm not sailing anymore," Sunny said before Agnes could leave. If she told enough people, then maybe it would be true. Yes, Herb had given her his blessing to stay ashore. He'd even said he would help her open a restaurant. Once she told him she'd lost her savings, however, he'd seemed inclined to return to sailing, if only to more quickly earn back what she'd lost.

"You got my letter then," Agnes said conspiratorially. "About the restaurant? What does Herb think of the idea?" Then, when Sunny didn't answer right away, Agnes leaned closer. "If he doesn't want to stay ashore, you can live here, with us."

"A woman's place is with her husband." The voice was Maman's. She appeared in the doorway like an apparition. She leaned on a cane.

"You're not—" Sunny coughed, a sharp pain in her throat— "with yours."

Agnes, her back to Maman, widened her eyes at Sunny's gumption.

"Send me early to my grave would you?" Maman didn't appear ruffled at all. "If Herb wants to sail again, Sunday Marie, you'll go with him."

"Let her be," Agnes said without turning around. "She's a grown woman. She can make her own choices."

How Sunny loved her sister. It'd been far too long since she'd seen her. In the time she'd been away Agnes had changed, somehow.

Maman tossed a folded newspaper onto the bed and, before turning to leave, said, "It appears the *Marguerite* didn't fare as well as the *Titus Brown*. If what the paper says is true, then Cordelia's a widow now. I suppose she'll be coming back to Port Austin to live."

Agnes picked up the newspaper. Sunny watched her read, trying to glean information from Agnes's expression. It was taking her sister forever to finish. "What?" Sunny asked. "What's it say?"

Agnes shook her head, her eyes still on the paper. "It isn't good. The storm was even worse than I thought." She handed Sunny the paper to read for herself:

United Press Leased Wire Service. Cleveland, Ohio, Nov. 12:

Never in the history of navigation on the Great Lakes has a storm claimed such a toll of human life and damage to shipping as the terrific blizzard which swept over four of the big freshwater bodies the early part of this week. Latest reports today place the number of missing sailors on shipwrecked vessels at one hundred and fifty.

There is a growing fear today that four steel steamers on Lake Huron, carrying crews of twenty men each, have been lost. The vessels are over sixty hours overdue and still unreported.

A score of bodies have already been recovered on Lake Huron, washed up with the wreckage of numerous boats. ... Among the ships known to have foundered on Lake Huron are the James Carruthers, Charles S. Price, Regina, *and* Wexford. *The total number of big vessels lost will reach twenty-five, it was estimated today....*

There was no mention of the *Marguerite*.

"It's further down," Agnes said when Sunny looked up. "Keep reading."

DULUTH, Minnesota, Nov. 12:

Fears today were expressed for the steamer Marguerite, *three days overdue here and never reported since leaving the Soo. Marine men believe she foundered off White Fish Point. The tug* Everett *made two searching trips but was unable to find any trace of the* Marguerite. *She carried a crew of twenty-six men. A body recovered near Crisp's Point Lighthouse has yet to be identified. It is unknown whether the body is from the* Marguerite, *or from the* Henry B. Smith, *which foundered near Marquette.*

"Foundered," Sunny said quietly. "Do you think Cordelia knows?"

"I'm sure of it."

Sunny stared at the snowy window pane. Poor Cordelia. Sunny didn't know what she would do if something had happened to Herb. She felt almost guilty, having already gotten thirteen years with the man she loved, and Cordelia didn't even get three months. It wasn't fair. And after losing Lewis!

"First Lewis, and now Edmund," Agnes said, echoing Sunny's thoughts. She poured more water for her. "I'm on my way to the telegraph office now. If it's as we fear, I'll offer to go to Cleveland to help her however I can."

When Agnes reappeared in the doorway later that afternoon, she had a blank look about her, like she was trying to focus on something that wasn't there. In her gloved hand was a letter.

"Did you send the telegram?" Sunny asked. Her throat felt somewhat better. It no longer burned to talk. At least, not as much as before.

Agnes shook her head. Sunny waited. Something in Agnes's expression sent a chill of dread down her spine.

"There was a letter at the post office. From Cordelia."

"What...?" Panic fluttered in Sunny's chest. Why was Agnes so slow to speak? "Out with it, already! What's it say?"

"She wrote to tell us she was going to join Edmund on the *Marguerite*."

"When?" And then louder, when Agnes didn't answer right away, "When did she go?" Sunny wouldn't accept this. They knew nothing for certain. "We don't know she was with him when it—" She couldn't bring herself to say *foundered*.

"They were to depart from Cleveland on the fifth," Agnes said. "They were bound for Duluth."

"Maybe she changed her mind," Sunny offered, hearing the weakness of her argument as she said it. Neither of them mentioned the body that had washed ashore on Shipwreck Coast. "Send her a telegram." Sunny's throat tightened. The room spun. She thought she might be sick. "Just in case."

Staring off into nowhere, Agnes spoke slowly. "Yes. I'll do that. And the shipping company. Do you know which one? They'd know if the *Marguerite* had any passengers."

Sunny gave her the name of the shipping company and Agnes left in a hurry. It was a hopeless errand, Sunny knew. Cordelia would never receive the telegram. Sunny cried until her pillow was soaked with her tears.

A telegram arrived the next day. It wasn't the reply from Cordelia they'd been holding their breath for. Instead it was a request to come to Whitefish Point on the Upper Peninsula to identify a woman's body that had washed ashore. The body had been found frozen to a life raft stamped *Marguerite*, and as the only woman known to have been on that freighter, it was suspected to be the body of the captain's wife.

The pale-yellow cottage by the lake was heavy with grief. Sunny and Agnes were in shock. Their sister's death was too terrible to be true. Maman took to her bed, inconsolable. Someone had to travel to the Upper Peninsula to identify the body. Agnes volunteered for the grim task. Sunny wanted to go with her, but her frostbitten feet wouldn't allow it. Nor would Herb's bad back. In the end, Lizzie Duncan went, so that Agnes wouldn't have to make the awful journey on her own.

December 1913

Port Austin, Michigan

"I guess she's perched up there pretty good," Sunny said to Agnes as they looked toward the reef. Today would have been Cordelia's twenty-first birthday, and the two sisters had just visited her grave at the church cemetery. It had been Sunny's first walk of any distance since her frostbitten feet had healed. From their backyard, the sisters looked out at the lake that seemed to go on forever. The *Titus Brown*, apparently determined not to go under, still lay broken on the reef more than a month after its stranding.

The *Marguerite* should have been as lucky. Sunny silently cursed Captain Blythe for leaving Whitefish Bay that terrible Sunday night, and she cursed the shipping companies for offering captains bonuses for late-season trips, and she cursed the weather observers for not predicting the storm's ferocity. Curse them all, because that made more sense to her than to shout at the wind and the water and the snow.

Weeks ago, when Agnes and Lizzie returned from Whitefish Point with Cordelia's body, Agnes had told Sunny the sorrowful story of how their sister was found by a Vermilion surfman. He'd been on patrol Tuesday morning, November 11. Cordelia lay on a life raft, frozen to death and alone, mere feet from the beach. And while scores of bodies had washed up along the eastern shore of Lake Huron, from Port Franks to Goderich, Ontario, none of the *Marguerite's* crew had come ashore on Michigan's Upper Peninsula. That was the difference between Superior and the rest of the Great Lakes, people said: Superior never gave up its dead.

In the days following the Great Storm, as the newspapers were calling it, the sisters had learned the enormous reach of the destruction. On Lake Huron alone, eight large steel freighters had gone down with all hands and seven more stranded on reefs or beaches. And while Lake Huron had seen the most casualties, lives were lost and vessels sunk on every Great Lake except Ontario.

In total, twelve big commercial freighters went down with all hands, and thirty were stranded on rocky shoals. Dozens more were badly damaged. More than two hundred and fifty sailors perished. And that didn't include the unknown number of sailing vessels, tugs, or powered barges that foundered. No one knew for certain how many commercial fishermen, hunters, or anglers had been taken by the storm. It was hard to comprehend the devastation, the loss of life.

Sunny stared at the serene lake. Today only a faint winter wind breezed in from the northwest, not enough to form even the smallest of whitecaps. This quiet lake was the same body of water that had raged and swelled and wrecked their freighter along with so many others.

"I'm glad you're not going back out there," Agnes said, as if reading Sunny's thoughts.

"I'm not sure what's next for me." Sunny had already told Agnes that she'd lost her savings in the storm.

"You'll make your restaurant happen someday," Agnes said. "I'm sure of it."

Sunny smiled at her sister. Having someone believe in you made all the difference.

"I want to go into business myself," Agnes said. "If I get my captain's license and find a bigger boat, I could give tours of the area. Take people to the lighthouse and Turnip Rock, let them see the rock formations and caves up close. Lizzie wants to help."

"Is that so?" Sunny studied her sister. Agnes seemed different, somehow. More at ease with herself. "I think that's a fine idea. And Lizzie seems like a nice girl."

"She is. She's wonderful." A pause, then, "I've invited her to come live with us. The situation's difficult for her at the station, you see. She turned down an offer of marriage from one of the lifesavers and he didn't take it too well. She thinks it's best if she's not around, at least for now. I was thinking she'd stay in my room. I have the extra bed, and besides, the sleeping porch is too cold in the winter. You and Herb can stay where you are, of course."

Sunny knit her brow. Agnes was talking too quickly and explaining too much. There may be more to her friendship with Lizzie than she was letting on. Well, Sunny knew how to mind her own business. "It's good you can help Lizzie out," was all she said.

Agnes nodded in the direction of the *Titus Brown*. "There must be thousands of tons of coal out there."

Sunny pretended not to notice the abrupt change of topic. "Over nine thousand tons, in fact."

"Doesn't do anyone much good out there on the reef, does it?"

Sunny narrowed her eyes at her sister. "It's supposed to be a real cold winter."

Agnes sighed. "Too bad I've put away my skiff."

"In the spring, then. I could help you. Restaurant or not, I'm sticking around."

Agnes smiled and reached for her sister's hand. "It's good to have you home, Sunny."

"Glad to hear it, 'cause I ain't leaving."

Agnes squeezed Sunny's hand. "I couldn't bear to lose another sister."

Port Austin, Michigan

One week before Christmas, Sunny was in the kitchen preparing the candy fairies for Agnes's daughter Aimee, who was arriving the next day, when there was a knock on the front door. Maman was resting and Agnes was at work, so Sunny put down her spoon and went to see who it was. When she opened the front door there stood Captain Hanna, snow dusting the shoulders of his wool coat. Sunny's mouth fell open. What on earth was he doing here?

Recovering from the surprise and remembering her manners, Sunny invited him inside to warm himself by the woodstove. He removed his hat and followed her into the parlor. All the while her mind churned with possible reasons for his visit. "Herb's out with friends," she said preemptively.

"That's all right. I came to see you."

If he'd come to see her, his purpose could be only one thing. She would have to nip this in the bud. "I'm sorry, Captain Hanna. I can't sail with you next season. My mind's made up to stay on land. Herb, on the other hand, I don't know." Sunny gestured to two chairs by the hearth and they both sat.

Captain Hanna assured her he had not returned to Port Austin in an attempt to dissuade her, that he'd resigned himself to the fact that he would have to go without her baking. In the spring he would be captain of a brand-new straight deck freighter that was to launch in Lorain. "I've spoken with Cleve and he's going to be my third mate."

"Oh, I'm glad to hear it," Sunny said. It was hardly surprising that Cleve had no reservations about returning to the lakes after the Great Storm. He may have loved the water more than life itself. "A storm like that'll make a lot of sailors think twice. I know it did me."

"I myself can't stay ashore. I feel itchy if I stay on land too long." He glanced away, adding, "Lucky for me, my fiancée is very understanding."

"Your fiancée?" Sunny smiled. "I knew it. When you asked to have those gingersnaps delivered in Detroit, Herb and I wondered if you might propose." Maybe it wasn't prudent to admit to gossiping about their boss—well, it was too late now. "Let me offer my congratulations. I'm very happy for you both."

"Thank you," Captain Hanna said, reddening slightly. "We're getting married on the twenty-seventh. If she doesn't come to her senses first and decide to abandon ship." Then, after clearing his throat, he continued, "Sunny, I wanted to offer my condolences on the loss of your sister and brother-in-law. When I left Port Austin last month I didn't realize you'd had family on the *Marguerite*. I understand the conditions on Lake Superior were every bit as terrible. I've heard reports that the Three Sisters were sighted."

Sunny looked at the rug, shaking her head. "Thank you. I didn't know she'd gone up the lakes myself, not 'til after..." For the thousandth time, Sunny wished she could have stopped it somehow. If only Cordelia had delayed her wedding. If only Lewis's horse hadn't spooked. If only, if only. She snapped herself out of it. "Can I get you some tea?" she asked. Then, when the captain declined, she waited. Certainly he hadn't come all this way to offer his condolences. And he'd already said he wasn't there to convince her to return to sailing.

He reached into his coat pocket. "Have you seen the papers? I picked this up at the station in Detroit." He pulled a newspaper from inside his coat. "Mrs. Colvin, you're quite the sensation." He pointed to the headline:

WOMAN IS STORM HEROINE – Steward's Wife Feeds and Cheers Sailors While Wind and Waves Pound Vessel.

What on earth? Sunny took the paper from his hands and scanned the brief article. The chief engineer had been interviewed by a reporter. The engineer had sung Sunny's praises for everyone to read. Her cheeks warmed. "Hogwash," she said, returning the paper to Captain Hanna. "I was just doing my job."

"Keep it. I bought two. I hear the story's been picked up by newspapers across the country."

"Is that so?" Sunny fidgeted with the newspaper, folding and unfolding it. "Honestly I don't know why. My job was to feed the crew. And that's what I did. Why are people are so surprised a woman did her job?"

Captain Hanna laughed. "It wasn't just any job. And if they find it remarkable, I guess it's because they've never known a woman as brave as you."

Sunny grunted. "I'm no braver than most women I know." She adjusted her collar, thinking of Agnes rowing out to the *Titus Brown* in those terrible seas, and of every woman who'd ever stared down death to birth a baby.

"In any event, this article brings me to why I came."

Sunny leaned forward in her chair.

"I wanted to talk to you about what you lost on the *Titus Brown.*" Then, in a lower voice, "I understand you lost a great sum of money in the storm."

"Yes." Sunny looked at her lap, wondering who'd told him about the money. Cleve, maybe. "But I'm grateful not to have lost my life."

"Yes," Captain Hanna said quietly. Then, after a pause and in a more chipper voice, "The first mate and I got to talking, and we thought it wasn't right that the woman who kept the crew alive and in good spirits should lose so much herself. We took up a collection and I'm here to deliver it." He offered her an envelope.

Sunny held up her hand to stop him. "Captain Hanna, I can't accept this. Whatever it is, it's too much."

"On the contrary, it's not enough. We want to show our appreciation for your courage throughout a harrowing ordeal. It would mean a lot to me, and the entire crew, if you would accept it."

Sunny took the envelope and laid it on her lap. She swallowed hard to hold back tears. "Thank you. This means so much to me."

"I'm hoping it's enough to start your business."

Sunny jerked her head up. "How did you...?"

Captain Hanna only smiled and shrugged.

"This will make all the difference," she said, her voice rich with emotion. "There's a place that's become available, right on the lake. Now I can have my café—breakfast and lunch and all sorts of baked goods. I wasn't sure it was going to be possible! I can never repay your kindness."

"You can do one thing for me."

"Anything," Sunny said, putting her hand on her heart.

Captain Hanna smiled. "Promise me you'll serve snap doodle bread."

It was an inspired idea. She wished she'd thought of it herself. "I know just the thing," she said, clapping her hands once. "I'll make it every Friday, as good luck to you and anyone else setting sail. And I know just what I'll call it: Captain Hanna's Snap Doodle."

Epilogue

Three Sisters Café opened in the late spring of 1914. By the time the Pointe Aux Barques resort-goers arrived that summer, Sunny and Herb were running a brisk operation. Word of Sunny's baking skills spread quickly throughout the resort, and when vacationers came to the village they always stopped at Three Sisters. Herb was as cheerful as ever in his new role, making friends easily with their customers. And as she'd promised the Old Man, every Friday Sunny baked Captain Hanna's Snap Doodle. It soon became a customer favorite.

Sunny and Herb lived in an apartment above the restaurant, and both of them helped to take pressure off Agnes when it came to Maman. They often came by to sit with her in the evenings when the café was closed. Lizzie, whom Maman took to immediately, helped with the cooking and cleaning in exchange for room and board.

In a ceremony at the Port Austin Life-Saving Station that spring, the district superintendent of the U.S. Life-Saving Service presented Agnes with a silver medal for her "signal exertions in saving the shipwrecked." Keeper Duncan had recommended her for the award, for which he'd written a sworn affidavit describing Agnes's contributions. His recommendation had gone all the way to the Secretary of the Treasury for approval.

Agnes became somewhat of a local celebrity. Not long after that, she acquired the *Stalwart* from the Port Austin Life-Saving Station, which was replacing it with a new lifeboat. Agnes and Lizzie fixed up the *Stalwart* to make it more suitable for leisure passengers. With Agnes as captain, together they gave tours of the area from late spring until early fall.

Thumb Tip Tours launched from the Port Austin Harbor, just steps from Three Sisters Café.

Sunny kept her promise to remain on land. Mostly. Over the spring and early summer of 1914—on only the calmest days and always wearing her life belt—she had joined Agnes on her skiff for numerous trips to the wrecked *Titus Brown*, returning each time with a load of coal. Other villagers had done the same. It didn't seem right to leave nine thousand tons of coal sitting out there, where it would surely sink to the bottom of Lake Huron when the next big storm hit and finally pulled the broken freighter off the reef. As it turned out, the *Titus Brown* left its rocky perch not during a storm, but on a calm midsummer day when it was patched up, refloated, and towed away. Rumor was it'd been sold and the new owner planned to put it back into service under a different name.

Ten years after the Great Storm, on a crisp November morning, Sunny began her daily routine at the café. From a hook behind the counter she grabbed one of the white china mugs Agnes had painted: the words "Three Sisters Café" and a sunrise over Lake Huron. Into the firebox of the cook-stove Sunny scooped the last of the coal they had salvaged from the *Titus Brown*. Ten years their supply had lasted! As on most days, Sunny had risen before dawn, leaving Herb to sleep a little longer, so that she might dive undisturbed into the pleasurable work of making the baked goods her customers loved. Today it would be pumpkin muffins.

As she put on her apron she went to the window overlooking Lake Huron. Though it was still dark outside, she could hear and, when a breaker hit at just the right angle, *feel* the waves picking up. The hair on the back of her neck prickled, in remembrance of the storm ten Novembers ago. She couldn't help but worry about Cleve and Captain Hanna, out there on the lakes as the weather turned. She reminded herself that sometime in the last decade Captain Hanna must have availed himself of the wireless telephone, whether by choice or by regulation, and would therefore be amply informed of any foul weather. Catastrophes would be averted. Lives would be saved. Her thoughts turned to Stilts, whose life had not been saved. It saddened her that she could no longer call up a picture of his face.

No, it would not be pumpkin muffins today. Today she would make the butter tarts she'd promised Stilts all those years ago. Turning her back on the lake, she went to the pantry and reached for the raisins. Then the flour, salt, shortening, and butter. After making the pastry dough and rolling it out and cutting it to fit the muffin cups, she prepared the filling: brown sugar and corn syrup, egg and melted butter. Runny—that was how he said he liked the centers. The way his grandmother had made them. Into the bottom of the pastry-lined muffin cups she sprinkled golden raisins and covered them with the syrupy mixture.

Not long after the tarts started baking, the kitchen filled with their buttery scent. Sunny inhaled deeply. Butter tarts were just what the occasion called for. No finer use could there be for the last of the *Titus Brown's* coal than to fulfill her promise to Stilts. She was sorry it had taken so long. Ten years. Kind soul that Stilts was, he would not begrudge her tardiness. His voice echoed clear and true in her ear: Better late than never.

AUTHOR'S NOTE

I was inspired to write this novel by stories of my great-grandfather Walter Stalker, a captain on the Great Lakes in the early 1900s. He was at the helm of the four-masted schooner *Golden Age* at the time of the 1913 storm, a position previously held by his uncle. The *Golden Age* was a massive boat, the largest sailing vessel in the world when built in 1882. My great-grandmother Annabel served as cook and at least one of their children was also aboard. They sheltered for days in a cove on Lake Michigan's Beaver Island until the storm finally blew itself out. Traumatized by the ordeal, Annabel convinced Walter it was time to go ashore.

While the characters in my story are entirely fictional, the situations they encounter are based on actual events. The fate of the *Titus Brown* in my story mirrors that of the *Howard M. Hanna Jr.* Sunny and Herb Colvin were inspired by the *Hanna's* husband-and-wife, steward-and-cook team. The real-life cook, Sadie Black, was lauded in newspapers nationwide for her heroism during the *Hanna's* stranding.

The fictional *Marguerite* was an amalgamation of multiple vessels, including the *Cornell* and the *Sylvania* (although neither vessel foundered). While lifeboats were deployed during the 1913 storm, no one on them survived. For insight into what it might have been like fleeing a doomed Great Lakes freighter on a life raft, I read two mid-century accounts: that of sailor Frank Mays, in Pat Stayer, Jim Stayer, and Tim Juhl's *If We*

Make It 'til Daylight, and of sailor Dennis Hale in Andrew Kantar's *Deadly Voyage: The S.S. Daniel J. Morrell Tragedy*.

The course and chronology of the storm in *Sisters of the Sweetwater Fury* is based on modern reconstructions. For this I consulted the National Oceanic and the Atmospheric Administration website (www.noaa.gov), as well as David G. Brown's *White Hurricane*. Other works of nonfiction I found helpful, whether to my understanding of the storm or Great Lakes shipping in general, were Frank Barcus's *Freshwater Fury* and Frank Boles's *Sailing into History*. Ann M. Lewis's recollections in *Ship Captain's Daughter* inspired the scenes of Cordelia climbing aboard the *Marguerite* and attempting to steer the freighter.

The U.S. Life-Saving Service operated throughout the Great Lakes and along the Atlantic Coast from the mid-1800s until 1915, when it merged with the Revenue Cutter Service to form the U.S. Coast Guard. Immensely helpful to my understanding of the U.S. Life-Saving Service was Frederick Stonehouse's *Wreck Ashore*. Port Austin, Michigan was the location of an actual life-saving station, and that station's crew rescued the sailors stranded on the *Howard M. Hanna Jr.* The lifesavers in my story, however, are purely fictional.

I want to thank Laura Jacobs, professor and archivist at the University of Wisconsin-Superior; Bruce Lynn, executive director of the Great Lakes Shipwreck Museum; and maritime historian and author Frederick Stonehouse. These individuals were so kind as to answer questions from a total stranger about particular aspects of early twentieth-century straight deck freighters.

Finally, I'm thankful to so many in my family. My father, William Stalker, who fostered my love of learning and whose genealogical research inspired this story. My mother, Diana

Stalker, for encouraging my writing from a young age and for taking me on regular trips to the library. My stepmother, Laurie Stalker, for reading and commenting on multiple drafts of this novel. My children for their patience while I was tucked away in my office. And my husband, Mike, for his storytelling insight and support, and for making everything possible.

ABOUT THE AUTHOR

Kinley Bryan was born and raised in Northeast Ohio, and counts numerous Great Lakes captains among her ancestors. Her love for the inland seas swelled during the years she spent in an old cottage on Lake Erie. She now lives in South Carolina with her husband and three children. *Sisters of the Sweetwater Fury* is her first novel.

Made in United States
Orlando, FL
06 December 2021